I've travelled the world twice over,
Met the famous: saints and sinners,
Poets and artists, kings and queens,
Old stars and hopeful beginners,
I've been where no-one's been before,
Learned secrets from writers and cooks
All with one library ticket
To the wonderful world of books.

© Janice James.

The wisdom of the ages
Is there for you and me,
The wisdom of the ages,
In your local library.

There's large print books
And talking books,
For those who cannot see,
The wisdom of the ages,
It's fantastic, and it's free.

Written by Sam Wood, aged 92

CURTMANTLE

Henry, Duke of Normandy and Count of Anjou, shortly to become Henry II of England, married at eighteen the divorced wife of Louis VII of France. She was the beautiful and already notorious Eleanor of Aquitaine, by then aged twenty-nine. Henry was an able ruler; restless, cunning, ruthless, said to be descended from the devil; but he had great charm. This story is told by three of the women, who, in their different ways, both loved and hated Henry. They are Margaret, princess of Scotland; her daughter Constance, who married one of Henry's sons; and the woman who signed herself at last 'Eleanor, by the wrath of God Queen of England'.

Books by Pamela Hill
Published by The House of Ulverscroft:

DIGBY
VOLLANDS
TREVITHICK
ANGELL & SONS
SUMMER CYPRESS

PAMELA HILL

◆

CURTMANTLE

Complete and Unabridged

ULVERSCROFT
Leicester

First published in Great Britain in 1996 by
Robert Hale Limited
London

First Large Print Edition
published 1997
by arrangement with
Robert Hale Limited
London

British Library CIP Data

Hill, Pamela, *1920 –*
Curtmantle.—Large print ed.—
Ulverscroft large print series: general fiction
1. Henry I, King of England — Fiction
2. Great Britain — History — Henry I,
1100 – 1135 3. Historical fiction
4. Large type books
I. Title
823.9'14 [F]

ISBN 0–7089–3757–8

Published by
F. A. Thorpe (Publishing) Ltd.
Anstey, Leicestershire

Set by Words & Graphics Ltd.
Anstey, Leicestershire
Printed and bound in Great Britain by
T. J. Press (Padstow) Ltd., Padstow, Cornwall

This book is printed on acid-free paper

Part One

'Eleanor,
by the wrath of God . . . '

1

AS my golden-haired brat of a grandson has most impudently laid siege to me in this castle of Mirebeau, there is little for me to do at my age but sit and await the outcome. I have done what I might in posting archers about the towers and ensuring that one gate for supplies remains secretly open. However I brought only a small following with me, in haste, from Fontevrault. They said it was unsafe for me to remain there and pray for my dead, but it would have been safer than here.

I am almost eighty years old, though I seldom feel it, and the thudding of mangonels and clash of arms is unchanged since I heard them in Palestine more than half a century ago. I had not expected to have to hear their clamour again, and am not going near the window-slit to see how matters fare; I have no wish to have a chance arrow shot in my ancient eye.

I am trying, instead, to make myself think with calm philosophy of the whole affair, which when one thinks of it has its amusing side. I used to indulge in this practice during my sixteen years in prison, kept there by Curtmantle. This army, led by young Arthur of Brittany, is made up of forces supplied by my first husband's son by his third marriage, to wit Philip Augustus, as they call him, of France; but Augustus himself would have shown more wisdom than to anger England. The lesser part of Arthur's following belongs to Hugh de la Marche, out of pique because my son Lackland took away his bride. The whole business is unnecessary, and if they capture my person they will do themselves no good.

In plain fact, I have not been as angry since Henry Curtmantle, king of England largely by the benefit of his marriage to me, removed my favourite troubadour by taking him away to that chilly island midway through our marriage. That also is unimportant now. The lays of Bernard de Ventadour will outlast all of us. He used to delight in overdressing, favouring rich hats in particular. I enjoyed his wit as much as his music. Henry, naturally, was jealous of a situation he did not understand, having been reared in Anjou. No doubt it seemed disturbing to have a minstrel — the English think of minstrels as lesser beings — call me his Aziman, his magnet, and to offer to divest me of my shoe when I retired to my chamber. Henry put an interpretation on the matter which did not apply, and was too stubborn to be reasoned with. Although he spoke the *langue d'oc*, having been educated by his handsome father in all necessary tongues, he had a lawyer's mind and not a poet's, and could not understand that a troubadour's lady remains of necessity out of reach.

They are firing arrows at the walls again: the impertinence! An arrow killed my beloved son Richard at Chaluz, four years ago now; its tip entered his spine at the shoulder, and although they said that on his crusade he was frequently stuck all over like a pincushion with these and took no harm, this shaft killed him. Perhaps it was destined; Richard always swore that he would die by metal. Had he been alive, he would have marched instantly to my relief. As it is, I have to hope that John Lackland, my last and only son left out of all five I bore, will perhaps allow filial piety, and remembrance of my years, to stir his sluggish estimation of what is fitting and get him out of bed with his child-wife. I understand that at present he remains in it with her till midday. He took leisure to have Isabella crowned at Westminster, but is at present with her at Rouen. Possibly this fact adds venom to the arrows of Hugh de la Marche, whom she was to have married by the arrangement her family had made earlier. However as Lackland was their overlord there was no argument: he could have taken away their lands.

Lackland. He is always called that, after a jest of his father's, who had at the time given away so much land to Henry, Richard and Geoffrey, some of it his and some of it mine, that there was none left for John, who for some reason his father loved best. I love him least, having seen through him from the beginning. I cannot conceive why Curtmantle preferred him to Richard or even Geoffrey, after little William and Young Henry were dead. The last two — Young Henry was crowned by his father's order when he was still a lad, not foreseeing that he would die first, at twenty-eight — reached manhood. William, the child of our love, died when he was three.

It was unlikely that we would have failed to quarrel, Curtmantle and I; both of us were strong of will and high of temper, though I myself have never rolled on the ground and chewed straw after pulling off my clothes in rage, as he used to. John Lackland was conceived during the last reconciliation attempted between us, my husband and I. He was younger even than Joanna, lately dead with her child at Fontevrault. The peace between us did not last longer than the conception of Lackland. It was then, as we lay together almost as strangers, that I heard Curtmantle's voice, cold as if he sat in council and addressed some clerk. He had this lawyer's coldness as the other extreme from his ungovernable rages. To have endured both is to have experienced living. Until he said what he said to me then, I had loved him, despite everything. Thereafter, I hated him till I heard he was dead at last. Well, there it is; and I remember well enough.

"My father advised me not to marry you, madam, because he and you had committed adultery with one another long before. As it was I took no heed, but instead have kept you close and bearing yearly children to occupy your time. Perhaps you will bear one again after this night's work; contrive another son, if you may."

After that I hated him, as I say; and bore Lackland in that same hatred. By then, I was fifty. After that my fixed determination was that each son I had borne to Curtmantle should have revenge on their father; and by the end, this was done. Nevertheless we had loved once.

My own favourite among the sons I bore Henry II is known to have been Richard, crusader and king; but I have never loved even my glorious Lion Heart as I did little William, my firstborn son who died as I say at three years old, after I had been crowned England's queen. I had called William not after the

Conqueror, or the boy William Audelin, England's former heir who later drowned, but after my own grandsire, William X of Aquitaine, the tales about whom are legion. William himself, sturdy and full of laughter, was the pledge of our love, Curtmantle's and mine. We had known of it instantly at sight of one another in Paris, while I was still wife, after a fashion, to Louis VII. I can still recall the stocky freckled unkempt youth with red hair who was brought to me then, his big hands rough with riding, and three rings on them he always wore, one his father's. It is true that I had known his father Count Geoffrey somewhat too well. By then, the latter was newly dead. I knew his son was the man for me, as Geoffrey Le Bel also had once been. Henry at eighteen knew likewise, no doubt, that I, at twenty-nine, was the wife for him. It would have happened even had I been ugly; I could bring him broad lands in Aquitaine, I, the queen of France. The ambitious young devil! He had planned it all, as was his way.

They say that to become queen of France is the highest peak any woman may hope to attain, though the position has its drawbacks, as I had by then found in the course of fifteen years of dull marriage. To have become queen of England after my divorce was thought to be nothing, for England had been taken by Norman pirates earlier who had had themselves crowned there after a battle had been won. I am therefore supposed by all the world still to loathe France because of my great fall from one state to the other. However from being the wife of a monk to becoming that of a man, more of a man than any I have ever known, is not to fall but to rise in one's own estimation if not that of others. I dislike narrow pious France in any case; Philip Augustus is as bad as his eventual father Louis, though coarser by reason of his mother's Champagne blood. The etiquette of Paris chafed me from the beginning after the freedom of the south, and it was partly to get away from that that I rode off with poor Louis at last on crusade. I craved the sun and songs I remembered from my girlhood, and knew the company of my young uncle Raymond, who had been like an elder brother — there were only eight years between us — would be there waiting at Antioch, and that we could talk and laugh together as we had used to do in young days in the Ombrière. However when I was fourteen years old they married me to a bridegroom most of whose manhood appeared to have been drained off into his long hair.

Louis used to keep it uncut like that of the ancient Merovings, who were latterly unable to do anything but be trundled about in carts by their subjects. I will say that to prepare for the crusade, Louis agreed to have it lopped to his shoulders. This still did not turn him entirely into a man, but he wore a helmet, and on top of that his crown, despite the increasing heat; and the armour they fashioned for him gave him a great curved belly he never possessed. It was painted with lilies, which suited him.

★ ★ ★

We rode off in a great train, and I was to meet very different men then and after; in Byzantium, the Emperor Manuel

11

Comnenus looked at me with onyx eyes that understood women. He was weighed down with ropes of pearls and a dalmatic so stiff he could scarcely move, but he would have made love to me had I agreed to it; I did not, though the forbidden desire stirred in me. I was sad to leave that matchless city, Middlegard as the West called it, but its name, as all know, is Constantinople. I like the earlier name of Byzantium best. We had to leave, after Louis had venerated the relics. He and Manuel Comnenus were still on good terms then.

★ ★ ★

The other man I could readily have lain with was different, and all his power was given to God. I had spoken with Abbot Bernard of Clairvaux before we left France, for I desired a child by Louis lest it be said I was barren. The Abbot did not look at me at all, for he dared not. He had in his youth been handsome, with red hair which by the time I met him was turning white, and was in any case tonsured. His flesh was a skeleton's by then with fasting, and he kept his fiery glance cast down, as was to be expected. He had forced, I knew, all his brothers into convents and monasteries, thinking like St Paul that the world was about to come to an end; and the one sister who had dared to marry he refused to receive, though she had travelled a long way to visit him. He had also been harsh to Abélard, the great teacher who had dared to love a woman, and who was by then alone and castrated in a bleak remote community in Brittany. I do not think Christ was as harsh as Bernard, but the castration itself was not Bernard's fault. He distrusted love, however; and young King Malcolm of Scotland would later on not make heirs because he followed the thought of Clairvaux, as did others. I did not. It was by then seven years since my marriage with Louis, and I was still childless. At the beginning there had been what they had called a hope, but it had come to nothing. I tried to tell the Abbot how I thought my husband was mistaken in thinking love a sin, the original sin of Adam; had not God told the beasts to multiply, and why should man not do likewise? Nevertheless Louis still knelt in prayer before and after, and haunted the confessional though he said constantly that he loved me. If I could have persuaded him that it was not sin, we could I thought have made a child together: but it was hard to talk with this stern chilly skeleton in its white robe with its averted eyes. The robe was girded with a rope to scourge itself from sins of the flesh, so I made myself say little; and heard the abbot promise that if we would bring peace to France, which at that time was disturbed, I would conceive a child. The mellifluous doctor, as he was known, then dismissed me; and later preached war himself, namely the second crusade, at Vézelay.

Nevertheless I did conceive my child that year, but it may well have been by Curtmantle's father, Geoffrey Le Bel of Anjou. In any case, it was a girl, and in France they cannot inherit. I called her after the Mother of God.

★ ★ ★

Count Geoffrey deserved his name, being so handsome he would have been noticed in rags, and certainly naked. As it was, he wore a black surcoat sewn with golden leopards, and was tall and slim, with broad shoulders, and the most compelling gaze I have ever seen. It was hard, light and sharp, with a kind of ironic amusement; he was a notably shrewd young man. His mouth was engaging but prudent, and his talk well-informed. He had been knighted in England by King Henry Beauclerc, who had chosen him to marry his daughter Matilda, which happened. He was in France now to pay my husband homage for Anjou.

After the plodding attentions of Louis, and his journeys back and forth to the confessional, I was strongly drawn to the Count; he would, I knew, be different. I will not deny that when we rode out hunting, I edged my palfrey near to his. We rode on at speed; it was one occasion when I could escape my women. As we went Count Geoffrey told me first about his ancestry and secondly about his marriage, which was unhappy. He himself was descended from the devil.

The English marriage he had made out of a desire for advancement, which is natural. His wife was not only royal, but haughty, widow of an emperor, and older than he was. At that time, till she should have mended her manners, he had sent her packing out of Anjou.

I met Matilda later on, but under different circumstances; she was by then my mother-in-law. She was also the Lady of England and empress of Germany; the only legitimate daughter and heiress of the Conqueror's son Henry I, by then thankfully dead. His own two sons had drowned and he had been able to get no others by a new wife, which soured him as he had fathered bastards without difficulty on numerous occasions.

"He stank so much," the Count said, "that when he had been dead two hours they had to wrap him in a bull's hide and sew it up. Nevertheless he was a good lawgiver, and it was thought fit to examine his brain. The surgeon then died of the stench."

"The king himself died, they say, of eating too much fish," I remarked politely.

16

"He was a noted lecher as well as a glutton. That first is one state of mind with which I have sympathy at this moment."

The light compelling gaze was on me. I knew I looked my best, although my hair, which was then a bright red-gold, was hidden by my riding-hood. However my gown fitted closely, and I saw Geoffrey Le Bel's gaze lower itself to my breasts, whose shape survives still after the bearing of ten children and at that time showed beguilingly through the silk. I resolved to have an affair; why not? I was tired of abbots and monks and of being queen of France, forever sewing altar-cloths and growing weary of my husband. We broke into a gallop and in the end came to where the forest cleared to a place full of low rocks, where hounds used to nose rapidly after low prey such as hares, but we had left the hounds behind. The rocks were covered, at that season, with yellow broom blazing in the sunshine. The place itself is called Fontainebleau. The kings of France have hunted there since, no doubt, the days of Clovis. Count Geoffrey gazed for moments at the yellow broom.

"I always," he said, "stick a branch of that in my hat when I hunt at home in Anjou. It is the *planta genista*, which is why they give me the name of Plantagenet. It will descend to my sons."

His eyes returned to me. "Let me lift you down," he said. "Help me to choose a sprig." He was smiling his prudent smile.

★ ★ ★

We picked the yellow broom together; it was like a pledge between us. I stuck a sprig in Count Geoffrey's hat and he placed another in my bosom. Then we coupled enjoyably without delay among the rocks in the sun. This was what I had always known love should be; a glorious fulfilment. I can remember it yet; it was the first time it had happened to me.

There was no sign of the hunt till later on, and by the time they came upon us we were seated talking decorously. It was mostly, I remember, still about old King Henry, the Lion of Justice in England, called so because he had made good laws after subduing that land and Normandy; both by rights belonged to his brother Robert, whom he imprisoned and took the throne. "He snored at night so loudly it could be heard all through his palaces," the Count reminisced. He had not loved his father-in-law, but like everyone else dared not disobey the edicts of that thunderous presence. Henry's widowed daughter he disliked thoroughly, but felt it prudent to marry her because of the closeness of Normandy to Anjou. Also, Matilda would inherit England, or so then it was thought; afterwards, King Henry being dead, her cousin Stephen of Blois seized the throne. "He used the excuse that a man must rule, and was hustled by his half-brother across the Channel to be crowned. No one could have foreseen it," said Geoffrey. "The old king's barons had sworn fealty to my wife as Lady of England at his orders before he died, as her two brothers — the elder, William Audelin, was newly married to my sister and she mourns him still — had been drowned in the Channel. After Henry Beauclerc died a tale was got up to the effect that he had withdrawn the vow of allegiance and had left the crown instead to Stephen, who was his sister's son. *He* reigns still in England, after a fashion; his barons do as they choose. I will not involve myself beyond keeping Normandy as best I can; hence I am here, and have met yourself. It was worth coming for that." He smiled again, but already as though the episode between us were past. He began then to talk of his eldest son Henry, aged eleven, whom two years before he had sent into England, carefully guarded, to show him, a red-haired freckled urchin of parts, to his mother's people. "My wife herself made a fool of her part in the war; she alienated the Londoners, who are the very ones she should have cozened, and they chased her out. She will never reign in England, despite the support of her royal uncle of Scots and her bastard half-brother Robert of Gloucester. She sent often for help to me, but I do not waste time or men. Henry my son is different; he will win England at leisure."

His mouth had hardened. "Tell me of

your knighting by the Lion of Justice," I said, for I heard the hunt approach. I had brief space to hear from Geoffrey Le Bel of the handsome sight he must have made at fifteen, having been bathed at dawn after kneeling in vigil all night. A fine linen shirt was put on him, finer than he had ever known, for the English weavers are famous. "Then there was a robe of cloth of gold, and a cloak dyed purple," he said. "They gave me silken slippers I have yet, and on top of that shoes sewn with golden lions, and a magnificent Spanish horse, and a coat of mail the like of which I had never then seen, double-meshed so that no sword or javelin could pierce it. Then," his voice grew reflective, "they put golden spurs on me, and hung a shield with more lions on my shoulders. Old Henry liked the symbol of the lion for himself, though he is known mostly as Beauclerc since he died, because he wrote a fair hand, his father the Conqueror having intended him for the Church."

"He would not have made a contented prelate. They say his bastards numbered twenty-one."

Henry I **21** is son of William Duke

"You have heard that, have you? At any rate, the court of England was very rich then, whatever it is now; they put a helmet on my head that shone all over with precious stones. Then they brought me a lance of ash wood, I recall, and a sword from the King's treasury. The old devil had seized that at the beginning while his brother was abroad, and gained the throne by means of money. I was only a boy from Anjou, astonished by all this splendour, as you may imagine; but — " and he laughed — "I could still show them how to leap into the saddle, weighed down as by then I was, without touching the stirrups. Even my haughty bride was impressed, which is not easy."

I could well picture the magnificent young knight made at the hands of Beauclerc; nevertheless I preferred the Count with the sprig of broom stuck in his hunting-hat. That is the only time I have committed adultery.

Count Geoffrey died in the year before I married his son Henry, who was by that time aged eighteen and had carved out most of his own inheritance, with by then, also, the promise of England, King Stephen's heir Eustace being dead. I was twenty-nine by then as I say, but felt like a young girl. In fact I have never felt any age in particular. One remains oneself, as I do to this day.

* * *

To go back seven years before that, after Count Geoffrey had left Paris that time I found myself pregnant. It might, after all, have been Louis. I had reminded him of the good abbot's promise once France should be at peace, and largely because of the count's renewed homage for Anjou, this was by then the case. Later, there was however the crusade; but before that my little daughter Marie had been born, and was taken away from me to be reared as a Child of France. A girl as I say cannot inherit, but Marie's existence raised hopes that I might yet bear Louis a son. I never did; it took three marriages to get him one, which must have taxed his piety. In the meantime, we listened to Abbot Bernard's preaching at Vézelay, where the

23

crowds were so filled with enthusiasm for the new crusade that they tore fragments from the holy man's very cloak to form rough crosses to pin on their shoulders. Richard's crusade, since then, has been in its way more civil; each country has its separate colour to keep to. Meantime, I chose my wardrobe and the women who were to go with me to the East. I saw no virtue in entering Antioch other than suitably dressed for the joy it would bring me.

★ ★ ★

I have known three saints, when all is said; Abbot Bernard himself, who was canonised a decade since; Thomas Becket, of whom I was jealous in the early days when he was Curtmantle's friend and chancellor, and my husband used to leap across his carefully disposed London dining-table unkempt from the chase and unexpected. My husband Louis was no doubt a third saint also; he had much to endure, and he loved me.

He never burned hotly about anything, and merely felt it his duty to go with the others on crusade. I myself went out of ennui and a desire, as stated, to see my uncle Raymond again and laugh with him about his marriage. That had been made because he was so handsome that the dowager Alais of Antioch, ruling for her nine-year-old daughter and greatly desiring a second husband, sent for him and at sight, would have had him in her bed very shortly. However he slipped round to the church and married the nine-year-old heiress instead, thus becoming Prince of Antioch. Alais, enraged but powerless, had to retire and, no doubt, console herself elsewhere; both she and her sister Queen Melisende of Jerusalem had hot tails, as I was to discover when we got there.

I had meantime filled so many baggage-carts I was blamed for delaying the progress of the crusading army, which lacked proper direction in any case. After many adventures we came to Antioch, and I saw its palaces shining in the sun, and the slopes of silver olive-groves, and knew I had come home. My uncle Raymond and I greeted one another joyously; as I have said, we had been like sister and brother in Poitiers, and were the same in Antioch; how could we be expected to do anything but talk and laugh far into the night? Louis' prim mind however was disturbed, or perhaps his advisers remembered the rocks at Fontainebleau: there had of course been gossip. When I said that, for the army's convenience, I would stay where I was, Louis forbade it, with a face leaden as penances.

"Your thoughts are like a cesspit," I shouted at him, with other things. I saw the tears begin to run one after the other down his face; all he would answer to my shouting was "My darling wife! My darling wife!" I hardened my heart.

"You have no notion how to use a wife," I told him. "You should have let one of your brothers rule, and stayed in the Church, as was intended, despite the death of your elder. How dare you tell me I cannot stay? I will do as I choose." But he had the resolution to order them to drag me away after only ten days, and Raymond shortly thereafter lost his life in battle and his head, as I remember hearing with sorrow, was sent to the Caliph in pickle to Baghdad. I have had masses said ever since for his soul.

How the arrows shower out there like rain! There seems to be a fresh attack, perhaps from La Marche. There is no sign yet of Lackland. The day is wearing on and by night, anything may happen; but if they take the castle they dare not harm me at my age. I will go on sitting here, remembering. I had many years later in which to learn to reflect.

* * *

Louis and I were meantime outwardly reconciled, and after the crusade — it had been unsuccessful, like all the rest — the pope came to bless us in bed together, an experience I found embarrassing. As a result, Louis was inspired to conceive either a first or a second child on me, this time again a daughter. He called her Alais, a name he seems to fancy; there has been a girl named Alais from each of his three marriages. I never liked my Alais as well as my Marie, who became my delight long after, in Poitiers, when again I held my court there, having separated from Curtmantle for the time.

* * *

Louis had no wish to divorce me; he wept as many tears as he had done at Antioch. Nevertheless it was becoming urgent to have a male heir for France, though the reason given for the annulment — both my daughters remained legitimate — was consanguinity discovered late. I knew already that I would marry Henry Fitzempress as soon as I was free, and galloped through the night to evade the embraces of his brother Geoffrey, aged seventeen, who lay in wait, as had Theobald of Blois, King Stephen's brother, who had missed the throne of England and no doubt hoped to console himself with the duchy of Aquitaine instead. I can remember drawing great breaths of free air on the ride, away from Paris at last and all narrowness and piety.

* * *

Henry in those days was as I say known as Fitzempress, and there is no doubt that he was his mother's son. I met her soon after I married him. She was a handsome woman still, and it seemed strange that she and the equally handsome Count Geoffrey should have engendered between them at last, after five years, so uncomely a creature as Curtmantle. He was virile, had charm, brains, learning and statesmanship; but in appearance he might have been a stonemason, and he never cared what he put on or what he looked like. Empress Matilda herself liked ceremony, to which she had been reared carefully in Germany with her first husband the old Emperor Henry the Lion, to whom she had been married as a child. As a widow of twenty-seven she had been forced to receive into her bed a boy of fifteen by order of her royal father. In addition to this, she was in love at that time with her cousin Stephen of Blois, who was to usurp her throne. It would have been a trying situation even for any woman of less haughty temper, but the empress, as she still liked to be known, had mellowed by the time I met her and made a wise regent later for Curtmantle in Rouen, though England, her heart's desire, had never accepted her except in the west parts. "My son has gained my inheritance for himself," she said placidly, "and I can live content as long as I may." She was no longer in good health since the birth of her third son William, the one who died of love. That does not seem like an Angevin, kin to the devil as they are; yet love no doubt ran somewhat in the veins of the Conqueror's own descendants. He himself married in too much haste to wait for papal sanction, being kin to the bride by way of the royal house of France and an earlier Fleming. This gave Beauclerc, the youngest son, the excuse that he was the first among his brothers to be born legitimate, and as he was also born in England this appealed to the sentiments of that nation, or at least was said to.

Beauclerc's loves are notorious, yet he no doubt loved his wife, who came of the old royal house by way of the Scots; however she was pious, like her mother. Empress Matilda can hardly have known the Good Queen Maud, as she herself left

England for Germany when she was eight. A letter from her to Stephen that I have heard of read *You know well enough what passed between us two*, but that of course was long after. If Curtmantle was indeed Stephen's son and not Count Geoffrey's, he said nothing of it, being anxious for Anjou as well as Normandy and England. He gained all three, by persuasion rather than warfare, though he conducted at least one knowledgeable siege in England after I had married him. Nevertheless it was his good fortune that Stephen's heir, hot-tempered Eustace, died mysteriously as the result of the curse of certain monks after setting fire to their corn.

Love. Henry loved Rosamund Clifford, after all, not myself: it must be so, as she brought him no advantage except beauty, which I had then also as well as lands. I will not allow myself to think of that; it is long over, and both he and she are dead, though I did not kill her.

★ ★ ★

A silence has fallen outside; the arrows have stopped. They must be parleying, the two leaders of this army sent by Louis' son and led by my grandson and, also, by Lackland's rival. I will go to the window-slit after all. Heaven and earth, how my bones ache! Yet I made the journey recently into Spain, to betroth my daughter Eleanor's daughter to Louis' grandson and namesake. Blanche of Castile is pious enough to suit France, and also has wisdom at her young age. I chose her in preference to her sister.

It is inactive, the great encamped host, like Henry's once outside Toulouse; he was never, at heart, a warrior. I should say there are a thousand men below, outnumbering by far my handful brought in haste from Fontevrault. Blanche's late betrothal has after all made me angry; after arranging that, and doing homage to Philip Augustus at my great age, kneeling and placing my hands between his — what a head of shock hair he has! — he now accepts homage instead from this impudent boy, son to my fourth son Geoffrey and Constance of Brittany, who herself took refuge at my court in England as a child with her Scots mother. Now, this Arthur of theirs will, if let, destroy what is left of Curtmantle's empire by causing it to lapse into the hands of France. He has done homage for Poitou, as if I did not exist; also for Brittany, Anjou, Maine and Touraine. Normandy is already virtually Philip's in any case. The ghosts of Curtmantle and his father rise to taunt me, boasting, as I used to do, of my great possessions.

A thousand men, and two hundred hand-picked knights, sent alongside that slim figure I can see well enough, for my eyesight has never failed! Arthur of Brittany stands like an angel in shining armour, as they say he did lately on the walls of Angers so that the people cheered aloud, seeing in him their saviour, instead of the destroyer of all my husband built. The second Arthur, son of my fourth son and of that strange half-Scottish creature with her silences or else old long-drawn tales of forgotten legend! Today is today, not yesterday. I must not look on Arthur long.

Lackland has spread the tale that Constance, Arthur's mother, died a leper. That may well be spite for having put her son early out of his reach in France. She certainly knew much misfortune. Her mother Margaret was easier to understand.

He has put up his vizor, that boy, no doubt thinking himself safe, or else hoping to inspire his men by the sight. He is only sixteen. I can see his flushed young face, and a lock of the bright Plantagenet hair straying across his forehead. It is the only time I will look upon him. I have no wish to soften my heart. Beside him stands a sturdy dark young man who must be Hugh the Brown of La Marche. Lackland reft away young Isabella from him, and he is vengeful. If my son would wrench his attentions away from her himself for the moment, he might come to my aid.

Well, I have placed my archers about the walls as I say, blocked up the entries, reinforced the gates and bridges and posted men on the turrets. I can do no more, and what happens next is the will of God. Having seen as much as I need see, I will go back to my chair, and think again of Antioch.

★ ★ ★

It is useless to try, after all; the image of that most delicious of cities has faded, and my uncle Raymond has become a soul in purgatory for whom I have these masses said monthly. The sound of the *langue d'oc* they still spoke there, in that place of earlier and most valiant victory, is heard no longer in my ears; there are only the sounds of war. Sound should, after all, be welcome to me; I spent my sixteen years in prison at Curtmantle's command, after causing his sons to betray him. I passed the time there in reading a great deal. It is important not to let the mind rot. Beauclerc's brother Robert, whom he had blinded and who spent twenty-eight years in prison, learnt Welsh to pass the time. That time was not, after all, as long for me; when Curtmantle was dead, my son Richard freed me at once.

Curtmantle, at least, had not had me blinded. I suppose I owe him that.

★ ★ ★

Curtmantle! How I remember that man, my husband, beyond any, despite the heartbreak, the humiliation, the years of imprisonment, the betrayals of my bed! There is a link still between us that can never be broken, a strong chain forged of iron and of gold. I know, I knew then, that Henry wanted me also for my lands, but there was more; far more, a loving between us for the first years I can never forget and no other woman can remember. After the divorce from Louis, after my flight to avoid other avid suitors who would have seized me till I married them — that young devil, Geoffrey of Nantes, had already refused to let Le Bel's corpse have Christian burial until Henry ceded him Anjou, but of course Henry did not, and Le Bel was buried in decency — after my gallop through the night to Poitiers, my own city, the proposal from Henry Fitzempress was waiting as I had known it would be. I staggered to my chamber, stiff from the saddle, and got my women to comb out my hair and make me seemly. It was dawn by then, and no time to sleep. Then he came; and I moved towards him with both arms outstretched, and we stayed together as one. He said, I remember, one word only; my name in the *langue d'oc*.

"Aliénor."

It means eagle of gold. I do not remember our marriage ceremony, which had to be quiet because of the scandal. We had in any case gone to bed at once.

★ ★ ★

The encamped army is astir again now; something has disturbed them. It cannot be Lackland arriving already; that would mean he had made the journey in only two days. His father would have done that, however; when Curtmantle was dying, he nevertheless rode two hundred miles in less time. I do not want to think of that dying, but of his intense and forceful living; of our life together, so long ago.

★ ★ ★

I bore William before his father gained England, then when I was already pregnant with my next I was crowned at Curtmantle's side at Westminster, with the fools of people gaping at the new victor king. I could see Henry's big neglected hand, which by then had caressed my breasts often, wearing the Confessor's ring for the time, and we were both anointed. He was also wearing the Confessor's breeches, a thought which made me smile. Thereafter I bore Young Henry, and William being dead soon after, my husband began to dote on Henry and to say he would have the boy crowned in his own lifetime, for a crown means certain inheritance, and his friend Becket had already done him a favour by preventing the Lateran from allowing the crowning of dead Eustace in the remaining lifetime of Stephen. By then, I was full with Richard; and when that last was born he was so glorious I could think of nothing else for long, and used to have him with me always, watching his golden strength grow. There was young Matilda by then also, and I was yet again pregnant when it happened, the discovery I made about Fair Rosamund. I had hardly noted my husband's absences, so taken up was I with my future Lion Heart; but one day I saw, from the window, Curtmantle pick a rose in my Woodstock garden I had planted, and which he did not bring up to me. I knew in any case that there had been a woman before he met me, a whore who had borne him two sons early; they were both about Court, and one, freckled Geoffrey, resembled him greatly. That did not matter; this, though, was different.

I made enquiries, and shortly had the young woman brought to me. She had evidently come from the Brecon country, and had provincial manners. She was beautiful and delicately made, and I myself was big with child. However she trembled as though I had been a lion, and cast her eyes down, full of tears.

"Why do you presume so with the king?" I asked her directly; there was no point in mincing words. I saw her pink mouth tremble; she did not answer for moments, and then as though she was in the presence of God.

"Madam, forgive me my sin: I love him greatly."

The tears were running down her cheeks; she reminded me of Louis at

Antioch. "They tell me you are pious," I said coldly. "Leave me now, and reflect chiefly on your sin."

They took her away, still weeping, and shortly my husband came. I could see that he was angry, because his eyes, which were grey and prominent, had become bloodshot; it was always a sign, and could herald the chewing of straw.

"How dared you?" he said. "You speak of presumption, I believe; correct your own. It is I who rule in England, not yourself." His voice had a hoarse quality always; I had already noted it. I made my hands into claws, and went then for his bloodshot eyes. He seized my wrists, imprisoning them.

"By the wrath of God, you use me as a brood-mare," I shouted. It came to me that I had borne him five children in six years, counting the one in my belly: there had been Matilda as well.

"The mare must submit to the stallion," he said with smoothness, which enraged me further. I began to struggle against the grip of his wrists, which remained like iron. I shouted still that he gave me no right at all over my own lands, and governed them himself. I shouted many things.

"Have a care lest you harm the child you are carrying," was all he said, and he turned on his heel, having dropped my hands, then left. I stayed where I was, drawing deep breaths of anger; I am not one to fling myself on my bed sobbing at any time. Perhaps that is the reason why I never had as much affection for the next son, Geoffrey, whom I then bore, as for the rest. After that Curtmantle got Eleanor on me, then a third daughter, Joanna, whom I loved as she resembled me more than any; and after that Lackland, as I have related, and who is late now and, no doubt, still enjoying his young wife's bed at Rouen.

* * *

Perhaps we women can be vengeful, after all, Eleanor, my second daughter, has had her husband's Jewish mistress murdered in Toledo. She had borne Alfonso eleven children, including Blanche. I bore Curtmantle eight, and might have saved myself the trouble, except for this young girl lately from Castile.

I have misjudged Lackland after all; he has indeed come in time. I can see his banners waving, and a great host, by far superior to young Arthur's, pouring in. There is noise and confusion already among the besiegers. The only entry I left open for supplies seems to have been undefended. Arthur of Brittany lacks foresight at sixteen: I cannot see him any more. I do not know whether my son has made haste to come out of love for me, or hatred of his rival; his two rivals, for Isabella did not want him as a husband, they say, preferring Hugh de la Marche, who was her own age or nearer it. However hatred, and fear of loss of his lands that remain on either side the sea, is more likely now Lackland has sampled Isabella's young body to his satisfaction. England's king, such as he is, is here, and will shortly relieve me.

★ ★ ★

It is over. They have raised the siege. My seneschal is at the door now, bowing and

42

saying the king of England has come, as if it were an ordinary reception of mine at Poitiers. It has been a quiet enough victory, hardly worth the name of battle. The boy Arthur was trapped, after all. I must not think of it. He should have acted with less presumption in the first place.

Lackland is before me now, and we are making the prescribed gestures of acknowledgement to one another. I must remember that King John has been crowned and anointed, like his brother Richard; like the young Henry himself, in his father's lifetime. It did not prevent that young man from being a handsome fool, and it will not save this one's soul. Here he is, with his remembered sly yet bold glance and his wide flaring lecher's nostrils, bending over my hand. He is smiling. I congratulate him mildly on his qualities as commander.

"Madam, there were few needed. The King of France is as amenable to the gleam of silver as the next man, and I had secured my father's treasure earlier from Chinon."

Richard might never have reigned. It

is he who took the Chinon treasure. Lackland helped himself instead to much of the money raised by the English for the Lion Heart's ransom, delaying Richard's release from prison in Austria thereby. Why should I not loathe John, why not support the boy who is by prior right the heir of England? Lackland was the fifth son; Geoffrey, Arthur's father, was the fourth. Richard had named Arthur his heir, then changed his mind on his deathbed, having quarrelled with Philip Augustus; quarrelled with France, who had Arthur in guardianship. Lackland himself is a most unworthy king.

"Madam, I have your young enemy bound below stairs. Will you see him for yourself before I take him back to Rouen?"

I have steeled myself. I will not look again on the golden creature they say surpasses all princes in beauty. If he had surpassed them in wisdom, he would not be here, besieging me, his grandmother. Curtmantle my husband's empire once stretched from Scotland to the Pyrenees. While I live, I must do what I can to save it from the clutches of France. Otherwise, when we meet soon in the shades — will it be in heaven or hell? — he will not greet me except in anger or else coldness. Even while I was in prison he sent me a furred scarlet gown, one Christmas: why do I remember that now?

"I have no wish to see my grandson," I hear myself reply. "Take him away."

Having heard the party ride off and the army begin to depart, I return to my chair, at last feeling old. Presently the women will pack my gear and we can ride back to Fontevrault, this autumn of 1202.

b, 1122

Part Two

The Geste of Duchess Margaret, 1167 – 1171

1

"QUEEN MELISENDE, my dear Margaret — she married my present husband's grandfather, whom she thus made King of Jerusalem, not that that lasted — was a bitch," announced the queen of England, spreading out her elegant shapely hands and regarding her rings. She was not embroidering with the rest of us in the solar as she disliked this form of passing the time, having no doubt been caused to fashion too many altar-cloths while still queen of France.

"Why," she continued, "I can remember Melisende as an old woman when I was in the Holy Land after my first husband King Louis took the cross — *he* ought of course to have been a monk, as nobody knew better than himself — and Melisende was still taking lovers in an abandoned fashion, as well as trying to rule on behalf of her son, who was by then more than capable of doing so in person. One of the lovers was stabbed unsuccessfully by a Breton knight, I remember, and went to live in Apulia for his health."

Her eyes, which under their hooded lids seemed dark until she opened them widely, when they revealed themselves as being many-coloured like strange jewels, dwelt on me in a kind of friendly malice. I met her gaze squarely, being her equal in rank if anything was to be measured between us. I am a princess of Scotland, until recently a more certain title than any in the south, because during the civil war it had been somewhat uncertain whose kingdom England had by then become. Also, Queen Eleanor might be duchess of Aquitaine in her own right, but I was duchess of Brittany by right of my husband. That situation, granted, was precarious at present, and no doubt accounted for Eleanor's subtle mockery. Moreover, she was near her time and one must make allowances. However it remained my duty to take an interest in the welfare of my absent lord's subjects. I smiled and asked "What became of the Breton knight, madam?"

"Why, they cut off his arms and legs, as is customary, but spared him his tongue, so that he could make a full confession before he bled to death. He used it to save the honour of King Fulk, whom Melisende had hoped would be blamed for the whole episode. As I say, she was a bitch. Why Black Fulk remained devoted to her — after all an ancestor of the same name in that family had burned his first wife, who had borne him several children, alive at the stake in her wedding gown for far less — I cannot conceive. The Angevins were always unpredictable. They are said to be descended from the devil, which hardly surprises one."

She shifted a little in her chair, revealing the fact that her lithe body was almost unaffected by what was after all a tenth pregnancy by one husband and then the next. "Well," I heard myself say, "the Angevin you have married now is no monk. That is one compensation."

My voice, which has never lost its downright accents of Lothian French, fell into a devastated silence; nobody but a Scot, I knew they were all thinking, would have spoken so to the queen. However Eleanor gave her hearty laugh, patted her abdomen and told everyone the child was moving again and would be here in time for Christmas. She always gave birth with the ease of a cat. Those creatures, like the queen herself, had come back from the Second Crusade along with still more carpets, and caught mice with greater ease and speed than the little furry genets I recalled from our castles in the north.

The court was at Oxford, and outside the high narrow window-slit it was snowing, making it difficult to see fine work, and the Provençal oil-lamps the Queen preferred to candles did not give enough light. The dull daylight fell on the silver-fair curls of Constance, my six-year-old daughter and the heiress of Brittany, who sat at my feet disentangling coloured silks to hand up when I should be ready. Beside her sat Princess Joanna, who was her friend though younger.

★ ★ ★

There had been no royal children born since Joanna's arrival, and this awaited event was the fruit of a temporary reconciliation between the king and queen, who had been on bad terms for some time. King Henry himself, whom everyone called Curtmantle because he wore the short hunting-cloak of Anjou and they said often slept in it after a hard day's riding, when he would fling himself down in some forester's hut for the night without ceremony, was not here. He had ridden off earlier in the day despite the threat of snow and the bitter cold; we had heard the jingle of harness and the great winding of hunting-horns of his departing following, although he himself might well return alone. He was, as his wife had lately said, unpredictable. He had of course inherited his passion for the hunt and for hawking from both his parents — I reflected that it must have been the only thing they had in common — and his talent for sound government from his late grandfather, King Henry Beauclerc, so known afterwards because he wrote in a fair hand, to the relief of those who had the task of trying to settle

53

matters after his death, not that it made any difference in the long run.

I set another stitch in the banner I was sewing for my lord duke's Breton war, not that the man who had become my husband might ever summon the resolution to fly it. I had discovered, in the brief time we had been together, that Conan, fourth of the name in Brittany, was almost incapable of making up his mind; and this makes the rule of turbulent subjects impossible. In any case they had disliked him from the outset and would greatly have preferred the rule of his half-sister Alix.

He had told me all this, but of course in his own way, when we first met in the saddle and with falcons on our wrists, flying them on our moors where Conan's then fief of Richmond adjoined ours of Huntingdon, which the Scots had held in honour since the time of King David my grandfather. Conan was a small man with dark hair. He said he had loved me at sight because I was beautiful and kind. I think I had loved him, or thought I did, because I was sorry for him and the tale he told, which was that he had crossed seas to ask for aid from Henry II because his grandfather, the late Conan III, had disinherited him and had preferred Alix, whose parents' marriage he had arranged after young Conan's own father, Alan the Black, had died. It sounded most unjust to me, and while our hawks flew back to hand after fluttering up in the cool sky, bringing back a snipe and a woodcock, I had agreed to marry Conan of Brittany if my brother, the king of Scots, by then just of age, would agree. Malcolm, who had ridden out with our party and came up shortly on his white palfrey, with his yellow hair flying, agreed eagerly and too hastily, doubtless thinking it would give Scotland power abroad. He was also, by that time, aware that Curtmantle was making a fool of him by demanding, after the Toulouse expedition, that assistance was again needed in the Welsh wars. The wars in the end killed Malcolm, as the damp in the mud-flooded valleys of Wales attacked his lungs, which were never strong. My second brother William inherited, as Malcolm had taken a vow of chastity and had no heirs.

Curtmantle was furious when he heard

of my Breton marriage, saying his permission should have been asked both as overlord of Richmond and of Huntingdon, and, he nearly added, of Scotland as well. Malcolm replied by marrying my elder sister Ada shortly into Holland, which enraged Curtmantle even further as the counts of Holland are in a stronger position than the dukes of Brittany, also richer and with prospects of trade with Moray and Inverness. By then, however, I was abroad with my own husband and had already given birth to Constance, finding the moors of Brittany much akin to the moors of Richmond, good for hawking and also with the strange dolmens rearing from a time no one remembers. However there was no great sprawling fortress such as had been ours in the north of England, ever since another ancestor of my husband's, Alan the Red, had raised the siege of York in his time for the Conqueror and gained Richmond, which later on Curtmantle took back, as was his way.

Matters sped badly for my husband, for Alix's father, Eudo de Porhoët, was in rebellion. The fault was Curtmantle's.

In course of the war, Alix herself had been handed over to him as a hostage. She was very beautiful, and shortly the fate of all personable young females left in Curtmantle's large neglected hands befell her. Indignation was rife through Brittany, fomented by her father, and war again broke out against my husband and his supporter the lecherous king of England and duke of Normandy; Curtmantle of course is both. Meantime I wanted to return to Scotland with my child, but when we reached safety at the English court we were detained with smooth courtesy; Constance, with her father's consent, had by then been betrothed to Geoffrey Plantagenet, at that time still the youngest prince. The surname — even the kings of Scots to this day still only have my mother's, which is de Warenne — had come about from the habit of Curtmantle's father, Geoffrey Le Bel, of sticking in his hat, when out hunting, a sprig of the *planta genista*, the yellow broom.

★ ★ ★

As might be expected, I remember Constance's birth. It took place in the lower tier of the curious double beds they have in Brittany, with the advantage that each partner may turn at ease without disturbing the other, except for marital encounters. When the child was born I was thankful that she resembled the Athelings; fair and beautiful, with a skin like a rose, and the fine features of my brother King Malcolm, still alive then, whom everyone called The Maiden from the brightness of his complexion and also, which greatly troubled our mother, by reason of this vow of chastity, which as I have said prevented his marrying and making heirs for Scotland. This was partly the fault of the Cistercians, who were spreading their inconvenient notions about at that time, and also the fault of the Arthurian legends, a book about which was dedicated to Queen Eleanor. The figure of Galahad attracted several hopeful young men and they tried to imitate him in purity of living, which is all very well if one is not a king. As it is, my second brother William has inherited the crown of Scotland and calls himself the Lion. Many men think themselves lions and, accordingly, fail to resemble Galahad: one evidently cannot be both.

★ ★ ★

I raised my eyes and met those of Queen Eleanor's French daughter-in-law, the wife of her eldest son Henry the Younger. Marguerite was herself a queen, as her husband, young Henry, the eldest surviving son, had been crowned in Curtmantle's lifetime to ensure a smooth inheritance at the latter's death. Marguerite, I thought, might well have resented the queen's late remark that King Louis VII ought to have been a monk, as King Louis was her own father by a second marriage. However as she had been sent across to England at three years old, it was unlikely that she remembered him. She had a gentle and biddable nature, was beautiful, and gave me her serene smile.

The solar still seemed empty without the presence, even briefly in passing, of Curtmantle himself. I wondered how he was faring in the forest and the snow, with the cold flakes — he would never admit to feeling them — drifting down between his cloak of ruby scarlet and his tunic collar of Lincoln green, trickling at last down the back of his thick neck beneath the closely cropped red hair. He never wore gloves unless for a hawk, and his big uncared-for hands would be cold, with the three rings always on them, one being his royal grandfather's seal. The second was a sapphire, and the third had belonged to his dead young father, Geoffrey Le Bel, and bore the gold pard of Anjou.

★ ★ ★

I was well aware, even then, that I must keep a curb on my thoughts concerning Curtmantle. He was, God knew, a manly man, and my blood is half Norman and my husband was elsewhere. Fortunately the pious Atheling half redeems such inclinations, but for the time I could not even resent the fact that Richmond itself had been seized back again by Henry II as a fief of the English crown. It seemed also that Brittany might be absorbed into

60

Normandy, of which last Curtmantle remained duke; and for Constance's sake I did what I might to try to prevent this from happening and to try to remember my duty to the man I had after all married. I compromised meantime by thinking not of Curtmantle himself, but of his parentage; that at least was at a safe distance from present events.

★ ★ ★

"His mother may have been by right Lady of England and Beauclerc's heir after her two brothers were drowned in the White Ship disaster, but Matilda the empress should have made quicker shift to get herself crowned. As it was, Stephen of Blois her cousin had the crown put on his own head at Westminster, and a crown makes a king."

My mother's youngest brother Ralph de Warenne, who had never married and used to travel between England, Scotland and Normandy like a knotless thread, gazed into his ale. I was seated between him and my other uncle Reynald, whom I liked less because he was boisterous and shouted when he spoke. He spent most of his time fathering children on his Mowbray wife in Cheshire, but when he rode south was generally where trouble might be found; it was he who, a little later, cut off the tail of Archbishop Becket's horse on the prelate's return to England from exile. It was an undignified thing to do, and my mother Countess Ada was ashamed of him. The eldest de Warenne brother of all, William the third earl, was dead on crusade, having spent most of his manhood years in prison under King Stephen. Like Beauclerc, he had left only a daughter, my fair cousin Isabel.

★ ★ ★

Isabel de Warenne is the reason why I know as much as I do about Beauclerc's daughter the empress, mother of Curtmantle. My cousin Isabel was as I say very beautiful, and her husband, who was King Stephen's younger son, loved her dearly; they were very happy together, although William was said to be too fat to give Isabel any children. He was an amiable person like his father, and died of fever in the Toulouse campaign which Curtmantle waged on behalf of Queen Eleanor's rights to the city and, also, because it guarded the trade route to the Mediterranean. My brothers Malcolm and William were there, but came safely home.

It became a question of who was to become Isabel's second husband. It was necessary for her to have one, for she was the sole heiress, as the empress had been, of her father, my eldest uncle the third earl of Warren and Surrey, he who had died on crusade. It was said he had gone there on release from prison to escape the tongue of his wife, and his heart was brought home later on to be buried at Lewes. This was the chief English residence of the de Warennes, though my mother and my uncle Ralph were brought up together in the Norman one, from which they had all come; Bellencombre, built above the river Varenne from which the family takes its name. Long ago, Werma, a de Varenne woman, was handfasted to an invading Dane named Herfast, whose sister became Duchess of Normandy and great-grandmother to the Conqueror. The latter's daughter Gundreda later married the de Warenne descendant who fought at Hastings, thereby acquiring three hundred manors and more land in England than any other follower of William the Conqueror. This accounts, with the later title given in the time of Rufus, for Isabel's vast inheritance, also her close relation to the Empress Matilda and the latter's second son.

Curtmantle's youngest brother, another William, had in fact been in love with my cousin Isabel for years. On Fat William's demise he greatly desired to marry her. Their marriage was prevented by Thomas Becket, who intervened at Rome because of consanguinity; there had been the two earlier marriages I have mentioned, tying the de Warennes firmly by blood to the Conqueror's descendants. The union of Isabel and William of Anjou was therefore forbidden, and although such things can be settled in time by enough money, young William could not wait. Instead, he went back to his mother the empress's court at Rouen, and died there of a broken heart, the only Angevin ever to do so as far as is known.

Becket had already perhaps incurred the King's resentment by being the foremost warrior in the field at Toulouse, by which I mean the best equipped, with the finest armour, the most richly arrayed following, the loudest brazen trumpets to sound before a charge. Curtmantle himself had nothing like it. In the days before he became a churchman Becket had to outdo everyone in splendour when he was chancellor — the embassy to France to secure Marguerite for Young Henry was one example — and while they were still friends, the King used to love to tease Becket by leaping, straight from the hunt, across his chancellor's carefully arranged dining-table, and sitting down to eat without warning, hot, untidy and unpredicted. He also said, one day when they were out riding together "Tom, there is a poor beggar; would not he like a warm cloak?" and the end was that he pulled Becket's fur-lined cloak from his shoulders and threw it to the beggar. Such things must be remembered now Becket is become a saint, after his murder for which Curtmantle was universally blamed. Nobody had been more cruel than the same future saint on the Toulouse campaign; he massacred many by his personal order, though otherwise the bloodletting was small owing to the presence of King Louis, Curtmantle's overlord for Normandy, inside the walls.

At any rate, when Becket was struck down in his own cathedral on St Stephen's Day, 1170, one of the four murderers cried out "That for my lord William, the king's brother!" and hacked at the dying archbishop's already wounded scalp. Meantime, poor Isabel had been married to Curtmantle's bastard half-brother got on some woman by Geoffrey Le Bel; a man calling himself Hameline Plantagenet, a brute who gave her children yearly. He was however loyal to the King, and guarded the Norman marches for him from Bellencombre, where he and Isabel thereafter lived.

Le Bel, young and personable, had disliked his wife the empress thoroughly, and refused to come to her aid during the course of her wars with Stephen though he was careful of Normandy for their son. Nevertheless there is a human side to this, and it is that of the empress. I learned a certain amount from my mother, whose own marriage was arranged, to end the war, by King Stephen's wife, that other Matilda, niece to the empress's pious Scots mother Edith Maud, the first wife of Beauclerc, she who had washed lepers' feet and died fairly young, no doubt of that and other mortifications.

Matilda of England — she was in fact christened Aaliz — was sent meantime abroad to Germany aged eight, to marry, four years later, the old emperor. Henry the Lion was good to her and the German people loved her, and later on when she was widowed and her father Henry I ordered her return, begged that she might stay among them; but it was not permitted. Her forced marriage then to a boy of fifteen, at the orders of Beauclerc, would have been uncongenial in any case, as the English in their Norman pride looked down on Anjou, but old Henry had determined to secure his Norman borders. However, Matilda was by then passionately in love with the man who would shortly steal her throne; her handsome and easy-going cousin, Stephen of Blois, already married. A letter of hers has been found which proves this; *You know well enough what passed between us two.* It was said later that Curtmantle himself was in fact the son of Stephen, and this is possible; certainly the Angevin marriage had been unfruitful for the first seven years. Curtmantle, before he became king, used to refer to himself as Henry FitzEmpress. Certainly he was Matilda's son, but also coveted Le Bel's Angevin lands.

The barons of England — Le Bel did secure Normandy as I say — tried to think of reasons for disavowing the promise they had made Henry I before his death to honour the empress as Lady of the realm. Firstly they tried to say that Beauclerc had changed his mind on his deathbed and had willed the crown to Stephen, his sister's son. However there were no witnesses to this except a troublesome old baron in Norfolk who died at the age of ninety. Then they spread the suggestion that the empress was illegitimate in any case because her mother had been a professed nun. "That was nonsense," I remember my own mother saying. "King David told me that his sister Edith used to jump on her nun's veil in Romsey convent which the abbess, her aunt Christina, had made her wear; and he remembers his own father King Malcolm Ceann Mór tearing one from Edith's head her mother Queen Margaret had put on her in Scotland earlier, swearing no daughter of his should take the veil. Queen Margaret — you were called after her, my dear — had the notion that all her sons ought to be monks and all her daughters nuns, but it would have caused great difficulty in the matter of heirs, as is well seen with your brother Malcolm." Mother had always tried in vain to persuade Malcolm to marry, or at least to fall in love with one of the eager young women about Court. He was so handsome it was a pity he did not succumb, but he died instead.

★ ★ ★

Yet another tale was spread, probably when the young Curtmantle had successfully laid siege to a castle of King Stephen's and they had later parleyed on either side a ford. It was claimed then that the old German lion, Emperor Henry, Matilda's first husband, was not dead at all but had been on pilgrimage, or in one version had entered a monastery. He returned, or was awakened to events, later, and when the time came truly to die sent for Matilda to bid her farewell. It was true that her presence was unaccounted for at one time, but there may have been other reasons including the fact that Le Bel had once banished her from Anjou till her manners improved.

This tale may be true or not — probably not, as it resembles others of the kind concerning different persons — and by then it was already evident, as during Stephen's reign it had been said God and his saints slept, that Curtmantle and no other was England's salvation. He was therefore peaceably accepted as Stephen's successor, and Stephen obliged by dying in timely fashion in his bed.

Altogether the whole business, and

our relationships, begins to resemble a tapestry seen from the back; but it will be evident that I and my daughter Constance were not the least among those frequenting the court of England whether we would or not. Constance of course could remember little else. However I made certain that she was informed concerning our ancestry. It is as ancient as any, and as proud.

* * *

My great-aunt the Scots princess Edith, later Beauclerc's queen Matilda or, as she was always known, the Good Queen Maud, was steadfastly wooed in her convent at Romsey by two suitors, despite the vigilance of her aunt Christina the abbess. Edith had been placed in the convent as a child with her younger sister Mary, the one who later became the wife of the count of Boulogne and produced Stephen's valiant queen. The two girls, and their young brother David, had been brought to England after the deaths of their parents and the seizure, for the time, of the throne of Scotland by a rival. The result was that David himself was reared by Henry Beauclerc and married richly by him later on to a young widow who brought Huntingdon as her dowry. Later David succeeded his brothers as King of Scots, which made relations with England amiable, the more so because Beauclerc had been successful in his suit of David's sister Edith and my maternal grandfather the second earl Warren had failed, to his great chagrin.

He had always disliked Prince Henry, youngest of the sons of the Conqueror, whether or not because of this rivalry, and had called him in derision Deerfoot because in those early days, being without enough money to provide himself with a horse for the hunt, Henry had to run after it. Later, having helped himself to the treasury and the crown, he could well afford a horse, a wife and, later, as many concubines as Solomon. However for the time he tried to please his bride, whom he had induced to change her name to Matilda on the specious excuse that the English could not pronounce the other. Edith Matilda was used to Saxon ways, her mother Margaret having been an

Atheling, and Henry therefore at first grew a beard after the Saxon fashion, to please her.

A son William Audelin, and a daughter, who was to become the empress, were born to them, and meantime my Warren grandfather had made a disgruntled marriage with the widowed countess of Leicester, who had children already by a first marriage. The subsequent squabbles of her parents made my mother glad that she and Ralph, as the two youngest of the second union, were brought up separately at Bellencombre and not at Lewes.

Meantime Beauclerc, on a visit to Normandy, was mocked there by a prelate, who told him he and his courtiers resembled he-goats. Beauclerc therefore had himself shaved, and his courtiers, having grown beards unwillingly because he did, parted with them cheerfully likewise. Perhaps by then Edith Matilda's increasing piety made her hesitant as a wife; for whatever reason, the clean-shaven Beauclerc began to take to other beds. He was responsible to all his bastards, of which there were reputed to be over twenty, and married the girls well, one as I have said into Brittany, and she became my first husband's mother without any thanks. Meantime, Beauclerc's queen having died, his only legitimate son was drowned in the Channel: and the widowed empress was forced to come home.

★ ★ ★

That apart, relations with Scotland fared well enough till Beauclerc died himself, when King David, who had taken the vow to defend the rights of his own niece the empress, did so against King Stephen. The result was the beginning of terror at the name of Scots in the north of England, particularly certain warriors attired in what the English at first took to be the garb of dancing-girls until events proved otherwise.

★ ★ ★

"It was more than that," said my uncle Reynald, not shouting for once in case he was overheard; instead, he thumped his fist on the table where we sat.

"The Lady of England had to shift her stately backside fast enough after sitting down to a banquet she never ate, for the Londoners came at her in force, having been asked for gold, not civilly. That's why they favoured Stephen; he was civil. Also, his wife Matilda — God knows there were far too many Matildas — brought them the wool trade by way of Boulogne."

"Matilda of Boulogne our cousin was a brave woman," said my uncle Ralph reflectively. "She fought Stephen's war for him, in especial while the empress held him in prison."

"The empress was no doubt used to being obeyed in Germany," snorted Reynald of Poynton. "Geoffrey of Anjou should have beaten her; maybe he did. He had no time for her, but did his best for their son. Whatever they say, Curtmantle — " he looked over his shoulder — "will own no other father, because he coveted Anjou and kept it from his brother Geoffrey after Le Bel's death. He will own the world before he is done."

"Maybe," said uncle Ralph, and drained

his ale adding "Count Geoffrey gave the empress three sons despite her high-born ways. She had Scottish blood from the older race of kings, who did not take kindly to being ordered."

"Nor do our present nephews of the newer race," grunted Reynald, who was on the whole nearer them in Cheshire. I spoke up then for my brothers, of whom by then only William and young David were left. Malcolm had died in the year before I and Constance took refuge at Curtmantle's court. I knew Curtmantle was determined to make his kingdom again as it had been in his grandfather's day, and disputes had soon arisen over Northumbria and Huntingdon. "The King here," I said, "should remember that King David was one of the few to honour his vow to the empress, and not only fought for her at Northallerton, losing many men, but almost got himself killed fighting on her behalf at Winchester itself." I sat back and remembered what mother had told me of the Battle of the Standard, as it was known, when my father Henry of Huntingdon rode back unharmed with his vizor down among the enemy's cavalry, for in those times there were not yet devices on shields.

"Do not say, niece, what our liege lord should remember," shouted uncle Reynald, glad of an excuse to raise his voice. It was politic, no doubt, to voice his own support for Curtmantle, but by now nobody doubted it: nothing else was safe.

* * *

After they had gone I recalled hearing the requiem masses for Matilda the empress, which had been said in England after her death in Rouen the year after I left Brittany. Many years had passed since Matilda's attempt to gain the throne without success, for no woman had ever ruled England, though many in Saxon times had shown the ability to do so, mostly of necessity in convents. Norman England was however no convent, and needed a strong hand; and the memory of Beauclerc's Scots queen, beloved for her charities, was not enough to make the claims of her foreign daughter weigh against the accepted custom of a man's rule. Moreover, Stephen, as has been said, had got himself crowned.

Stephen of Blois was the second of three brothers, all of them sons of the Conqueror's strong-willed daughter Adela. The only one of the three to inherit her nature and his was the third, Henry, who would have made as good a king as his namesake Beauclerc; but he had already entered the Church. The eldest, Theobald, was idle and treacherous; Henry of Blois therefore passed him by, and instead entreated the middle brother, kindly and handsome Stephen with his gallant wife from Boulogne — that Matilda was also a descendant of Malcolm III and Margaret, therefore our kinswoman — to cross seas forthwith to Westminster and have himself crowned king. Thereafter, whichever way the fortunes of the civil war went, no one ever referred to Stephen without his royal title; a coronation settles all argument, and Empress Matilda should have thought of it in time.

However her unhappy second union with Geoffrey Le Bel of Anjou, no matter how she and the English looked down on it, had produced Curtmantle; and despite his plebeian appearance, which no doubt resembled that of the Conqueror's maternal forebears the humble tanners of Falaise, she must have known early that the thunderous spirit of her father Beauclerc lived on in her eldest son. As a stocky red-haired freckled child of nine, he first made known his claim to the heirship of England in person with the help of his father: the second attempt was made by his own will when he was sixteen. The third, partly owing to the recent death of King Stephen's unpleasant heir, was successful; Fat William, Isabel's husband, had no ambitions to rule England, and Henry FitzEmpress was declared successor to the crown after King Stephen's death when it should occur. That brought Curtmantle to the throne of England the year after his scandalous marriage with Eleanor of Aquitaine. 1153 age 18 + 29

★ ★ ★

He had enough determination and intelligence for ten men, and had been the favourite of his young father Le Bel, who saw to it that his mind was not neglected. I can remember Curtmantle's talk later on, made in his strange hoarse voice and including anything from poetry or theology to falconry, for which he had a passion. He read whenever he had time. He could charm anyone, especially any woman; that is well seen by the conduct of Eleanor, newly divorced, much sought as a wife immediately thereafter by every fortune-hunter in Europe including the idle Theobald of Blois himself, who tried to entrap her by playing host on her journey south. "I had to kick him where it hurt, and get myself at once into the saddle to travel on to Poitiers," she would say, as if it had been no great matter; but she was already twenty-nine then, and galloped fifty miles by night after that: and, also, an attempt by Curtmantle's seventeen-year-old second brother Geoffrey of Nantes, as he was later known, to waylay her. Henry, duke of Normandy, already met with in Paris and by then aged eighteen, was already her choice, and they were married. The union of course caused comment, but at first was evidently rapturous, and produced a son named William who died at three years old.

King Stephen had been too easy a king meantime, and his barons did as they chose during and after the wars with the empress, which followed. Meantime, Curtmantle had been knighted at the Scots court in Carlisle by King David my great-grandfather. Henry II in turn made much more of a delayed favour in knighting, in the end, my young brother Malcolm the Maiden; that was ungrateful, to say the least, and may have goaded Malcolm into allowing my Breton marriage.

* * *

Geoffrey Le Bel himself is not much considered in England, where they still regarded the Angevin marriage of Matilda the empress as degrading. Possibly the rumoured descent of the House of Anjou from the devil is something to do with it; and an ancestress named Melusine flew out of the window in church, leaving her cloak in the hands of her husband's attendants, when he had particularly desired her to remain for the elevation of the Host; all that was left was the smell of brimstone. Nevertheless King Henry Beauclerc had considered Anjou, with its nearness to Normandy, important enough to provide a bride earlier on for poor William Audelin; as it happened she — her name was, inevitably, Matilda also — was not drowned with him, but left no heir. Geoffrey Le Bel was her brother, son of Black Fulk and descendant of the unfortunate lady who was consumed by fire at the stake in her wedding dress. This, and the evident disapproval of the English, did not affect the young man one jot. Geoffrey became in fact an excellent ruler, later also governing Normandy on behalf of his disliked wife, whom as is well known he resolutely declined to support in person during her descent on England. In course of this the empress was not only chased out of London by its citizens while about to sit down to her banquet, but also later forced to escape across the frozen Thames in a snowstorm, disguised in what is by custom politely described as a white mantle. There are however few of these outside Cistercian monasteries, and my present husband, who supported Matilda in his youth, insists with soldierly precision that it was a nightgown and he saw it for himself.

In the end Curtmantle's mother returned to her abhorred marital duties, and the three sons she bore Le Bel then and earlier were Curtmantle himself, Geoffrey of Nantes, as he is still called — he caused much trouble briefly in Brittany, but fortunately died — and William, Isabel's unlucky lover, after whose birth the empress was never well and in process of losing her health, gained wisdom. She became known as a restraining influence on Curtmantle in her later years, as his frequent untamed rages could have unfortunate results, including the murder of Archbishop Thomas Becket.

Curtmantle respected his mother, but was devoted to the memory of his father, who died aged only thirty-six. Le Mans, the place where Geoffrey Le Bel is buried, was always the king's favourite place of them all in his incessant journeyings to and fro. I myself have lost count of the number of times Curtmantle must have crossed the Channel, even in storms. Once there, he would cover unbelievable distances, never flagging in demonic energy, as usual hardly ever taking time to sit down to eat. Nevertheless his purpose held firm that, having at last gained England — Stephen's heir died mysteriously in the end after burning down the monks' corn at Bury, but of course Curtmantle had fought knowledgeable campaigns before that, and had spent some time with my parents at Carlisle, at King David's court, where as I have said he was knighted — having gained the land at last, he determined to make it again as it had been in his grandfather Beauclerc's day, to the last yard of soil. That accounted for his worsening relations with my kin in Scotland, though William, my brother, after he became king, used for a time to ride down and spend Easter, and young David was always familiar with the English court, where he had spent some years as a boy. However part of what they thought was theirs Curtmantle thought was his, which is the cause of most wars. Also, he had plans for his sons. The daughters he arranged to be married abroad while they were still children, as is often done; it is perhaps best for a bride to be brought up in her husband's country.

I wish I could remember Curtmantle as a young man at Carlisle. Perhaps I should have paid less heed, in event, to that other I met later on, flying his hawk at Richmond near York. One never knows.

* * *

"You are fallen silent, Margaret," said the Queen.

I replied that I was waiting for news of my lord out of Brittany. The last I had heard was that he had taken refuge in Guingamp, which was part of his appanage. The Queen shrugged, raised a jewelled finger and beckoned to her overdressed jongleur Bernard de Ventadour, whom she had brought from her native Provence and who sang in what I always found to be discordant sounds of the kind to which they are accustomed there: I prefer our soft Gaelic harps. Bernard sang, in what truly sounded like an ass's braying to me, a verse which had become popular at the time of the Queen's second wedding, and which I therefore understood although it was in the *langue d'oc*.

Did I own all lands from the Rhine
*   to the Pyrenees*
I would give them all
To have the queen of England lying
*   in my arms.*

Eleanor was still very beautiful, although her red-gold hair was greying beneath the veil. She never wore her crown. After their coronation together at Westminster soon after the marriage, she and Curtmantle, then still in great accord, laid the two crowns together before the high altar of Worcester cathedral, taking a vow never to wear them again. "In fact," Eleanor said to me once, "they were too heavy."

Much had gone amiss since then. The main trouble was that Curtmantle would give his wife no say in governing her great possessions, which increased his own beyond the extent of land in the suzerainty of the King of France, who remained his overlord as well as Eleanor's former husband and father of two of her children. It was a situation that would have required gentler handling than it received, because even at the beginning Curtmantle had summoned my brother Malcolm across seas in his time to aid him, as vassal for Huntingdon, at the siege of Toulouse, by right Eleanor's and occupied by a kinsman, also by Louis himself. That had come to nothing, except that Malcolm, and also my second brother William, became knights there at last. By now, though, Eleanor had become convinced that she had exchanged the dull narrow etiquette of Paris, and Louis' equally dull company in bed, for still duller Oxford, Winchester and Clarendon, where in every case she was kept strictly with her women and no longer consulted on high matters or any. The only other enjoyment besides Bertraud that she had was the company of her growing sons, and soon enough she began to mock their father to them, spreading discontent with his authority.

She could not be blamed, perhaps; she felt herself used yearly as a broodmare, though Curtmantle's company in bed cannot have been as unrewarding as that of King Louis in any case. However Eleanor of Aquitaine, despite all they say of her, was never lewd; she had too many other interests, such as painting, illumination, books, music and the world. Like the king, she could talk about anything; it is a pity they did not spare more time to talk together after the first. The gossip about the queen had been avid throughout Europe from the beginning, and may have been the reason why Curtmantle early decided to keep her close; it was said she had, while still in Paris, had an affair with his own father Geoffrey, which may well have been possible given the lack of awareness that she would later marry Geoffrey's son. I do not think however that the etiquette surrounding a queen of France would have permitted such a thing, though when she accompanied King Louis to the Holy Land there were still other rumours. It was said by then that Queen Eleanor had slept with her uncle at Antioch and had also visited Saladin himself in his silk tent dressed as a man, and he likewise had become her lover. With regard to that, I have certain information by way of my mother, then newly in Scotland, who received it in turn from her de Warenne kin, some of whom were on that crusade or else the next or the last: at any rate, they were informed. "Saladin was never inclined to luxury, and would not have had a silk tent in the first place," mother assured me. She added that although it was true that he had seventeen sons, the Saracen was strict with himself according to the rules of his religion, and no woman dressed as a man would have been admitted to his presence. As for Antioch, it is true that King Louis had Eleanor forcibly removed from that city, which was said to contain every possible delight. More I cannot say, except that Oxford and childbearing must, after so many adventures, have ceased to be altogether diverting.

She went into labour, I recall, shortly after the sewing session I have mentioned, when it had grown dark. On Christmas

Eve, a boy, the last, was born and they called him John. I have never before taken a dislike to a baby, but as soon as I perceived him I withdrew. It might have been the fact that his nostrils were already wide, flaring like a stallion's.

His father had no complaints. I heard, that time as others, Curtmantle's return from the hunt; he was alone. The slaughtered deer had been brought in earlier, their soft noses covered with blood, their feet tied together on long poles for transport. I heard the king come in, then his hasty footsteps hurrying to the birth-chamber. He must have been pleased with the baby, who became his favourite and for some reason still is so, despite everything.

★ ★ ★

It was my youngest brother David, riding down as he used to do from his great fief of Huntingdon, where he lived with far more magnificence than we did, who brought me secret word from our mother in Scotland. She herself had been ailing for some time and seldom now travelled, and I had not seen her since my marriage. Smooth excuses were still given which prevented my travelling to visit her or to show her Constance, on whom she had never set eyes.

The news David brought was to be kept entirely to myself. Our brother William, King of Scots, had entered into a private alliance with the King of France, Louis VII.

I had seen Queen Eleanor's first husband on one occasion when the Court was at Argentan. I thought then that he was the kind of man who can never have been young. Piety was in every feature except his eyes, which were those of a bewildered child. It is said that he had loved Eleanor in an almost childlike way and grieved at parting with her, but despite his saintliness he would not have been human not to resent the fact that his former wife, who had borne him only two daughters in fourteen years, had given Curtmantle a posse of sons in six. Louis's own second daughter by Eleanor had they say been conceived in a state of deep embarrassment to both parties after a personal blessing in bed by the pope, following their disagreements on the crusade and the forced removal of Eleanor herself from Antioch. All was supposed to be, again, as it should, therefore; but still the only result was a further daughter, and no woman can by law inherit France.

It had been unfortunate for Louis from the beginning that his elder brother Philip, who should have been king after their father, died when his horse stumbled over a pig. Louis was compelled to accept the throne despite having several extremely fertile younger brothers. He himself was not made for marriage, being steeped in the notion some unfortunate persons have that original sin is the same thing as marital intercourse. He was the laughing-stock of Europe when, after the divorce from Eleanor and his second marriage with a princess of Castile, only more daughters were born including Marguerite. The question of her marriage, at three years old, to the young son of Henry and Eleanor might not have been entertained, but Thomas Becket, still Curtmantle's great friend and chancellor, brought so magnificent an embassy to Paris to ask for the child's hand that the dazzled French could not refuse. "I should like to have seen the monkeys riding on horses," I remember Constance saying when I told her the tale.

However Curtmantle outwitted Louis again over the disputed Vexin, the land between France and Normandy, which was demanded as Marguerite's dower. At that time she was, as a bride for Young Henry, by far more important than she became later on when Louis' third marriage brought him a son at last, as well as a third Alais who was later sent to England.

Curtmantle was also, of course, duke of Normandy, and this alone would have made him a thorn in the side of the king of France. France had once owned the great coastal region, and had parted with it to the invading Northmen for the sake of being left in peace. That had been in the days of Charles the Simple, but the kings of France never ceased to hope to regain it. Nearby Brittany was the obvious place to start nibbling at edges, which is why Curtmantle spent almost a year in Brittany two years after I had taken refuge at his court.

Curtmantle's second brother Geoffrey, who coveted Normandy for himself, was meantime making trouble in Nantes. Their father Le Bel was by then dead, and there is a story, improbable to anyone but the Angevins, that young Geoffrey would not allow the handsome corpse to be buried until his elder brother had sworn an oath whose conditions Curtmantle was not permitted to know. These were, of course, the cessation of Normandy and Anjou. Curtmantle took no notice. Le Bel was suitably interred at Le Mans, and Geoffrey retired in dudgeon to Nantes, where fortunately he soon died.

It was about this point that Curtmantle seduced Alix de Porhoêt, whom he had demanded as hostage. He used the excuse that her father Eudo had betrayed his promises, but it would no doubt have happened in any case. The result was that the outraged Eudo joined Raoul de Fougères and the de Thouars brothers in the Breton rebellion and in the end, was forced to escape to Wales, a place whose unpredictable valleys had baffled Curtmantle already.

All this my brother King William would know, but at third hand, though he once visited Normandy, staying briefly with our cousin Isabel at Bellencombre. That no doubt is when he made contact with King Louis, though it is questionable if they met. It was in fact the commencement of a tremendous conspiracy against Curtmantle which took years to perfect. I think that had I known all that was to happen, I might well have betrayed my mother Countess Ada's secret to Henry II; she herself cannot have known entirely to what it would lead.

★ ★ ★

There was a further insult to King Louis which may have been fortuitous, but by that time he was sheltering Becket, already for some years Archbishop of Canterbury. Curtmantle had had one of the tidy notions peculiar to his mind, and had decided that he and Tom Becket between them would be ruler, chancellor and archbishop in one accord in England.

Unfortunately he had reckoned without the dedication Becket brought to any part he played. He had been the best equipped fighter at Toulouse, the most magnificent ambassador to France to ask for Marguerite, and now he would be the most devout archbishop of Canterbury since St Alphège, who was done to death by the Danes after a banquet when they threw meat-bones at him. Becket began by returning the chancellor's seal to Henry, who was then across the Channel. Shortly he had himself ordained priest. After his death it was found that, far from lining his cloak with fur as formerly, he wore a hair shirt and drawers beneath his priestly robes which he allowed to become pervaded with lice. He also scourged himself daily.

Such habits found no favour with Curtmantle, who was angry at the disturbance of his cherished plans. The friends fell out increasingly over other matters than the legal trial of clerics, which is the best-known clause. I take no sides in that matter, but I know Marguerite of France was delayed at the king's order with her mother-in-law

Queen Eleanor across seas while Young Henry, who had been Becket's pupil and was devoted to him, was crowned by another hand at Westminster in his father's lifetime. This was a habit copied from France and supposed to secure the succession, and Becket himself in earlier days had done Curtmantle a service by preventing the crowning of Prince Eustace, King Stephen's rough-mannered heir, which ceremony would have continued the civil war in England at that time. Eustace however, like Geoffrey of Nantes, died in any case, supposedly, as everyone knows, for having set fire to the monks' corn at Bury.

Marguerite and Henry were crowned together later on. They eventually had one child, who died. I liked Marguerite; I hear she has been sent even further away now, married a second time to King Bela of Hungary. No doubt Curtmantle used his influence in this way, knowing repayment of Marguerite's dowry would be unlikely to be insisted on at so great a distance. However perhaps I misjudge him. His other plans, by then, were in great jeopardy.

2

"I WILL wear the pearls," I said.

My Breton waiting-woman Berthe, whom I had inherited by way of Conan's late mother, her namesake who had brought her up, so that she had been educated, shook her head.

"That monster will be enraged," she said, speaking French. I myself had had small opportunity to learn Breton, although I encouraged Constance to talk with Berthe in that tongue. "He sent orders," she went on now, "that you were to dress plainly for this occasion."

"It is my daughter's occasion as well as that of her betrothed. I will wear the pearls as I say, also the Hungarian coronet which belonged to my great-grandmother."

I sounded defiant even to my own ears, and Berthe drew a shocked breath. "Duchess, you are wood-mad. The monster — " she seldom referred to Curtmantle as anything else since his alleged rape of Alix de Porhoêt, the briefly preferred ruler of Brittany, while she was his hostage — "will chew straw and divest himself of his clothes in his rage. It has happened before. The innocent Alix — "

I did not want to hear, yet again, the tale of how Alix supposedly died on emergence from Curtmantle's lascivious embrace. It was my private opinion that the young woman had enjoyed the proceeding thoroughly. She had been removed, disgraced and pregnant, after return to her father in a state no longer fit to be seen in public, and was probably by now, like him, in Wales. It had been, no doubt, one way of removing a possible rival to Breton dominion, but Alix's faction could hardly have withstood the combined Norman and English attack in any case, though there was still a determined rebel named Raoul de Fougères hiding in his own forests near Dol.

I was less angry over that — it did not after all concern me except that much of Brittany had been ravaged — but I was angry about the ceremony about to take place today when young Geoffrey Plantagenet, aged twelve, was to be enthroned in Rennes cathedral as duke of Brittany even though his marriage to Constance was not yet permitted by the pope because of consanguinity. It was as though her rights were of no importance, and I was determined that both she and I would be noticed both by the crowds on the way, and the invited nobility in the cathedral.

The rights of my husband Conan, I knew, had to all intents lapsed. He was still making half-hearted warlike sounds at Guingamp, but it meant no more than that he supported the Anglo-Norman invaders against his own people. I had contrived to send him the sewn banner, as was my duty, but doubt if he displayed it. He had in fact had his spirit broken as a child by the dislike of his grandfather, and lacked interest in anything at all, even, by now, our marriage: that in its time had lasted just over four years, till I left for England.

I said a prayer for Conan within my mind, and took out the jewels from my baggage. The coronet gleamed. It was of gold, curiously wrought in interwoven scrollwork, and had belonged to Queen Margaret Atheling of Scotland, my great-grandmother for whom I had been named and who was herself half Hungarian. My mother had given it to me at my wedding. Queen Margaret is remembered for her piety, but mother, who had it from King David himself, who was Margaret's own sixth son, told me he remembered, before his flight into England after she died, her palace at Dunfermline filled with colourful and beautiful things, woven hangings and embroideries, and the Black Rood in the chapel, gleaming with jewels of many rich hues. That last — she held it as she died — he reclaimed when he came back to reign as King, but much of the rest had gone.

The pearls had a history also; mother had sent me those at Constance's birth. No doubt they should have been saved for my elder sister Ada, but she was not then a bride; and when she married in the following year it was in any case to the rich Count of Holland, who could buy her other pearls. These were different.

I held them up, admiring their milky

perfection. They were pearls from the River Tay, and had been painstakingly collected and matched there in the time of King Alexander, King David's elder brother; three of Margaret's sons had reigned in Scotland. Alexander was famous for his love of rich fine things no one else owned; he had once led up, in gift to the altar, a noble horse in silver trappings, bearing a suit of Turkish armour. The pearls he gave to his queen, who was one of Beauclerc's twenty-odd bastards but who bore Alexander no children. I had carried Queen Sibylla's pearls back with me now into Brittany, and when my daughter Constance was made a wife they should be hers. At present she was only eight years old.

I let Berthe hang the pearls about my neck and saw them gleam against my gown, transforming it. Presently, after my hair was combed out and the veil set on it, I myself put on the coronet. I had not worn it since I was a bride. I am said to resemble Queen Margaret Atheling, as did my dead brother Malcolm and, in a sturdier way, my youngest brother David of Huntingdon, who often rode down to visit me in England. I studied my own reflection in a polished mirror, and was not displeased. The crowds would not entirely forget Duke Conan's wife and daughter, though no doubt they would merely look on Constance as the future mother of Duke Geoffrey's sons.

She herself was brought to me wide-eyed, having been permitted to wear a narrow silver circlet for the ceremony. Beneath it her hair, like a silver-gilt veil, by now almost fell to her knees. She was a strange child who never said much, and used to see things which had not yet happened. I discouraged her from speaking of this, as it is an inconvenient gift and no doubt came from the blood she has, on both sides, of the old Celts further back. She exclaimed at my grandeur: there were not many great occasions she could remember. In fact I think the last had been the crowning of Young Henry and Marguerite, years ago now when they themselves were hardly more than children.

"You look very beautiful," Constance said to me shyly. She was kept in her place too much by the sisters of her betrothed, who with the exception of Joanna were as cruel as the brothers. I was glad that Geoffrey appeared to be the most likeable of these, although he was, as the Scots say, too sweet to be wholesome. He had developed smooth ways in order to get his own, the elder brothers, especially Richard, being bigger and stronger. Richard in particular was a bully, and the Queen's favourite.

I told Constance she looked as beautiful as I did and bent to kiss her cheek; it was like a cool flower petal. We went hand-in-hand to where the escort waited to ride to the cathedral. There were crowds lining the roads, as I had foreseen, but they called no blessings on the Angevins who had ruined their country: only, when they saw me and my little daughter, there was a sound of pleasure. I looked at them as we rode past, the men shaggy and shy, some in the round hats they wear, the women with their heads in clouts. They were often thin-faced, having endured much. They are a tenacious people who remember the past more clearly than the present, and to this day, though the Danish raids are long over, the Vannetais will wade out and set fire to any ship which is seen to be approaching, partly because their pride is roused at having had Vannes declared no longer the capital, as it is too near the sea and invited attack. That however was over a century ago, and in the new inland capital of Rennes today, the cathedral's great bell tolled. It was a fine day, and the pale sun shone on other clustered circlets; young Geoffrey's, whose red-gold curls were contained in a gold one, and Young Henry, who was never without his crown. Homage had to be rendered to him today as well as to Curtmantle, of whom there was still no sign.

We dismounted at the cathedral door, and I saw the gleam of gold thread on the copes of two bishops, those of Rennes and of Dol, and the hastily contrived grandeur of the local nobility and their wives, who had been invited to be present. The procession formed, followed by the crowds as far as that might be done, for not all would be able to enter. We ourselves went in.

Curtmantle was waiting, seated on a

raised dais near the altar, which was made ready for mass. He must have arrived unannounced, although expected. I should have known in any case that, even here, he would be in command. He was clad as usual, as though this was no particular occasion, except for the rings he always wore and the shoulder-brooch which fastened his short cloak. His presence was so powerful that it was impossible to think of anyone else as being at the centre of events. Young Henry was far handsomer than he, and regally clad in white and ermine, but hardly anyone noticed him as he climbed up to his father's side to receive supposedly equal homage. I saw Curtmantle fix his eyes on my coronet at once, and on my pearls, regarding me with a red and angry light in them like that of a wild boar. I recalled hearing of the occasion, about a year previously, when Roger du Hommet, a churchman friend of my brother William's who walked in procession nearby, had been a witness of the chewing of straw and casting off of Curtmantle's clothes in one of the rages which had become accepted as evidence of the King of England's descent from the devil. "It concerned King William and Northumbria," Roger had said somewhat deviously: in fact, as I was to discover later, it concerned my brother William and the secret pact with King Louis he confirmed openly later on. If Curtmantle tore off his clothes now, I reflected, it would look like public penance. However it did not happen, despite my appearance. We took our places, and the ceremonies began.

Young Geoffrey, aged twelve and resembling the angel he was not, performed his homage in proper course, hands placed between his father's and then his eldest brother's. Although this act meant, in effect, that Brittany had now become the vassal of England, Normandy and Anjou, everyone in church seemed to regard Geoffrey favourably; he contrived popularity later on among the Bretons. There was the pervasive smell of incense after Mass, and singing; during the long ceremony, Geoffrey was invested with the dukedom in place of my husband Conan IV. As a gesture, Constance was finally allowed to place her hand on the raised wrist of her betrothed as the procession left the cathedral. She had been overawed by the necessity, but as they passed two shabby young men of the minor nobility who stood by the door, she dropped her formal stance, held out both hands and smiled in delight as though to friends not met with for long. I was behind her, and knew who the young men were; the de Thouars brothers, Poitevins whose great castle Curtmantle had long since levelled to the ground and had lopped their lands, leaving them penniless. They fell each on one knee, and kissed the child's hands and then my own. The episode puzzled and disturbed me; why had Constance stopped then? She could not possibly remember the de Thouars; their loss had taken place in 1159, the year before my own marriage to Conan.

"I do not know them as yet," she said later, "but I will."

I asked her no more then, for Curtmantle sent for me on our return. By that time he was striding up and down in impatience and anger, as though the only event of the day had been my forbidden wearing of jewels. I still had them on.

"You disobeyed me, madam," he grated. "I sent orders that you were to dress plainly. Do you suppose I do not have enough trouble already with this stubborn people?" He sounded like some Biblical prophet who has been offended in no godly fashion. "It was unfitting that anyone except my son should put themselves forward on this day," he said. "Moreover I expect to be heeded."

His eyes dwelt on the pearls. "By rights those are mine," he announced. "My aunt Sibylla left no children. If I took them off your neck and whipped you with them, madam, I would be justified, but for your position. As for the crown — "

I intervened; the prospect of being whipped by him with my own rope of pearls was strangely exciting, like a tale from the Crusades and Queen Melisende. "Sire, it is no crown," I said levelly. "It is no more than a dead queen's coronet, which my ancestress, whose brother Edgar should, as you know, have inherited the English throne, wore, I believe, on her daily rounds of doing good in Scotland, of which she had become queen. Our crown there is in any case richer by far." Through what I knew was my insolence — but it always paid to stand up to him — I remembered that crown which mother had had made in haste for my twelve-year-old brother Malcolm when King David died, my father being dead already in the previous year. Had he lived, he would have worn the crown instead and mother would have been queen of Scots. As it was, she had acted as regent.

"There were no coronations in Scotland till your mother took it upon herself to have her son crowned as well as being anointed on that stone they think so highly of," growled the King now, having evaded the question of Edgar Atheling, as well he might. "Many Scots," he shouted without necessity, "abhor your great-grandmother's memory and in her time disliked her thoroughly. She brought in the pope and Sunday observance. Before that the Scots were savages, and in most ways still are."

I remembered that he was having

trouble with the pope at present over the matter of Archbishop Becket, who showed signs of returning to England after six years' exile; there would be more trouble soon. The King grinned suddenly, showing strong wide-spaced teeth.

"You are a thrawn Scot yourself, woman; what induced you to speak with de Thouars at the door? Their castle was said to be impregnable and I took it in three days, and reduced it to rubble. They are no longer of any account, and should not have been inside."

"Neither is Ralph de Fougères of account, no doubt, but he is still alive and will be heard of again in Brittany; you reduced his castle of Dol also, sire, but castles can be rebuilt."

"Get out, before I forget you are a king's sister; nevertheless your brother William had best have an eye to his secret doings with France. Do you suppose I know nothing of that? Go now, and in the future conduct yourself in seemly fashion, as ordered by me."

"As your guest, sire, whether I will or not, what else can I do? I am only a

poor woman, with few protectors here."
I was not as abject as I sounded, and he
knew it.

The hard Plantagenet eyes surveyed
me, their red look gone. "Go," he said
again more quietly, and I made a deep
curtsey and left. I should have known
that his mind, which occupied itself with
every detail, was still partly occupied with
myself, despite the coming troubles with
Becket. I took off Queen Margaret's
coronet thoughtfully, and replaced it and
the pearls in my baggage. I did not know
where we would be ordered to go next,
but thought it might well be to Bayeux.
Marguerite had been left there long ago
in company with Queen Eleanor, in
order that her personal coronation might
be delayed; she and Young Henry had
wanted to be crowned by Becket, whose
right it certainly was. I let myself forget
the matter, and later, after the feast, went
to look at Constance, by then asleep
in bed, her stomach full and her hair
plaited for the night. She looked flushed
and beautiful, like other children. I went
to my own place and tried to forget
Curtmantle and the effect he had on me

and, probably, on all women including Alix de Porhoêt.

* * *

Although I was with the Court at Christmas in the King's hunting-box at Bures near Bayeux, I did not see four knights slip out of the hall after his celebrated remark made in anger about the man he by then called a low-born clerk. I heard, of course, of the murder of the archbishop at Canterbury as all Christendom did, and trembled for Curtmantle and what he had for once brought on himself without intention. The best that could happen now would be his excommunication, the worst war, or else interdict. However, with his usual cunning he avoided all such extremes by going off shortly to Ireland, where the pope's edicts, which take a long time to promulgate in any case, could not reach him, or at least not without great difficulty regarding storms and tides, which papal legates dislike notably.

I myself heard later, by way of mother's restless youngest brother Ralph de Warenne, who had never married and spent his days travelling incessantly with news from one branch of the family to the next, whether in Normandy, England or Scotland, that my elder remaining uncle, the third earl their brother by now being dead, had been first among those to insult Archbishop Becket as soon as he returned to England's shores, by cutting off the tail of his horse. "They had plundered his forests already while he was abroad, despoiling the game so that none was left for him," remarked Ralph, who had a kind heart, ruefully. That however was to prove the least of it, and Becket himself had been insulted in England years earlier. At Clarendon, where the King by custom hunted, he had been mocked in his archiepiscopal robes for almost tripping over a pile of faggots on the way out of a conference, carrying his crucifix. The mocker on that occasion had been Le Bel's bastard, Hameline Plantagenet, the loud-mouthed brute the King had forced my lovely widowed cousin Isabel to marry, failing his own younger brother William who had died of grief at Rouen because of Becket's consanguineous meddlings at Rome: at least, that was part of the argument. The marriage also conveyed the de Warenne title to the King's kin, a point all of us noted.

About the murder itself the Court talked in whispers, saying there were miracles already at Becket's tomb. The Young King Henry, who had been the dead man's pupil in early days, increased his smouldering resentment against his father, which greatly pleased the queen. "My son has bouts of piety fostered in his time by Becket, but like all Hal's other moods they do not last," she said, having summed up her eldest son long ago. Hal I knew was handsome and charming, but inconstant; his one enduring virtue was his fondness for his young wife Marguerite. Eleanor spoke of that marriage now, but not with pleasure; she loathed any mention of France. "Why, in the days when Becket was chancellor, and my husband's friend, he took so splendid an embassy to Paris as you know, with mastiffs and tuns of beer and monkeys riding on horses, and the rest, that the French said among themselves that this English king must after all be worthy of a Child of France, aged three, as a bride for his son not much older. In the nature of things they did not send one of my own two daughters by Louis from Paris; that would have been as incestuous as I was accused by Louis himself of having been at Antioch."

She set aside her paintbrush — she had been illuminating a script — and began to walk restlessly up and down the room, her body still graceful as an animal's although her face was ageing; but nothing would ever destroy the beauty of the bones. "Now, to send yet another French princess, a daughter of Louis' third marriage, over as a mere infant to be married to my son Richard is an insult to me," she said, staring at a wall-hanging of figured saints, I cannot now recall which. "Can you credit that this child is once again called Alais? There are three; the first my own, conceived with Louis in public in bed after the pope's personal blessing at the bed's end: can you imagine my feelings at the time, after having been removed from Antioch in such a way? *That* proved another girl, to Louis' great chagrin; then we made a laughing-stock of him, Curtmantle and I together, when I bore three sons in fewer years than it had taken Louis to make two daughters on me. That alone took fourteen years of marriage, if it may be called such. Louis divorced me accordingly in the end, not that he wanted to; but a girl in France cannot inherit. His second venture got only more girls, and all Europe laughed, for by then I was bearing sons to another husband: by God's wrath, I bore Henry Plantagenet five brats in six years, three of 'em boys; meantime Louis had his second Alais, evidently fancying the name he was used to, but the new wife died at a birth of one or other and within a fortnight, my monk was married yet a third time, and on that occasion got himself Philip. There is also this third Alais, who is to be sent over. It is an insult to me, I say, and my lord knows it. He gives me small pleasure since the birth of John, for there can be no others, as he is aware. I was fifty then, and by now feel a hundred."

She talked on, as if there was no

listener: I said nothing. As she often liked to do, she harked back to her adventures in course of the Second Crusade, when she had ridden by King Louis' side into Palestine with the Christian armies, after much travail on the way.

"France has shrunk by reason of losing my lands at the divorce, but in those days was considered great," she said. "Nothing had been lost then, except Normandy to the Northmen long since. Louis rode out having taken the Cross, on a horse with lily trappings, having also taken that flower as his emblem, and his great crown perched on top of his helmet, and his armour fashioned to show the belly he never had: I remember that well. We passed on the way by the relics of the poor who had ventured on a crusade by themselves the time previously, and never reached Jerusalem; their bones, piles of them, were still heaped by the roadside as we passed by, in the forests of Hungary. If they had had the sense to wait till other armies were made ready, they might have lived to enter the Holy City, or rather their sons might. As it is, Richard speaks of going on a third crusade when he is old enough, having no interest in this infant Alais of France."

To try and divert her, I asked if she had come across my eldest uncle the third earl of Warren and Surrey, who had been with the King of France's army and had been killed fighting the Saracens at Laodicea. Eleanor shrugged, and turned away from her staring at the wall-hanging.

"There were a great many fools out there alongside my first husband," she said. "I will never forget the day I and my women sat down to rest ourselves, for once, in a green valley full of fountains, rare in that arid land. Word came that the Saracens were surrounding us and would carry us off, and by then I would not have minded. Louis however thought it his duty to defend my honour, and ended by having to climb a tree to defend his own life." She laughed. "What a fool he must have looked, even more so than usual! Nothing happened, and would you believe that in the chronicles, they have stated that the King of France clung to tree-roots with one hand only on a steep mountain face, sweeping right and left with his sword and cutting off infidel heads with the other at every stroke? Louis, I am certain, never cut off a head in all his days; he would have entered the Church but for the death of his elder brother Philip, after whom he has named this son he has got at last. When I remember Antioch, the place where they found the Holy Lance deep in the ground after a vision on the First Crusade, and the talks I had with my uncle Raymond there about everything under the sun — *his* marriage was amusing — when I remember all of that, and the way I am kept now, narrow as the grave and strict as a convent, I do not forget certain things. Convents! Rosamund Clifford, who was the King's mistress for years, is in one now, for she began to weep with sin every time he lay with her. She is at Godstow on her knees, as anyone may go and see for themselves, although it is beginning to be said I made away with her as she is never now met with. That boy with freckles, the one also called Geoffrey, is in any case not hers; he is the son of a

Pictish whore my good lord met in youth at Carlisle, and she calls in once a month for her silver accordingly."

She talked on, and I reflected sadly that one thing was clear; by now, she hated her second husband even more than she had despised her first. Henry of Anjou, king of England and duke of Normandy, had made himself master of wide dominions whose lack made France herself shrink to a lesser power. Those lands were by right Eleanor's. There would be trouble, springing partly from the death of Becket which had shocked all Christendom; but perhaps more so from the hatred of Curtmantle's own wife, who he had deprived of any power and had used instead as a brood-mare, then left her alone.

★ ★ ★

Shortly, word came that I also was alone, not by then that I was used to any other state. My husband Duke Conan IV was dead at Guingamp; not gloriously of fighting there, but miserably of a chill. This was like him, but I dismissed the thought as uncharitable; sent for Constance, who did not remember her father enough to grieve; and had masses said for Conan's soul, hoping it rested in peace.

3

OUR litter swayed and jolted over the unspeakable roads. It had started to rain and they were deep in mud, which made the going slow; the horses dragged their hooves out each time with a heavy plopping sound, and carried us perhaps a yard further on. A leak of water had begun to drip, then trail, down between the supporting corner-poles and the leather roof. I shifted the cushions carefully to save them from being spoiled, anxious at the same time not to wake Constance who was asleep against me, tired out with the journey and with her hair covered in a green hawking-hood. At the other end of the litter were the two serving-women, Berthe as usual with my immediate necessaries, and Ykenai the king's Pictish whore.

The latter was returning to her own people, we were told. Berthe did not, as might have been expected, look down her nose, as the woman's Gaelic, which I also understood, was akin to Berthe's Breton and they could follow one another's speech. However in the nature of things this remained sparse. It was said at Court that Ykenai was capable of all filthiness, but that was the churchmen. She seemed harmless enough, and could never have been beautiful; she had a face with high cheekbones and small black eyes, expressionless beneath the headclout; she had long lost her teeth. Now that her son, the other Geoffrey, was grown to young manhood it was doubtless advisable to leave him with his father for his own advancement. Curtmantle spoke of putting him into the Church.

Without intending to stare openly at Ykenai I could not help watching her from beneath my eyelids. She would remember, I knew, Curtmantle as a young man, hardly more than a boy, at my grandfather's town of Carlisle where he had taken refuge in the civil wars and where King David had knighted him. She would have seen my mother, Ada de Warenne, the Norman bride who had come north to marry the handsome and devout Prince of Scotland, Henry Earl of Huntingdon, my father who had died when I was nine years old. There had been six of us children, but only five left orphans, for my young sister Matilda had died at the same time as my father, of a sudden fever that took them both. Great had been the mourning in the land, for the king of Scots had no other living son. He himself died, no doubt of grief, the year after. I remembered all of that; and wished I might talk with Ykenai, but not here; it was the place of neither of us.

Nevertheless she could have told me of how the folk had lined the roads to see the bride, my mother, pass by to end the war. The marriage itself had been arranged by Queen Matilda of Boulogne, King Stephen's plump and gallant wife who had fought his battles for him, King David having taken the side of his sister's child, the empress. Mother herself — I had not seen her for eleven years — used to tell me how when she travelled north she was sad and alone, not knowing how she would fare with a young man said to possess the virtues of a monk as well as a king. "We loved one another, however," she would say in her placid way. "I was an orphan when I came to Scotland; my father the second earl had died the year before, and my mother had been dead for eight years, but I hardly knew her; she was as a rule with the others at Lewes, while Ralph and I, being the youngest, were brought up together at Bellencombre."

Bellencombre I knew was the old castle on the river Varenne in Normandy, from which the family took its name; they had been there long before the coming of the Conqueror's forebears, the invading Danes. I gave up trying to remember as far back and recalled how saddened mother must have been at my brother Malcolm's early death; he had been her pride, and she had been anxious for him to marry and had had scant sympathy with the Cistercian vow he had taken. Nevertheless since his death she herself had founded, I knew, several Cistercian nunneries. No doubt she had changed in other ways as well, and aged. I might not know her again. As for William, no doubt he was the same as ever; big-boned and grim, laughing seldom, his chief pastime lechery. My youngest uncle, David of Huntingdon, I knew and liked better, as he rode down the oftener of the two to the English Court, and had spent a part of his boyhood in England as hostage. As our father and Malcolm had been he was handsome, though sturdier, the picture of a chivalrous knight; but no Galahad, and like William already had several bastards, although not enough between them to begin to rival King Henry Beauclerc in his day.

I wondered why they did not marry and decided they enjoyed their freedom. William was at present enamoured of a young woman in Eskdale who had borne him daughters. There seemed a dearth of sons.

I looked down at Constance, who had turned a little in her sleep. She opened her eyes suddenly as the litter jerked to a standstill. The curtains parted and a man's great figure appeared between them; the earl of Hereford, our escort to the north. He was a big solid man no longer young, who had supported the empress, Curtmantle's mother, in her wars, in the Marcher country. More de Bohuns had also fought at Hastings than any other Norman clan. Otherwise I knew nothing of them or of him, except that he was a man of few words. He had a square jaw and blunt features, seen now as he removed his vizor out of courtesy. Behind him, the pennants bearing his device hung limply in the rain. I recalled idly that it was William who had set this fashion, with his lion rampant. The de Bohun device was a talbot, a white hound's head.

"We are crossing the ford. You must all leave the litter. We will carry it over, with the baggage brought out from under, then yourselves."

I was pleased that he had taken the trouble to come in person and say so; one of the outriders could well have been sent. He vanished into the rain and I made ready to emerge, and we got ourselves out into the pouring wet, huddling in our cloaks. I wrapped Constance inside mine against my body: she was prone to chills. She snuggled against me. "When will we reach Scotland?" I heard her ask. She yawned, being still half asleep, and did not hear such answer as I could make, which was as well, for I knew no more than she.

Curtmantle had agreed, with surprising ease as his mind was no doubt occupied with the blame pouring in on him from all sides regarding Becket's murder, to let us return to my own kin after my husband Conan's death at Guingamp. I was pleased that the king had even allowed Constance to accompany me, not that I would have gone without her.

Curtmantle might however well have insisted that Geoffrey's betrothed be kept at the court of England. No doubt, I reflected uncharitably, he was close-fisted enough to be gladly rid of the charges of two guests.

I tried to pretend to myself that I looked forward to the company of my brothers and, when I got to Haddington, of my mother. Nevertheless Malcolm was dead, my sister Ada overseas, and everything would be different. Also I knew I would miss the barbed wit of Queen Eleanor and the occasional glimpses, which were all anyone had, of Curtmantle as he came and went. It would be cold in Scotland; cold and strange. Nevertheless I had asked to go.

I tried to remember old days in the Border country where my grandfather King David had built his great abbeys, and where we children had been happy together in company with our parents in Roxburgh, the king's own town, or at Slipperfield which now belonged to the Augustinians. At such times, in the warm green summers, King David himself would ride down to be among us, with his grey beard and sad eyes beneath the crown. He had used to watch my handsome father with pride; Earl Henry was the hope of Scotland and would reign on his father's death. Long ago his elder brother, the king's first son, had been strangled as a child by a rival to the throne, and that sadness had never left the king's face. However Earl Henry had been born then, and lived to be a fine knight, and was married now with heirs; all seemed hopeful, and then that summer of 1152 a fever took my father Earl Henry and our little sister Matilda as I say, and both were dead within hours. Great was the mourning in the land for the man high and low had loved, and had hoped would be king in time; now, there was only my brother Malcolm, a boy of eleven, to inherit.

Old King David did not die at once; he made arrangements for the boy to be escorted through his kingdom, guarded by six earls, in order that all might admire Malcolm's beauty. Then the king died, leaving my widowed mother to rule Scotland, a wild land made up of diverse peoples, for her son. It would be no wonder if I would find my mother aged.

Malcolm was dead now too. I would miss his slim splendour-loving beauty and his company. We had had much in common.

I stared at whatever place we had come to, watching the men lift the baggage, stowed as it had been on long poles under the litter, over the brown river, fording it where it ran least high with rain. I asked one of the men where we might be. He said we were near the Welsh border.

"Why so, when we are going to Scotland?" I asked. I had never before travelled by land, having gone to Brittany, at the time of my wedding, by sea from

Berwick. The man gaped at me, with two teeth missing from an old sword-cut, and mumbled something about the Roman road saving time. I began to be ill at ease: there was one, I knew, which ran to the north, but we appeared not to have taken it.

"Where is the earl?" I said. "Pray him to come to me." The man went away, then came back with word that my lord would attend me shortly. I stared at the brown hills seen dimly through the rain. We were soaked, lost, abandoned, and might well be hostages for all I knew. I should not have trusted Curtmantle; I should have waited for my uncle David of Huntingdon to come and escort us north.

It was a strange mysterious country we were in now, in a valley with hills on either side. I remembered how my brother Malcolm had lost his health down here in the King's wars, also the goodwill of his barons for coming at all. Many Bretons had taken refuge here from Curtmantle nevertheless, including Eudo de Porhoët and, doubtless, his daughter. Berthe had a tale she often repeated of how the monster — always that — had blinded the little Welsh boys and had cut off the ears and noses of the little Welsh girls on his campaign long ago. I had made her stop, as it frightened Constance to hear the tale when she was small. Later, to put matters straight in my child's mind, I had discovered the truth, which was not quite so bad; Curtmantle had indeed blinded twenty-five Welsh hostages, including two sons of a local prince, largely because the weather had been like it was now and had prevented the advance of his armies through the mud.

We watched, as it seemed interminably, while the baggage was unloaded from the litter and conveyed across the ford, then the litter itself, swaying, soaked and empty, its leather roof and curtains sagging with wet. I made as if to get back into it with Constance for such shelter as it provided when we could, but the earl rode up.

"They will bring your gear in that, and you yourselves will ride," he said. "It is quicker."

He hoisted me up before him in

the saddle, and I saw Constance taken up likewise by a de Bohun brother bearing the same talbot device. The two women rode before the men-at-arms. The day was beginning to darken as we travelled on. I asked my solidly armoured companion, who had at once wrapped his great cloak about me, how soon we would reach the Roman road.

"It is not far, but we will shelter tonight in my stronghold."

He spoke already with the intonation of Wales; regions have altered the French the Normans brought with them over a century since, that having in its time been already altered from the French spoken in France.

The earl was a man of few words, however, as I had already noted. I gave up attempts to talk with him and instead, wrung out my wet hair, which plastered my face as we rode. In the near distance I was then able to make out a fortress rearing, built of cream-coloured stones. It was unlike the wooden erections that mostly remained, even now, in England, except at strategic points where the King had ordered watch to be kept, having destroyed King Stephen's unlicensed castles long ago. This left only their rearing mottes scattered up and down the land; we had seen some already on the way.

"Where is that?" I asked, staring now at the great keep. It occurred to me that no prisoner could win out of it, once inside.

"Hereford," he said. He sounded pleased. No doubt it was a sign of power, and of the king's trust, to be lord of so strong a place. I said no more while we clattered into the courtyard, thankful to be aided down from the saddle at last; my wet clothes clung to me. A smouldering torch by the great door sputtered with rain, giving little light.

The woman Ykenai appeared then, evidently none the worse for the rain; she wore a garment of thick grey felted stuff and no doubt slept in it. She had evidently been given the task of looking to my comfort, while Constance was taken elsewhere in charge of Berthe. I made no demur about this arrangement; the main point was that we would be dried and fed, and had a roof for the night.

I was shown past the hall fire up winding stone stairs to a wall-chamber. In the old fashion the bed was not standing separately but was a mere alcove in the stones, with a great bull's hide flung over for covering. However there was a lit brazier, which was a comfort, and two flat rush-lamps glowed on the walls. I let Ykenai peel off my cloak, gown and shift, wring them out dripping and carry them away. We did not take that opportunity to talk. She would no doubt go down to where the great fire blazed in the hall; drifts of its acrid smoke came up here, but not badly. She would be able to speak with the Welsh retainers, some of whom might be almost kin. No one knows a great deal about the Picts; they were driven in the end to the far north and the south-west in my brother's country.

I slid into bed with my hair still damp, and covered myself with the bull's hide, which gave surprising warmth. When presently food was brought I managed to swallow part of it, though it was somewhat burnt; stockfish, a platter of stirred eggs, a manchet of bread and stoup of small-ale. I asked the servant if Constance was being looked after, and was told that she had had her supper and that Berthe was with her. I settled down and tried to sleep, noting that everything seemed disposed, more or less, for my comfort; there was a curved chair of wood which folded away if not wanted, a towel and ewer, and further off a privy covered over with black cloth. The rain had lessened outside and hardly now beat against the walls, and one could hear the accustomed comings and goings of a castle, also smell the smoke as before, and the burnt food. No doubt the earl of Hereford did not greatly care what he ate. I myself had taken more of the small-ale than anything else, and for this reason had to get up soon to make use of the privy. I looked to see if Ykenai had left a shred to cover me, but she had not; everything would be drying out in the kitchens, no doubt, or before the great hall fire.

I called out, but no one answered. In the end I spread out my hair, which had dried, like the fabled wife's of Leofric of Mercia, should any come. I went then to the privy, used it, and cleaned myself afterwards by means of the ewer and towel, having replaced the black cloth. It occurred to me that Humphrey de Bohun must have few women in his castle; no doubt he took Welsh peasants as he needed them. My chamber resembled a soldier's tent, with bare necessities only, and no floor-straw. I called out a second time, for someone to come and bring fresh water and if possible, to empty the privy. This time a voice replied, and from close nearby.

It was a man's, hoarse and unforgotten. Curtmantle and no other was standing by the wall, regarding me expressionlessly where I stood, naked as Eve. I covered my breasts with one hand and my privy parts with the other. He must have seen them in any case while I was relieving myself, and my cheeks flamed. How long had he been here, watching? What was he doing here at all? He was supposed by everyone to be in Ireland. My thoughts whirled; what would happen now? I thought I knew; with Curtmantle and a naked woman there was as a rule only one ending. I prepared to fight; he would not take me easily, I remember telling myself, believing I meant it.

He strode over, scooped me up in his arms and carried me to the bed while I struggled, aware of the smell of rain from his cloak. "Leave that," he said. He cast me on the bed, heaved the great bull's hide over me, and went to the curved chair, flinging himself down in it. "I would have speech with you, Margaret of Scotland," he said, smiling. His smile had charm.

★ ★ ★

"I have no doubt you thought me in Ireland," he began, still amiably. "I would have it kept in secret that I am here; the tides running to the Welsh coast are easier than those to be encountered on the way back. Also, my good De Bohun is one I can trust; and you yourself will have no chance to tattle as women do."

I remarked that some of us were silent by nature, but why would I be given no chance? He made no reply, smiling still and sitting at ease, the bowed horseman's legs planted squarely to display his grey woven hose, which he never took the trouble to cross-garter. He looked much as he had done that day two years ago in Rennes, when Constance's betrothed had stolen her birthright and I had worn my coronet and pearls. I wondered if this visitation was to be my punishment in some form; if so, it was a long way to have come to avenge one woman's disobedience. I said this, coldly, pulling up the bull's hide so that my breasts were hidden. Nevertheless he had the kind of glance which sees through bedcovers. The hard eyes surveyed me.

"Do not indulge in your known ancestral piety," he remarked. "It is not to disarrange that that I am here; I could have done so any time these past six years, since first you came to my court at Woodstock. It is your market worth, now that you are widowed, that concerns me. Did you suppose," and his voice rasped angrily for the first time, "that I would let a Scots princess, free to marry again and proven fertile, out of my hands? My rival William, who is my vassal but calls himself the Lion at least for the time, would make haste to arrange a foreign marriage for you, his sister, doubtless with France. Old Louis is himself wed for the moment, but one never knows what may happen, and he has brothers, and the brothers have sons."

I was growing angry myself; he spoke of me beneath my bull's hide as if I were a cow or a mare. "King Louis has a son also," I reminded him. "The marriage of infants is a habit in which you yourself indulge, sire. Why deny me the prospect of young Philip? They say he has parts." I knew I talked foolishly, but I also knew I had been tricked; the ease with which Constance and I had been allowed to depart from Woodstock had been no accident. I thought of her for instants, with a terror I knew was misplaced; the King would not harm his son's guerdon for Brittainy.

"They also say he is sickly," remarked Curtmantle of France's heir. "Better men may serve your need. As, for your daughter" — he had evidently read my thoughts — "tomorrow you shall see her to say farewell. Constance my son's future wife will be conveyed back to Woodstock, with her Breton woman and Ykenai, to the care of the queen. You would not have set out lacking her, which is why she was brought on an unnecessary journey. She will do well enough after a night's sleep."

I lay silent for moments, realising how he had prepared even the matter of the women, and knowing that I had lost my daughter. He had after all bartered his own to foreign countries early, without pity; it was a quality he lacked. I decided not to gratify him by asking what was to be my own fate. "What was it you desired to say to me, sire?" I asked instead. "If it has brought you in secret all this way, it must be a matter of some moment."

"It would give me pleasure to thrash your impudent backside; bridle your tongue. What I want to say is a truth which must stay in your mind, as if I had burnt it there with a brand. This realm is mine." He leaned forward a little, hands on the rests of the curved chair. "My grandsire the first Henry won it by his sword and by guile. It is my intention to restore it as it was in his day, despite your brother in the north, who is my vassal, or any other man."

"For no more than Huntingdon," I said of the vassalage. He could thrash me if he liked; I would not, by word or look, agree to surrender Scotland's rights as I knew them to exist. "Moreover, King Henry Beauclerc strengthened his claim, which was shaky, by a royal Scots marriage to my great-aunt Edith, whom he then caused to change her name to Matilda, saying the English could not pronounce the first. That was a lie," I said. "All Margaret Atheling's children were given Saxon names, most of them from Edward the Confessor's time, after him and his queen. Never tell me the English did not pronounce the name of Edith with ease; it is only that all traces of Saxon royal rule had to disappear under your Norman yoke, even the tongue being degraded to be spoken only by peasants and villeins. My great-aunt would have been happier by far left to marry my other grandfather, the second earl of Warren and Surrey, who greatly desired her. He disliked your grandsire, who could not then afford a horse, and called him Deerfoot because he used to have to run after the hunt. Later he grew too unwieldy to do so and they say he snored at night, and was so unfaithful my great-aunt was reduced to washing the feet of lepers. The English called her the Good Queen." I knew my talk grew wild.

"If she had washed fewer lepers' feet he might have paid more heed to her bed," shouted Curtmantle. I knew I had been somewhat unjust to King Henry Beauclerc, who was a good lawgiver and whose thunderous presence meant that no order of his was ever disobeyed by those who heard it. I returned to the subject of Scotland. "My brother William is liege lord of all his land, from Caithness to Northumbria," I said. I knew William had never in his life yet been to Caithness, which is a remote part peopled by wild tribes, but I had mentioned Northumbria in order to increase Curtmantle's anger, knowing that for once I was being less reasonable than he; but I was well beyond trembling at what he might do. As if he knew this, he contented himself with drumming his thick fingers on the rests of his chair, speaking evenly enough.

"In the reign of King Cnut, the King of Scots swore to be his man. It took place in a boat, and is recorded."

"That was Maelbeatha," I replied, "who was not of the rightful line, and in any case he merely swore to aid Cnut in time of war. Later my great-grandfather, Malcolm Ceann Mór, killed the usurper in battle and won back the inheritance of his ancestors. Had Edgar the Atheling my kinsman had as much fighting spirit, you would not now be reigning over England." By now, I was enjoying myself; he liked, I knew, to reason in argument, but it was seldom anyone answered him to the extent I had done and was still doing.

He stared at me now. "By God's eyes, you yourself have such a spirit," he said. "For longer than you know I have been minded to serve you, Margaret, and I do not think you would have been unwilling. Six or seven years without a man in your bed, as I know you have spent them, is a long time for any woman unless she be a nun." He sounded almost thoughtful, but I broke resolutely into his thoughts.

"You had a nun raped," I told him, angry again at the assumption he had that any woman would become his whore without protest. "Mary of Boulogne, King Stephen's daughter, was abbess of Romsey, and you sent Count Matthew of Flanders to ravish her in her own parlour, despite the cries of her sisters in religion beyond the door; then she was forced into the saddle, with the veil torn from her shaven head, and dragged elsewhere to the altar, and all because you wanted to secure Boulogne from the King of France." I knew well enough about Mary of Boulogne, a plump young woman who was close kin both through her grandmother, Queen Edith Matilda's sister, and through her dead brother's marriage to my cousin Isabel, later forced by Curtmantle to marry the brutal Hameline Plantagenet. Remembering all of it, I tried to hate the man who sat there, and could not. He himself was by then quite evidently consumed with rage.

"There is no straw on the floor here, and if you divest yourself of your clothes it will be improper in my presence," I said, again pulling up the bull's hide which had meantime slipped. His face had turned plum-red beneath the freckles and he began to breathe heavily. "Your ancestor the Conqueror, once he was dead, they say burst," I remarked unforgiveably. "As for King Beauclerc, they wrapped him in a bull's hide such as this is at that time because he stank, and when the surgeon came to open his brain the man died, they say, of the stench. That story is known to all. The King himself had died of eating too many eels." I was using my tongue because it was my only weapon; Scotswomen are apt at this exercise, more so than in England.

He was still clutching the curved chair, but under the circumstances exercised praiseworthy self-control. "You mock my forebears," he grated, "but when we are dead all of us stink. One day the flesh will fall from your own lovely bones, and long before that you will be wrinkled and grey. Nevertheless I am here in your chamber now, and if I do not leave till dawn it can be said in any case that you are the King's whore. Your fire-eating brothers will then harry my northern lands, thinking I have harried your parts as I would still not be loth to do, except that I would not deprive your bridegroom of that pleasure." He spoke now with deadly courtesy.

"My bridegroom?" I said. "You can force me to marry no one. I am neither your vassal nor an heiress in your charge." My voice had however grown faint; I was greatly disturbed, for he could certainly do as he chose with me, one way or the other. I pictured myself, helpless and naked in a Marcher castle, surrounded by his men; there was no help for whatever he chose should happen, and already I knew it.

"This is a man of honour and high birth, who will satisfy you; and your brothers, on hearing of such a marriage, will be the less inclined to make war," Curtmantle said. I knew already who the bridegroom would be; Humphrey de Bohun, earl of Hereford. It occurred to me even then that I could at least improve matters in his kitchens once I had forgiven the part he had played.

Henry's face had grown smooth, having got his own way. "Best be married while there is time in England, for the land may soon be under interdict," he said. "Make your choice between being made wife or whore, Margaret. There is no other."

★ ★ ★

The priest came presently, carrying candles; by then it was almost light. He was trembling, for none of the clergy knew where they were since Becket's murder and, before that, the dispute with the King himself regarding the laws of clerical punishment. With him was De Bohun, rocklike as ever, clad now in a bedgown of red stuff. I lay helpless, my hands clenching in resentment against the bull's hide. A brother of the earl had come in as a second witness.

"You will marry them in bed," directed Curtmantle. "It is almost day." He was evidently chafing to be off; he had sat in the chair for longer by far than was his custom anywhere.

I felt, rather than saw, Humphrey de Bohun divest himself of his bedgown and climb in beside me. The priest began to recite the Nuptial Mass, still nervously.

De Bohun's chest was broad as a lowland plain, covered with thick grey hair. I took the vows sullenly and received the Host passively, without prayers or confession.

When it was done, and a ring on my finger which like everything else had been ready provided, Curtmantle said, "I will kiss the bride," and came over and did so, hands gripping both my shoulders, his mouth pressed hard against mine. It was bruised next day, and he had gone, back to Ireland on the difficult tide. Later we learned that he had spent Christmas in a mud and wattle palace he had had built there and had taught the Irish to eat roasted cranes, which were plentiful in that country but which they had not before thought of.

Meantime I had heard my husband say, gently enough, "It must be done between us now, as the King has ordered it." He never questioned Curtmantle's orders, then or later. It was done, despite me: this time I found I could not claim to have been married to a man who lacked decision. The earl did not then, or on any other occasion, use me unkindly, though there was no gainsaying him. I heard, by the end, his grunts of satisfaction; soon it was day. Not long after, I was allowed to say farewell to my little daughter. It was difficult to contain my tears.

In such a way, I became countess of Hereford. Later, I was able to interest myself in the lives of my husband's Marcher tenantry, learning in such ways that there were women a great deal worse off than I. Most especially there were the poor Welsh, wives of the men Curtmantle took away without warning to fight in his foreign wars, including those waged in Brittany. My little lost Constance I never forgot, and continued to pray for her, together with the soul of my first husband Conan, as there was nothing else I could do for either of them. I would send Constance my pearls upon news of her marriage.

Curtmantle himself I tried to banish from my mind, but it was impossible; he continued a part of everyone's lives, in all of the lands he governed. He and I were to meet in person once more, only once, years hence and for the last time. However I was not, like Constance, able to predict the future, and that is as well.

Part Three

The Geste of Constance, 1167 – 1201

1

I CONSTANCE, duchess of Brittany, am about to bear a child for the fifth time; not to Geoffrey Plantagenet, who is long dead, or, thank God, to my second husband, Chester, but to my third, Guy de Thouars, whom I love dearly and whom I have at last been freed to marry. Nevertheless my health has never fully recovered from Chester's beatings, I have a certain wasting disease, and in the way I know such things I am aware that I shall not long outlive this birth. It is the birth of de Thouars' first legitimate child although she is the third we have made together. I know also that she will prove yet another daughter. This takes no skill; Merlin prophesied from his tomb that I should bear one son only. Arthur is fifteen years old now, safe in France. That accomplished, I can die with a clear mind and a heart full of thankfulness that I have at least not lived without purpose. I am at peace

155

to remember while I can, being alone in my room; even old Berthe my waiting woman is elsewhere.

I can just recall my father, Duke Conan IV, known as Le Petit by contrast with his terrible grandfather. We left him, my mother and I, when I was four years old, as there was civil war in Brittany. He had black hair, which made him different from us: that is all I remember of him. He held me to him before we parted, and after that went out of our lives. He does not seem to have been greatly liked by anyone except, briefly, mother at the time of their marriage; she seldom spoke of him and I have gathered most of what I know from Berthe, who helped to bring me up after my mother was taken away also and married again. By then I was ten years old.

Father should by right have succeeded his grandfather, Conan III. The name itself means king, but it is a long time since there were kings in Brittany. The first of these, long ago, was Conan Mériadech, which mother, who was a princess of Scotland, used to say scornfully meant no more than King

Murdoch as he was probably a Scot fleeing from the Saxon invasions. That apart, Conan III himself was a grandson of the Conqueror. His mother had been Constance of Normandy, after whom I am named, and who died in giving him birth; this fate overtakes many of us women. Possibly through having been motherless, he grew up into a tyrant, which at least kept his dukedom quiet. King Henry Beauclerc, who by then had seized the English throne from his brothers and was engaged in marrying his numerous bastard daughters as favourably as possible, chose Conan as bridegroom to one of the many such Matildas: these had been obsequiously named for Beauclerc's wife, his deceased mother, and his heiress, the mother of Curtmantle. The particular Matilda I mention inspired in her Breton husband a profound distrust, and when she gave birth to a son named Hoël, old Conan announced that the boy was not his and had him disinherited. On the next occasion, although the child was a daughter, she resembled the old duke so closely that denials were useless. This was Berthe my grandmother, and there is more to the tale.

When Berthe was grown, she was married to Alan the Black, and together they produced my father. On the surface this would appear satisfactory, but the difficult old duke took a dislike to his grandson at sight. He made the boy's youth miserable, which may partly account for my father's lack of decision in manhood; mother used to say that he bit his nails to the quick. As soon as his father Alan the Black was dead the duke forced my grandmother to marry again, this time to a Breton noble named Eudo de Porhoêt, much her junior. He told them to get a better heir without delay, but my poor grandmother, being no longer young, could only produce one girl, who was however very beautiful. She was named Alix, and became the apple of our grandfather's eye; he also saw to it that the Breton people adored her, and on his death decreed that she should take the place not only of my father, but of father's disinherited uncle Hoêl, who naturally caused trouble of his own over the matter. Between them, they made peaceful succession impossible for my poor father, who in the end fled across seas to Curtmantle, Henry II of England, for aid. Curtmantle, who was father's overlord in any case for the fief of Richmond, was happy to meddle in the affairs of Brittany, as he was also duke of Normandy, which adjoins, and was likewise concerned lest internal divisions should mean that Brittany herself was claimed by France, supposedly Henry's overlord for his dukedom. At that time Curtmantle had however milked away large possessions from King Louis VII by means of marrying Louis' divorced queen Eleanor, the heiress of Aquitaine, Guienne, Gascony and Poitou. He was thereafter determined to build up what has since become known as the Angevin empire for their sons, to one of whom I was promptly betrothed.

"She is perhaps a little young," mother had remarked drily, as I was only a month old by then; but the thing was done. The pope forbade the arranged marriage meantime, which meant that he wanted money. However there was certainly a complicated relationship not only with the Conqueror by way of the earlier Constance, but through the marriage of the latter's youngest son King Henry Beauclerc to a princess of Scotland. The Conqueror himself, an impatient man born bastard, had refused to wait for papal sanction for his own earlier marriage to Matilda of Flanders, herself nobly descended from Charlemagne. Apart from the couple's being made to build two abbeys at Caen in penance, this meant the births, too rapidly for full legitimacy — this was one excuse Beauclerc employed for seizing the throne from his elder brother — not only of Robert Curthose, as the latter was called, and William Rufus, but also of the eldest daughter Gundreda, whom the chroniclers politely record as the youngest. She was the grandmother of my mother's own mother Ada de Warenne, who herself married the son of King David of Scotland and bore him the present king, my uncle William the Lion. King David himself, being son to Malcolm III and Queen Margaret Atheling, was also brother to Queen Edith Matilda who married Beauclerc, mostly to her sorrow. Altogether our pedigree resembles a tapestry seen from the back, as been said.

Meanwhile, in 1160, my mother was married without delay to my father, to the extreme annoyance of Curtmantle. It is odd that the pope did not notice that Conan IV's grandmother was Beauclerc's daughter and his great-grandmother the Conqueror's, but no doubt he was not given leisure, as my uncle King Malcolm hastened the marriage. All things considered, it is as well that I did not turn out to be a son; I might have had to marry Curtmantle's daughter Eleanor.

★ ★ ★

She was particularly unkind, and used to stick pins in me and pretend the marks were fleabites. All this naturally happened after mother was taken away to be married to the earl of Hereford. After that I was obliged to see rather more of the other children at Woodstock, which is where we chiefly stayed when in England, though sometimes, mostly in order that the straw might be changed, the court would move with all its baggage to Winchester or to the King's hunting-lodge at Clarendon, depending on the season. Occasionally, we would cross seas to Normandy.

I disliked them all, except Joanna who was much younger than the rest including myself. Also, one of the king's sons who was not the queen's was brought up among us; his name was Geoffrey, like that of my betrothed, and I wished the two could have been exchanged. Geoffrey the Bastard was the image of the king, even to having Curtmantle's freckles, though taller and not at all given to outbursts of rage. He was in fact a gentle obedient creature and his mother Ykenai, who had come with me on the journey to Hereford and back again, continued to call in for her silver once a month. Tacheté, as I called him, being in fact the eldest of any — he had been got at the time Curtmantle was a young man as King David's guest at Carlisle — was less often among us than the younger boys, being away training in knightly exercises and also, in his case, clerkly ones, as he was half-heartedly intended for the Church and later on became a bishop. Ykenai's name, mother had told me, was Pictish, but when I said this one day in the presence of young Eleanor she nipped me unkindly and said "You think you know everything, Constance of Brittany. The word means Iceni, and they were a tribe whose queen led them in person against the Romans. My brother Henry heard that from the late Archbishop Becket, so it is bound to be correct." She walked off with her nose in the air and I was glad, and gladder still when she left to be married into Spain, but sorry for her husband, whose name was Alfonso. That made two crosses for him to bear.

I was in fact lonely and unhappy without my mother, even though Berthe my woman was still there. When I heard mother had given birth to a little son in Hereford who was to be named Henry after the king, I was more than ever certain she would forget me. At the beginning I used to cry at night, secretly as I thought, but as we often had to share a chamber, the others knew about it and mocked, so after that I began to keep my feelings to myself.

I was always different from them in ways I shall describe, but meantime I must remember them as they were. There had been five boys and three girls, but William, the eldest son, had died when he was three years old and I never knew him. Matilda, the eldest girl, I scarcely recall till later on: she left soon to be married into Saxony, followed by a grand train of pack-horses with scarlet cloth saddles and much gilding, and lengths of samite to make gowns as she grew, and furs to wear in the cold German winters. That left Eleanor and my little friend Joanna, who later went to Sicily. Curtmantle used his girls like pegs on a board, for foreign alliances.

Of the sons, my betrothed Geoffrey Plantagenet was a pretty little boy with red-gold curls and guileless blue eyes which concealed the fact that truth, even at eight years when we first met, meant nothing to him at all. He had no doubt developed slyness early in order to get his own way against his bigger and stronger brothers, especially Richard whom the Queen adored, Richard — he had been called after one of the drowned sons of Beauclerc in the White Ship, got on a Berkshire widow was tall, handsome as a god, yellow-haired, broad of shoulder and a bully, also cruel. Geoffrey, my betrothed, was afraid of him. The baby, John, was in the nursery for a time after I arrived, and when he emerged had become an unpleasant little boy who picked his wide nose furtively and already looked down our dresses.

I have left Young Henry, the Young King, to the last. Like all the rest he was handsome — none of the children were plain like their father — with golden hair, and so winning he could charm a bird off a tree; he even took the trouble to try to charm me, a small girl and a stranger. He did not contrive it, because I had already heard from Berthe the story of what had happened at his coronation, which had taken place in his father's lifetime in case anything should go wrong; the habit had begun in France. At the subsequent banquet the king himself had knelt to serve Young

Henry afterwards with ewer and towel at the high table. Someone remarked how fortunate he was to be served by his royal father. "It is no particular honour," remarked the Young King idly. "He is only the son of a duke. I myself am royal from both parents." It is true that there was already bad blood between father and son over the matter of Archbishop Becket, who by rights should have set the crown on the young man's head and who had been his tutor of whom he was fond, and who was by then in exile and, later, murdered. Nevertheless the remark was arrogant, and I continued wary of Young Henry despite his gilded good looks and celebrated charm. His French wife Marguerite was fond of him, however, and he of her. She had been sent over on condition that King Louis' former wife should not bring her up, and this was done by Robert of Newburgh, who later became a monk at Bec.

The feathers of the prime bird shine
in gold,
And in her third nest shall rejoyce.

166

It is true that, by the time I myself knew Eleanor of Acquitaine, there was no longer unalloyed joy in the third nest. No doubt she had been thankful at the time to exchange gentle monkish Louis VII for the young and virile duke of Normandy, having set eyes on Curtmantle in the first place when he came to Paris to render homage to her existing royal husband. This had been the custom since old pirate Rollo, first patrician of Normandy, had wrested the coastline almost two centuries earlier from the then king of the Franks, Charles the Simple. Rollo was said to have seized Charles's foot and jerked him backwards in the very act of homage, but at least he did not steal away Charles's wife. It is possible that the determination as to that came from Eleanor's side; here at last was a prince who would not be dull in bed. She had been reared in the warm southern land of the troubadours, loved freedom, philosophy, splendour and power, and no doubt assumed that she could pursue all four of them as the wife of a boy of eighteen, she herself being then twenty-nine, mother by Louis of two daughters only, and hopeful of bearing sons to a second husband who spent less time in the confessional than he. Moreover, the prospect of becoming queen of England was by then certain, as Henry had been recognised as King Stephen's heir before the latter's death.

Eleanor's disillusionment may have begun when she found that she was bearing one child after another to Curtmantle yearly, had very little say in the ruling of her own dominions, and was kept strictly at Woodstock and elsewhere, also Normandy, without much money being spent; Curtmantle was careful of it except at Young Henry's coronation. Also, he was unfaithful; not widely, but mostly with respect to one particular mistress, a young woman from the Brecon country named Rosamund Clifford. There was also still the presence of young Geoffrey Tacheté in the nursery among the others from the beginning, and there was a bastard named William elsewhere.

Eleanor knew well enough that she was part of a fable, the double eagle of Merlin's prophecy, as Curtmantle's mother had been the eaglet: but this was small comfort day after day. It was no doubt worse, as I heard not from her but from elsewhere, than having been removed forcibly from Antioch because King Louis was suspicious of the hours she and her young uncle Raymond kept in that delectable city and the way they laughed together. There was less laughter, fewer sons were made, in England; and after the only occasion when she herself was permitted to govern briefly in Curtmantle's absence during the Welsh campaigns, he personally told the queen her orders were ignored from the beginning and that he could have managed matters better for himself. As far as I was concerned, her brief regency gave the queen a knowledge of affairs in Brittany which later I was to find useful. In general, also, I enjoyed her company. She taught me her own cool judgement, even imparted, if such things can be handed on, a certain portion of her indomitable will. Otherwise, I had one thing Eleanor of Aquitaine had not; my Celtic inheritance. It did not however take the extra sense this gave me, an awareness of what happened once and of what will happen again, to tell me that disturbance in the third nest was beginning to be rife, and that Curtmantle's sons who were growing up to resent their father, purposely taught to do so by their mother.

★ ★ ★

I should have known less about the ancient things my own darkly running blood would tell me in time to come, had it not been for Berthe. My mother, though like myself she had the Tanist Celtic inheritance from the old Scots kings, had been brought up with the robust common sense of her Norman mother Countess Ada de Warenne and the remembered piety of her father, Henry of Huntingdon. That last had come from Henry's father King David, who had had it in childhood from his mother Margaret Atheling, and she in turn had learnt it at the court of King Edward the Confessor, who had taken a vow of chastity. When Queen Eleanor heard the Confessor's name she would throw her head back

170

and laugh. "It needed no vow," she said. "He could by no means have mounted a woman. He had a wife and never visited her bed."

Nevertheless Margaret Atheling and her brother Edgar, by rights the heir to England, with her sister and their Hungarian mother, had been driven by storms to the coast of Scotland while escaping from William the Conqueror after the Confessor's death, and King Malcolm III, then a widower, had fallen in love with Margaret and had married her despite the fact that, under the earlier tutelage of the chaste Confessor and his patient queen, she had intended to become a nun. "She recovered enough to bear six sons and two daughters, they tell me," remarked Queen Eleanor. I replied that Margaret had called all of her children after the Confessor and his queen and the former Saxon kings, except for Mary, the youngest, who was named for the Mother of God. "Best not mention any of that here," said Eleanor. "All is Norman here now, or rather Angevin. The devil is in greater favour than God, accordingly."

She looked discontented, and Joanna and I and Marguerite, who was old enough now to be present and who were all that were left by then except for Marguerite's snivelling little French half-sister Alais, who had been sent over some time before to marry Richard and who had only just emerged from the nursery to join us in the solar, tried to cheer her with tales. Marguerite began with some gentle story or other I forget, because in the midst of it sounds came from outside and below which announced the king's sudden arrival; he might come up to visit us or else might not. Marguerite fell silent and I knew there were two stories I myself would never tell, one of the nine sibyls of Sein, the other of the drowned city of Ys; for I would not have either mocked at. I therefore launched instead into the story Berthe had told me of a Breton king named Conamor who ate his wives. The queen was entertained. "He did not deserve his name," she said. "Such habits denote an excess of love, perhaps. What became of him?"

I said he had fallen in love at last with

a Christian princess named Triphine, who however would not agree to marry him until he had promised to be baptised and not to eat her. She also asked to be allowed to return to her father if at any time she felt the need.

"A wise provision," said the Queen. "We should all exact such promises."

"It did her no good, madam. When she found herself in that state ladies are said to be in who love their lords, which was when the rest had by custom been eaten, she understandably fled to her father during the night. Conamor was furious, and pursued her with his sword, and killed her in the forest. Next day her father found her corpse, and beside it the son to whom she had posthumously given birth. He was brought up by a saintly abbot, and became a monk."

"That was poor-spirited: he should have avenged his mother, slain the cannibal and occupied his throne."

Alais was meantime pretending to be affrighted at the tale of being eaten. "Do not be foolish, child," said the queen sharply; she had been angry at the arrangement for yet a second daughter of

France to come to England, especially as the bride of Richard, on whom she doted. Richard however had hardly noticed Alais and it was doubtful if he ever would; she was a thin drooping pallid creature with the melancholy Capet features, although she might fill out later. However King Louis had meantime, by a third marriage made in unseemly haste after the death in childbirth of his second, got a son at last, who was Alais' full brother. This made the earlier marriage of Marguerite with Young Henry of less importance, though in any event no woman can inherit the throne of France, even Curtmantle's daughter-in-law. In early days he had no doubt hoped that France would be added to his empire by the marriage.

I soothed Alais by relating the tale of St. Corentin's fish. "He used to go down to the river each day from where he was being a hermit in Brittany, and there was always a fish waiting for him to catch and eat. He would catch it and eat half, then throw the rest back. Next day the fish, recovered, was waiting again with all of itself miraculously restored, and St. Corentin would eat half again, and again throw back the rest. So he lived for many years.

"He must have been as fond of fish as my husband's grandfather, who died of it," said the queen. Alais begged for another tale of a saint. She had an ostentatious piety in which I did not believe, and so I told the story of St. Ursula, knowing quite well what the queen would make of it.

It was well known enough, but what most have forgotten, or perhaps in England cannot pronounce, is the bridegroom's name; King Conan Mériadech, no other. He had become a Christian, so fierce in fact that he did to death everyone who was not similarly inclined. When his queen died he wanted a second wife, and having heard that the King of Cornwall had a beautiful daughter named Ursula, sent across seas to ask for her hand.

It is curious that, in the way lands are made and altered over the ages, Cornwall and our Cornouaille are mirror images. The great archangel flew over both, so there is St. Michael's Mount on one side and Mont St. Michel on the other; and a place we have named Carhaix, where once a wicked princess lived, echoes Caerhays on the other side. The tongues are also similar, but that is because at the time of the Saxon invasions Celts fled in all directions to Cornwall and Wales and Ireland and Brittany, and everyone from all of those places can still understand one another, with slight differences which can be overcome.

"Tell us your tale, Constance," demanded the queen. I had already told two, but she had no doubt forgotten; she was listening for the sound of hasty footsteps on the stairs, which might or might not come.

I related how Ursula was sent by her father in a ship with eleven thousand virgins, and as I had hoped she would do the queen threw back her head in the way she had, and laughed.

"They would not find that number of virgins in all England, let alone in Cornwall," she said. "It must have been eleven; that would make a round dozen to be shipwrecked and violated at the mouth of the Rhine."

"Madam, Ursula was not violated; the Hunnish prince who led the barbarians was so struck by her beauty that he offered to marry her if she would surrender her honour, but she refused, and so he put her to the sword and she became a saint."

"I think that in the circumstances I would have yielded," said Queen Eleanor. Alais asked what violated meant. The answer was never given, or not then, because like a hurricane into the room, after taking the stairs two at a time, came Curtmantle, unkempt as usual, his short red hair ruffled by the late ride from wherever it was. He strode to me first and picked me up, his large hands hard about my body.

"You are growing to be a beauty, Constance," he said. "My son is fortunate."

He rumpled prim Alais, kissed Marguerite and Joanna, and only then, having never any heed to ceremony at any time, saluted his queen.

I remember that day particularly, I do not know why. It was one like any other, except that the king rode so constantly up and down the country that no one knew for certain where he would be found next. Apart from the saddle he never sat often, even to eat. He soon left us, to go off again somewhere else. As I say, I do not know why I remember that day so particularly, even now.

★ ★ ★

I could remember his kneeling earlier at Avranches, however, outside the cathedral there, in token penance for the murder of Archbishop Becket. He kept still long enough on that occasion for a cluster of cardinals to pronounce absolution, their broad hats nodding together so that the scarlet tassels swung in unison. I had still been child enough then to be fascinated by this sight, and by that of the king's thick neck bent in submission which Geoffrey, who was with me because he had lately been enthroned at Rennes, said meant nothing except that his father had by this means avoided getting himself excommunicated.

"That's why they don't flog him," he announced from his place in the saddle beside me. We both rode inferior mounts, because Curtmantle would never spend money on fine ones for his sons, even Young Henry, or give them enough to buy these for themselves. I looked sideways at my betrothed and wondered why he sounded complacent at the idea of anyone's flogging his father. This in fact happened later on.

By then, Becket had already begun to overtake St. Edward the Confessor as England's favourite saint; miracles continued to multiply at his tomb, which soon became as richly jewelled as my grandmother Countess Ada's abbey of Haddington, the Lamp of Lothian itself, which she had begun to build.

★ ★ ★

I myself had three reasons for remembering St. Edward the Confessor rather than the by then already popular St. Thomas of Canterbury. For one thing, King Edward had been canonised in the year of my birth, 1161. Curtmantle himself, when we became more closely acquainted, told me how he had stood by the coffin at the time when it was opened. Although it was almost a hundred years then since King Edward's death, the body was found to be incorrupt. "His hair was pale," Curtmantle said, marvelling at the remembrance, "and his flesh pale also, as if he had never known colour or youth. There was an enamelled crucifix of great beauty lying on his breast. We left it undisturbed with him in the new tomb." He himself had helped to shoulder the weight of the coffin as it was carried back from the high altar at Westminster.

Secondly, I was doubly related to the Confessor by earlier ties than the Athelings; his great-grandmother was Breton. She was a peasant girl named Sprota with whom William Longsword, son and heir of old pirate Rollo the Patrician, fell in love. They had a son who inherited as Richard the Fearless, by then named duke of Normandy. Longsword's unpleasant French wife Liutgarda — I regret to say that she also was related to me by my own Vermandois great-grandmother — was later furious that Sprota's bastard should inherit, and when Longsword was murdered she married his murderer. So much for that; but my third reason goes back to the days of the Danish invasions in England.

Edward the Confessor's father was King Ethelred the Redeless, a word which means an inability to do anything at the right time or in the right place. He was nevertheless held in affection by his subjects, being a descendant of great Alfred, despite the fact that he himself tried to buy off the Danish invaders with gold so that they kept coming back for still more, and when that failed mistakenly massacred large numbers of them on St. Brice's Day including the sister of Sweyn, the Danish leader. Sweyn had a son name Cnut. Ethelred, by his first wife the Lady Ithelgina, had himself a son who for his fighting qualities was known as Edmund Ironside. He was my ancestor. He fought twice with Cnut, first in a battle so fierce no one was certain which side was the victor. The two leaders, both young men, thereafter challenged one another to a duel which they fought at once. Again the result was drawn. They then agreed to divide England between them, and for the space of a day Edmund Ironside was king of half England. However his death — I know the manner of it — may have meant that he was a ritual victim, like Rufus later on in the new century. This victim has to be royal and male; there should be one again shortly after this year of 1201. After the duel, Edmund Ironside was relieving himself, and one Edric of Kent came up behind him with a spear and thrust it up his fundament. It was an ugly way to die, and he was carried to Oxford and the manner of it hushed up. His two sons fled to Hungary, where one married and the other died. The three children of Edward the Stranger, as the first was known, came with their mother back to England in the Confessor's reign and as I have said were reared by him and his queen. One was Margaret Atheling my great-great-grandmother, who became Queen of Scots. The others were Edgar Atheling, who should have inherited the throne of England at the Confessor's death but lacked the will to fight: and the third was Christina, who became abbess of Romsey, and was given charge of the two Scots princesses Edith and Mary, later countess of Boulogne, when the younger children of Malcolm III and Margaret fled south after their parents' deaths. They were shepherded there, out of harm, by none other than their uncle Edgar Atheling, who was himself so harmless even the Conqueror did him none.

That David, the youngest boy, grew up at the court of Beauclerc, who grew fond of him and later found him a bride, was of course important as far as future friendship between England and Scotland was concerned, also for the possession of the great fief of Huntingdon, brought by Earl Waltheof's daughter, David's queen.

To return to the Confessor, by then still remembered as England's saint, his mother had been King Ethelred's second wife, Emma, the Gem of Normandy. She was the daughter of Duke Richard the Fearless and the most beautiful Danish Gunnor, from whose brother Herfast the de Warennes are descended. Emma bore Ethelred two sons, the elder of whom was murdered. The younger, Edward, she disliked; and after Ethelred's death completed the confusion by marrying

Cnut the Dane, king by then of all England and much her junior. Afterwards, the Confessor was called back from Normandy to reign; he was forced, in gaining the throne, to marry the daughter of his brother Alfred's murderer, which may be one reason why the marriage was never consummated. Queen Edith Godwinson's brother was Harold, who perished at Hastings.

Altogether the Confessor was much in my thoughts, with that other English saint brought home from the Crusades and named St. George, although he seems in Arabian lands to have been called the Khidr, the green one who brings harvest. I was greatly interested in the older forms of religion taught me secretly by Berthe. Curtmantle and I would talk about most other things at a later time when he made the leisure, but never that. He was in fact devoutly Christian, especially after the murder of Becket which he did not fully intend. He was however interested in many other matters than money and the increasing grasp of power, but had little time to pursue them.

I can recall one time only in early days when he had leisure both to talk to me and to listen. The Court had attended mass at Winchester, and the King, as always, had heard it carefully, receiving the Host humbly in his turn; it must have been after Becket's murder, because I was about twelve years old; yet we were not by then at Chinon, nor was the king yet in Ireland. Truth to tell he moved so rapidly from place to place that my memory grows confused after so long. I only remember his charm, which was so manifest that his courtiers forgave him much inconvenience; having to stand for meals because he stood by habit; doing without a bed for the night because Curtmantle had suddenly changed his plans, and would cast himself down, wrapped in his short cloak, in the only place to be had in some forester's hut, while the rest might make shift as best they could. They forgave him this, and he kept his friends; but not his sons, still less his wife. That day it was evident. The queen had not come with us. I had sent Berthe back with the rest. I went afterwards to light a candle at the tomb of Emma of Normandy, where few prayed despite the fact that her son the Confessor was a saint. She had not been liked in England, but her mother's brother, Herfast the Dane, had after all been my ancestor through the de Warennes. Also, I knew that she loved her second husband, King Cnut, better than her first, King Ethelred, or either of her sons by him; and instead loved best of all the only son of the second marriage, Harthacnut, the last Danish king of England, buried here with both his parents. That all of these were dead bones now I knew, but I liked to linger near them; they had been foreigners, and so was I.

I became aware then of two figures beyond the glowing candles, one standing uncertainly, the other kneeling further off. The first was Geoffrey Tacheté, as I called him, the King's freckled bastard son whom I liked better than Geoffrey my own betrothed. Tacheté was looking down at the plain dark coffin-shaped tomb of Henry of Blois,

Bishop of Winchester, brother to King Stephen, without whose advice Stephen would doubtfully have had the enterprise to make the swift journey across the Channel to get himself crowned. Bishop Henry's tomb was deserted these days, none wanting to offend Curtmantle, son of Stephen's rival, by being seen to pray for him. Of such things are promotions made; but Tacheté seemed not to care, and had lighted a candle for the dead bishop's soul. I remembered that his father intended him for the Church; would he succeed Bishop Henry one day? It was possible, no doubt, for a king's son. As if he knew eyes were on him, Tacheté turned away and walked slowly up the nave, and out. This left me my view of the other presence.

It was that of Richard of Poitou, the King's second son, kneeling with head bent; but one knew him by his breadth of shoulder and his yellow hair. He knelt by a flat black stone without candles, and had lit none. I began to tremble, partly because I disliked Richard, but also for a reason I could not at first understand; and yet I knew well enough who lay deep beneath that stone, buried so far down in the earth that men now alive and in time to come might forget him; William Rufus, sometime king of England, victim of an arrow fired in the New Forest in the new century, who they said had gone to his death laughing and prepared. His lost soul, they also said, could not be saved by any prayer; he had denied the Church and had given himself to the devil. Richard resembled him, rumour had it, exactly, both in hair and high complexion. It might have been Rufus himself, kneeling at his own tomb. The rest had gone.

I felt a hand on my arm then; it was the king, alone and frowning. "Come out into the daylight, both of you," he said, jerking his head at his son, who scrambled to his feet, not gracefully. Outside, Curtmantle gave Richard a blow on the ear with the flat of his hand. "Go to the others," he said without explanation. Richard went off, with an ugly expression on his face. I did not fully understand what had happened then, though I do now, after the arrow shot at Chaluz, in the year 1199. An earlier

Richard, son of the Conqueror, also a third, his nephew, had each been killed long before by an arrow in the New Forest likewise: not many remember that, or care greatly.

★ ★ ★

"You are a strange girl, Constance, to linger as long by tombs," remarked the king now, evidently having regained his temper with the blow. "Why did you light a candle for the Lady Emma? Never tell me it was because she was my great-grandsire's great-aunt, and his excuse, or one of them, for invading England. You are half Scot and half Breton, and can care nothing for that. In ways you remind me of your mother, but there is a hidden quality she had not."

"Sire, you are part Breton yourself," I retorted; he liked us to speak up to him, I wanted to conceal my hidden part, and I was thinking not only of Sprota but of Judith of Brittany, mother of Robert the Devil who was himself father to the Conqueror. The king asked me to explain myself, and I found my tongue relating the old tale of Duke Richard the Fearless and how, young and handsome, he had been riding once through Normandy and had stopped for the night with his seneschal of Sècheville near Arques, and supped with him and his wife Sainfrida, who was sister to Herfast the Dane my ancestor. Sainfrida, like all five of her sisters, was very beautiful, and by the end Duke Richard had drunk so much wine that he asked his host to put his wife into bed with him. The poor seneschal demurred, but Sainfrida herself had a practical notion, and substituted her young sister Gunnor for herself. In the morning the duke was so pleased with Gunnor that he went to Sainfrida and thanked her for saving him from mortal sin. Curtmantle roared with laughter when I told him this tale, which I had heard by way of my garrulous old great-uncle Ralph de Warenne: Berthe would not have related it.

"Gunnor became the mother of Emma of Normandy, among others," I said, "and after they had had five children Duke Richard thought it time to marry her, as his first wife had meantime died."

"I have heard of Duchess Gunnor, and that she was beautiful indeed," said Curtmantle. By this time he had tossed our respective reins to the grooms, had taken my arm in the unceremonious way he had, and walked about with me in the market there happened to be in Winchester on that day; they were selling the usual wares, round cheeses and brown eggs, great sides of salted pork, oranges from Spain, ribbons, hot spiced bread, woollen cloth. There was a juggler, and the crowds ate bread or else oranges while they watched his antic play. Curtmantle produced a coin and bought bread for himself and for me, and we stood munching it together while we watched idly, still talking. The people did not stare; they were used to the sight of the king among them when he came to Winchester, familiar in his short cloak, mounted as a rule, clad as always in his scarlet and Lincoln green.

The bread was hot and good; I was hungry after mass. The King was talking half as if to himself, remembering a script he had seen, relating how Emma of Normandy came over the sea to marry

King Ethelred long ago. "*In that year the Lady, Richard's daughter, came to England*," he quoted. "There were no queens known here then. She had reason by the end to hate the powerful Godwins and the thought that Harold might become King. His father, Earl Godwin, had blinded and unmanned her eldest son Alfred the Atheling, then forced the younger, Edward, whom he well knew to be no man, to marry his daughter Edith in order to secure the crown. By then Emma herself was dead; but during the earlier time they fled back to Normandy, she and Ethelred and their sons, she would leave enough for my great-grandsire to feed his mind on when in time he bethought himself of the conquest of England. It was not only a matter of having made Harold swear accordingly on unseen saints' bones, when he was shipwrecked over there."

The juggler finished somersaulting, and came round to collect his dues. Curtmantle moved on, as he seldom gave away coins freely, and I had none. Such money as I possessed was from Brittany, which had been ravaged so often it yielded little enough, and half of that went in any case to Geoffrey my betrothed, and the whole when he could persuade the pope to our marriage. However in the meantime other matters came between, notably the flight of Young Henry at last to his father-in-law King Louis in Paris. The reason was chiefly that Curtmantle had given him a crown and titles to certain lands, but neither money nor power to maintain them. Also, Queen Eleanor had as I have said wrought harm steadily among the sons; Richard and Geoffrey, still hardly more than boys, soon followed the Young King, and after that there was war. It was not only the blow on the ear that rankled with Richard of Poitou; as I have related often, he was his mother's favourite, but presently there was the business of Alais, supposedly his betrothed.

One way and another, therefore, it was the last time for many years that Curtmantle had leisure to talk with me.

* * *

He had spoken of my hidden quality, but I had not been anxious to dwell on this. It arose partly from the fact that I still missed my mother, and even when, once, I had been taken up to Richmond, which Curtmantle had by then caused to revert to the crown, and allowed to fly a hawk up into the cool sky before the great sprawling fortress, there was no question of letting me either go west and south to Hereford to my mother, or north to her people; my grandmother the countess was still alive then, but I never met her, and only had news of her and sometimes letters, when my youngest uncle, David of Huntingdon, rode down as he often still did. He was a reminder of what mother's own young days must have been, different from my own; in the midst of a cheerful family of brothers and sisters, with the company of her father, the loved and admired Earl Henry, till she was old enough to remember him, and thereafter that of her mother till her own marriage into Brittany. I on the other hand was alone, with only Joanna as my friend, and the presence of Berthe always.

It was Berthe who was responsible, no doubt, for a part of my strangeness which I could not make manifest to this Christian king descended from the devil. Berthe was herself almost certainly a daughter of the disinherited Hoël, my father's uncle whom Conan III had himself denied fathering, and for this reason had been brought up at her namesake's court and educated; she was something more, accordingly, than a waiting-woman, though she was adept at mending and at the combing out of long hair. She had a twin brother who was a monk in the community of St. Corentin, he who had daily eaten half a fish, so she had the rudiments of the new religion as well as the old. But the old was in her bones; the inherited memory of the days of the Druids, long banished or killed by Conan Mériadech; their knowledge and their strange gods, kin to the gods of Rufus, the green men and forest victims, the mistletoe which is the fruit of lightning, and the oak which is the heart of wisdom. I myself learned from her the names on which to call; Esus for force, Taranus for vengeance,

Teutates for providence, Belenus for powerful promises, Nehalennia for the light eternal. I can remember them still, but do not now call on them. My devout Bretons obey the Christian teachings, and I would not sadden and alarm them by failing to respect their saints and their God. It may be that, in any case, he is the summation of all the rest.

Some Bretons can hear Merlin still, as I have done. Like them I have as I say Celtic blood from my father Conan as well as from the old Scots kings, Malcolm III and those who went before him, and who inherited through daughters. My own secret running of the old blood is partly from these Tanist kings who resented Margaret Atheling and her sons, and partly from those who earlier fled from the Saxon invasions into Ireland and Brittany and Wales, having come in the first place from none know where, long before the city of Ys was drowned deep or the wicked princess lived at Ker-Ahés, now Carhaix.

They were Christians early, but not according to Queen Margaret and her Romish reforms; they adhered to the teachings of Columba, nephew of St. Patrick, whose monks shaved the forehead but not the crown. There were of course other differences: a man could marry his stepmother. My uncles David and Ralph, both used to riding up and down the country, used to say these Culdees were to be found for far longer than anyone supposes, hidden in island and forest places, in the north and near the border.

My uncle David, later Earl of Huntingdon, as I say came to court often in friendship before the great war, as he knew England and Curtmantle well enough, having been held hostage by him as a boy. He was handsome and valiant, the very image of a true knight in the gestes, and talked of going on crusade long before he did so. Others talked but did not go: among these was, at last, Curtmantle.

2

I ONCE saw a strange thing at Woodstock; a very beautiful woman passing into the thickness of the great labyrinthine hedge they called the maze. It was as though she was a ghost, and yet I knew she was not dead. The hedge was thick and dark, as old as the Confessor's time or perhaps his father's. Having seen the woman's draperies vanish I went to tell Berthe, who was the only one I knew would not mock me.

She was not surprised; no Breton fails to believe that such things happen. "It is Rosamund Clifford," she said. "She came from the country near Wales. When *he* — " she would never name Curtmantle except as the monster — "was a young man, and later not so young, he loved her, they say, if he can indeed love. At the beginning, they say also, she did not know he had a wife. When she found out that she was no more than a kept whore, she repented over the years, and in the end went into Godstow convent, where she is still. No doubt her mind returns to the place where he would come to her, in the pavilion there. That is what you saw, little duchess; do not let it trouble you."

It troubled me in a way Berthe would not have condoned; I was fifteen years old then, and jealous that Curtmantle should have loved some unknown woman. He had married the queen out of ambition, as I surmised: that mattered nothing, but pride at fifteen is unaccountable. In time I found out that Fair Rosamund had been with the king less often in the heart of the maze than at Everswell, not far off. There are stone buildings there through which a stream runs, and lovers, by casting twigs into the water, can send messages to one another from room to room. I tried it myself once, but had no lover.

A year or two after, Fair Rosamund died in her convent. It is not true, as they say later on, that Queen Eleanor poisoned her. The queen was a woman of the world, and would be the last to complain of manhood in her second husband after its evident lack in her first. She had interests in too many other matters — music, verse, illuminating books — the *Geste of Arthur* was dedicated to her — and in the vain pursuit of power, to trouble about a young woman who did not interfere or presume. Rosamund, after some years of repenting her sins on her knees on a stone floor, died of a wasting disease accordingly, and the king ordered her coffin to be covered with silk cloths and kept before the high altar, where the nuns continued to place candles and fresh flowers. No doubt it is true that the king loved her. Much later his vile youngest, John, perpetrated a Latin epitaph on Rosamund's tomb, with a play on her name. *Once rose of the world, now stinking.*

Curtmantle changed very little over the years since he had been Rosamund's lover, except to become somewhat corpulent, like many of the Conqueror's descendants, and to begin — this was always his dread, so that he kept his hair shaved close — to grow bald. None of it altered his charm for women other than his wife, who by that time abominated him.

That was after the second Child of France, Richard's betrothed Alais, had come. I have spoken of her already, but there is somewhat more to say.

I stumbled on the matter unwittingly when we were all, except for Matilda who had gone to Saxony by then, playing hide-and-seek at Woodstock for lack of anything to do. It was Alais' turn to hide, drooping about as she usually did at the edge of the company, hardly taking part; none of us liked her, and the fact made me draw closer to the others than I had done before she came. I knew she had gone into the maze, where most people lost themselves; by then, I knew the way. I went to search for Alais not only because of finding her, but because I thought the witless creature would lose her way and be frightened. Had I known, I need not have troubled myself.

I wound my way through the elaborate pattern of dark hedged paths some Saxon gardener had copied from a Roman pavement, and came at last to the wooden pavilion at the place where by custom, Fair Rosamund used to wait for the king to come and lie with her. The king was there now: I had not seen him arrive. On his knees sat perched young Alais, and his hand was up her skirts. Neither of them saw me. The prim expression on the Child of France's face had not altered and she might have been experiencing a mortification of the flesh, except for a certain discreet pleased writhing. I knew without being told that it was not the first time it had happened; by then, he had accustomed her.

I withdrew without being noticed, and told no one. By then the royal couple had been on bad terms openly for some time, and the queen was in Poitou.

Later I witnessed more, but by then could have expected it. We were at our embroidery, but Alais was absent for whatever reason, having lately finished a pair of garters for herself with the lilies of France her father King Louis had had blazoned on his armour and his horse's trappings on embarking for the Second Crusade. Her half-sister Marguerite, the Young King's wife, whom all of us liked as much as we disliked Alais, was busy at a surcoat for her husband Young Henry. By then they had both been crowned at

Winchester, the second coronation; the first had lacked Marguerite's presence because Curtmantle had detained her with the queen at Caen, it was said on purpose to insult King Louis. There had however been the Becket quarrel at that time, and Becket should have done the crowning. Marguerite sat serenely as usual among us now, stitching; I had laid down whatever I was at, and when she needed a certain colour of thread her half-sister Alais had taken, I offered to run and fetch it; it was a diversion from sewing, of which I am not fond. I hurried up the half-stairs to where Alais had a small chamber to herself at the end, not passed through by everyone like the rest but having a painted wall at the back. I envied her the chamber; it was private, and the wall itself was painted with flowers.

As I approached I could hear sounds somewhat like a puppy's yapping, but there were often hound puppies at Woodstock; they got underfoot. I moved the door-curtain a little, and fortunately did not call out as to why I had come. Instead, I stood there frozen.

On the bed was Curtmantle, his buttocks jerking busily. His face was hidden by the curtain, but his legs were unmistakeable; bowed, a horseman's, and clad in the grey woven hose he never troubled to cross-garter, so that as usual they hung shapeless. The lilies of France were below, trembling as if in a gale. I could see no more of Alais, but as I drew back silently she began to moan with pleasure, and something told me the king would soon be done, and might find me. I retreated hastily, went back downstairs and was sick. When I had finished it was still as if my knees had turned to water.

Berthe was waiting. It was probable that she had followed me; she was always my shadow, moving silently. "You will be better now, little duchess," she said comfortingly. "Do not be afraid to speak of it; all the court knows."

I never did speak of it, then or later. I made some excuse to Marguerite about not finding the silk. Her calm eyes raised themselves to my face and she said nothing. It was impossible to think of her as permitting the same situation, except with her husband. For the first time, I had sympathy with Richard. I wondered if he and the queen discussed it together; they were seldom apart and at that time, he was abroad with her. It was assumed from the beginning that in due course, Eleanor's inheritance would be his.

* * *

As the years passed Alais of France was seldom seen. She might have been less a ghost than a memory; but she was about the palaces, always in her own place, and the king continued to visit her. They say she bore him a daughter who died at birth. That birth must have been difficult; I never saw any alteration, on the rare occasions she was seen to pass by, in Alais's flat body, lacking as it did the curve of hip and breasts other women have. In fact she was so plain I used to wonder what the king saw in her; he could have had any woman he chose, except Marguerite.

Over the years, as I thought of it a great deal, a possible reason came to me. Alais was the daughter of Louis VII, whose wife Curtmantle had taken. It was true that Marguerite was Louis's daughter also, but her mother had been a chaste princess of Castile. Alais's mother was of the house of Champagne, with its hot lusty blood. Although Alais was the image of her father, with the creeping ways, the snivelling piety of the husband Eleanor of Aquitaine had despised, she had hot veins and a hot tail, perhaps from the beginning, though Curtmantle knew well enough how to seduce even young girls of narrow virtue, such as my half-aunt Alix de Porhoët whom Berthe never ceased to bewail. However to master Alais, outwardly so like her father, may well have meant in Curtmantle's mind the mastery of Louis himself, and of the quiet dignity with which he had outfaced Curtmantle on occasion, also the fact that the latter was still France's vassal for Normandy. It was all very well for Queen Eleanor to mock her former husband and relate the tale of how he had climbed a tree to defend himself when he thought he was defending her, in an unexpected green valley with fountains in Syria on the crusade; but Curtmantle must have read the chroniclers, for he was an avid reader, and have known the truth, which was that Louis had they said grasped at tree-roots above a precipice with one hand and laid right and left with his sword using the other. Such valiant adventures never befell Curtmantle himself, whose guile in war was greater than his wish for fighting, not that Louis had wanted so to fight; but Eleanor herself had been blamed by the French and others for her many unwieldy baggage-carts filled with carpets, perfumes and changes of elegant clothing, all of which delayed the crusading army as it marched to Constantinople and then Antioch. As for Antioch, she was still spoken of for supposed improper conduct with her young uncle Raymond; but they had been childhood companions, and by now he was dead. The nature of different loves is uncertain and interesting. Curtmantle may even have been jealous of Richard as his mother's favourite, and determined to outdo him as a man. For whatever reason, Alais of France remained his whore instead of marrying his son.

★ ★ ★

Other things had of course meantime arisen to fill the mind. I had not heard the great joyful clashing of bells at Canterbury on the return of Archbishop Becket, come home in 1170 to be slaughtered after six years' enforced exile in France. We ourselves were then at Bures in Bayeux, spending Christmas at the king's former hunting-box which had been so greatly enlarged it took the felling of four hundred oaks to finish it. I heard Curtmantle inveigh against the low-born clerk who had dared to defy him, and saw his eyes grow prominent and bloodshot as they always did when he was enraged; and four men I saw then slip quietly out of the hall. In the shock which echoed thereafter through Europe, in the two years Curtmantle prudently absented himself at that time in Ireland, I heard chiefly from Scotland itself by way of my two uncles, particularly old Ralph de Warenne, and knew war was preparing there before I learned of the rebellion of Curtmantle's sons, including my betrothed. The fact that it happened at the same time was by no means due to chance: everything had been planned over the years.

* * *

We were at Chinon, and something had made me wake up before dawn, when the mists still hung over the great ramparts and the hill above the river, both of which made the saying that the fortress owed its strength half to man and half to God. I threw back the covers and, moving softly not to waken Berthe who as usual slept on my pallet, went to the window-slit.

Nothing seemed other than as usual; nobody was stirring, and the castle slept. It was a cold night in March. I knew Young Henry was in another part of the fortress, sharing a chamber with his father. Curtmantle had seen fit to keep a strict eye on his eldest son of late; the young man was extravagant, and had complained about the giving away of certain of his allotted strongholds to help form a dowry for young John Lackland, so named because he had none.

I blinked myself half awake and stared

out into the spring night; there was a solitary glowing sign in the sky that heralds dawn, that of Mary Magdalene, steady and familiar on the low horizon as always. I thought of her and of how she had dried Christ's feet with her hair, which must have been long like mine. I was about to turn and go back to bed, when some matter, perhaps an increase of promised daylight from the still unrisen sun, alerted me. Something was sticking forwards and downwards across the great moat; the drawbridge. No doubt the king, with his usual suddenness, had decided to ride off early for some reason. I thought no more of it, and went back to sleep.

By full day, there was consternation; the Young King had stolen off in the night, and was well on his way to France. We had no time to learn more, only to look on helplessly; Curtmantle flung himself into the saddle, and galloped off after his son. We waited all that day for news, and the next; then he returned alone. He had missed the young man by a few hours, and Young Henry was over the border in his father-in-law's domains, by now with King Louis at Chartres.

His father acted with care and prudence, or tried to, perhaps not yet knowing the full extent of the conspiracy. He sent an envoy to Louis to ask courteously for the return of his son, when any grievances would be dealt with.

"Who sends the request?" asked Louis, with Young Henry tall and golden standing by; like many, the King of France saw only the charm, and was also aware of rising opportunities for himself.

He was told that the king of the English had sent it. He smiled. "The king of the English is here," he replied smoothly. "The late king resigned his realm to his son."

His pleasure at being able to make such a reply was perhaps pardonable. If I had run at once to raise the alarm about the lowered drawbridge in the cold spring night, would I have averted a war that soon threatened to destroy Curtmantle's very empire? It is pointless to ask such questions; as I said, I went back to bed at the time to get warm.

★ ★ ★

He had already suffered humiliation, but deliberately on that occasion. At Canterbury, to put himself right in the eyes of all men and the Church, he had walked at last in the rain and mud, with feet bare and bleeding on the sharp stones, to lie all night fasting before the high altar where Becket had been struck down. He was clad only in his shirt, and next day stripped this off to be flogged naked by seven prelates and eighteen monks, some of whom gave him five strokes each with rope scourges. I am glad that I did not see this happen. I had already heard a certain prayer of his, made on deck as we crossed over in storm to England, unheard, as he thought, by anyone. *St Thomas, guard my realm for me*. He had been standing alone at the prow: I, wrapped in my cloak, unseen behind him. The other women were below, as the crossing was rough.

The capture, on the same day as the penance, of my uncle King William the Lion, who had joined the conspiracy with his close kinsman Leicester and

Curtmantle's elder sons, was put down to the saint's timely intercession. If so, it was prompt indeed, and certainly unexpected.

★ ★ ★

Great-uncle Ralph de Warenne of course had much to say about it; my mother's brother David of Huntingdon, having ridden down the spine of England armed with hauberks and brightly painted shields, while his brother harried the north parts notably, was again hostage; and King William himself was held by then in Falaise. "I have seen that fortress," said old Ralph. "No man may ever win out unless the king wills: it is the strongest place in Normandy."

He spat into the floor-straw. "Curtmantle will wring the utmost from William of Scotland before setting him free," he said. "It's well known how he has always doted on the thought of making everything again as it was in his grandfather Beauclerc's day, and Northumbria was the least of it. Had my sister Ada's husband lived there would have been a strong king in Scotland when this Angevin came to power on Stephen's death. As it was, your uncle Malcolm the Maiden, God rest his soul — of what virtue is a vow of chastity that prevents a king making heirs? — admired this Curtmantle almost to the extent of being his dog, and all for the sake of a knighthood fitted out a great fleet to aid him that time at Toulouse. His brother William would have done no such thing, though he sailed with the rest; and this Becket, who is now a saint, made war more fiercely than any, with his grand bronze trumpets sounded before a charge. Curtmantle maybe started to be jealous then; as for King William, the same Curtmantle fell into a rage once when his very name was mentioned, tore off his clothes and chewed the straw the way he does. I heard of that from Du Hommet, who had spoken up for William. It is not likely now that there will be mercy shown, unless Scotland is signed away in some fashion at Falaise. There is no heir to inherit, and David is a prisoner."

He drained his wine-cup, and scratched his thinning hair. "My sister Ada will grieve," he said. "This wine is good, at least."

I told him the queen had begun the fashion of drinking wine from Gascony instead of English beer, and many were now following her example. "That is a notable woman," conceded Ralph. "They say Curtmantle's mother the empress was handsome also, but her haughty German ways were not liked by the Londoners or her second husband. It is strange that she and Geoffrey le Bel between them should have made a son so plain as Curtmantle; maybe he is Stephen's as they say, or in any case goes back to the tanners of Falaise."

It had been said before, and I remarked only that that was where the Conqueror had been born, and refilled his wine-cup carefully. He began to talk then, as old men do, about matters long forgotten except by himself.

"I can remember, when I was a child with your grandmother, my sister Ada, at Bellencombre, hearing of the White Ship's sinking, and we were made to say prayers for the souls of young William Audelin and his half-brother Richard, and Ada said one also for William's bride Matilda of Anjou, who lives still, a nun. Is it not curious that she should be the sister of Geoffrey le Bel?" The old man lacked guile in such matters by now, and opened his rheumy eyes.

"King Henry Beauclerc arranged both the Angevin marriages, first to his son and then to his daughter to preserve the Norman borders," I said. "The first was so happy while it lasted that after the drowning she — she had sailed in Beauclerc's ship with him, which reached shore safely to learn of the disaster — refused to marry again, and said she would become a nun and pray for her husband's soul." My great-uncle twirled the wine-cup; he himself was a man of the world and Normandy was as familiar to him as Scotland and England, for he still rode up, down and across all three. "She is abbess now, they tell me," he said, "at Fontevrault."

Fontevrault. The name aroused echoes in me. I did not know why, but soon became aware of some of it, and am still so, seated here alone at last with my flesh wasted, awaiting this birth while

I still live. My little friend Princess Joanna, the king's youngest daughter who set off long ago for Sicily with a jewelled wedding-gown and the finest pack-train ever seen, died two years ago at Fontevrault, a nun there herself only of weeks. How well I remember her pointed chin, like her mother's whom she resembled, and her gaiety and friendship! Her Sicilian marriage was happy, but the husband died. As a widow she was held to ransom for her possession and dowry by Tancred, to whose daughter my son Arthur is betrothed. That last was Richard's doing; I hope a Sicilian bride will not find the winters here too cold. Richard redeemed his sister, but had made an arrangement which Joanna declined with Plantagenet rage, namely that she should wed the brother of Saladin himself for the sake of general peace in the East. It would have been better for Joanna if she had; the man she did marry on the second occasion treated her badly. She gave birth to his son, then having been made pregnant a second time came to Fontevrault, demanding to take the veil. It was bestowed on her just before she died, and the child was born alive from her dead body, then after being christened died also. Old Queen Eleanor was present; how much she has endured! Joanna, therefore, is buried at Fontevrault; and so are others. I foresaw a part of it that time at Chinon.

In the epistles of Peter of Blois it is written that Solomon said there are four things a man cannot know; the path of an eagle in the sky, the path of a serpent on the ground, and the path of a man in his youth. Peter said that he could add a fifth; the path of the king in England. To that could be added Curtmantle's paths everywhere else. While we women were left at Chinon after Young Henry's flight, his father might have been anywhere at all; I do not remember him in the castle after his return from the swift pursuit he made in vain towards France.

It was of course said by the world that Henry II was accursed of God as the result of Becket's murder, even after having done penance for it twice over, at Avranches and Canterbury. Certainly, after that disasters crowded in on him from all directions, and did not cease with the capture of my uncle of Scots, brought down from Alnwick like a felon, with his feet tied under a horse's belly, then forced to sign the shameful treaty at Falaise. The war had broken out at three points, with King Louis aware of all of them; from the north, from Flanders into East Anglia under the leadership of our kinsman Leicester and his warlike Countess Peronelle, who wasted the land with mercenaries and was in the end captured half drowned in a ditch, bewailing the loss of her rings like any other woman. The commander sent against them was none other than my stepfather, Humphrey de Bohun, earl of Hereford; his loyalty to the king was unshakeable. I think my mother was happy enough with him, as far as I know.

The third outbreak, which began then and never ceased in Curtmantle's lifetime, was the revolt of the sons. To say this started because of Lackland's gift of Young Henry's supposed castles is to beg the question; it would have happened anyway. Lackland himself was with us at Chinon, being still very young. I disliked him more than ever, and the little Maurienne girl was fortunate to die soon before she had to endure him as a husband. He had, among other unpleasant qualities, a nature which pried into everything. One day we were talking idly about our ancestry. Marguerite and Alais had begun it, referring to Hugues Capet as though he had been the very Clovis who had received the holy oil from heaven, and who was in fact no relation of theirs at all. I retorted that I myself, through Matilda of Flanders, was descended from Charlemagne and, through my mother, from Edmund Ironside. Lackland broke in, having surreptitiously picked his wide bull's nose.

"Ironside didn't have an iron backside, ha, ha."

How he had heard about the manner of that death, which is kept most secret in our family, I know not; but it was not a remark to make in front of well-bred women. The two French princesses cast their eyes down and the little Maurienne girl stared. I rose and went out, making for the chapel. I knelt down and tried to pray for resignation to my lot, also for the king, wherever he might be. It was then I saw the thing which I knew had not yet happened; an old dead man lying, placed before the high altar, crowned with what I knew to be a petticoat fringe; it was my own. The old man was Curtmantle. When I crossed myself, the sight vanished. I mentioned the matter to nobody, but when we were all taken away from Chinon back to England, I found that, by accident, Berthe had left the petticoat, which had a gold trimming, behind.

I spoke of this matter to no one, as I say. Curtmantle by now is buried close by his son Richard, at Fontevrault. It is not far from Chinon, and the other things that happened I heard later, after much that befell me also, in Brittany.

★ ★ ★

I find that by now, with past events so like a dream, I look back on all that happened between Curtmantle and his sons with strangeness, as though I had not been myself then. As a rule my mind is clear, and clear it has remained in truth with regard to all that happened since; yet other events, some of them heard of many months after they had occurred elsewhere, I must recall at random. There were so many reconciliations after betrayal, then betrayal again after that; neither faith nor truth among the brothers themselves, trouble starting openly between them as soon as they were grown; only their father had constant affection for them, despite everything; it is true that he liked Richard least. All he received in turn from any of them was greed, ambition, treachery, the desire of each one to be first and to have the most. Whatever the Christian faith teaches they seemed to deny, these kin of the devil, by their actions. My husband was perhaps the best of them, but that says little.

There was the constant refuge of King Louis, and later his son Philip, beckoning to the princes in defiance of their father as they did homage to France for Normandy and the rest. It did not greatly matter to them who was king there, only that France desired Normandy, Brittany and

Anjou from Curtmantle. That gave them bargaining power such as merchants use as well as princes. Curtmantle was a match for them at least till the end, and whatever may be said against him, lacked vindictiveness; the only revenge he took on Young Henry was to make him look a fool, and he was one in any case. Being expected to rule England, being crowned, anointed and set aside for that purpose from a boy, he might have been assumed to have some notion of responsibility by the time he was of age. However there was none, although his charm and good looks, and his spending of money, made Young Henry many friends and supporters against his father. When Curtmantle acted, he ended by treating Young Henry as the child he still was, and at last publicly. A chronicler has described it as a father's gentle chastisement, but it must have made the Young King resentful to be forced to look foolish, reading abject retractions before an assembly of bishops and being dragged across the south parts of England like some Roman captive behind a triumphal chariot containing the father against whom he had rebelled. Had matters been as they should have between his parents, Queen Eleanor might have softened the chastisement; but by then she was in prison, having stirred the witch's brew to her own undoing.

The great war between them all began openly in 1173. It lasted, in the third aspect at any rate, for nearly fifteen years. Meantime my uncles of Scotland, having been forced into vassalage by the treaty made unwillingly at Falaise, were unable to marry without Curtmantle's permission and could get no legal heirs. I believe the whole matter killed my grandmother Countess Ada, who died in 1178, three years before my marriage. I had never met her, which is regrettable.

3

ALTHOUGH there was scant sympathy between my husband Geoffrey Plantagenet and myself, our marriage when it did take place hardly received much fostering, owing to the other events which crowded after that into both our lives. Geoffrey continued too smooth in manner for my liking; I have enough Scots blood to prefer downright speech. However his silken ways went far, later on, with the young son King Louis eventually contrived to get on his third wife, and who was called Philip, after Louis' dead elder brother who should have worn the crown. Later, by reason of his own considerable wiles, this young man with a mane of unruly hair became known as Philip Augustus. He and my husbands were birds of a feather, short as the time of their flocking together was to prove.

I try not to be uncharitable to the memory of my first husband; by contrast with the second, he was an archangel. It has to be remembered that Geoffrey was born at a time when his father Curtmantle was busied with arrangements for the marriage of Young Henry and Marguerite of France, with her important dowry of the Vexin. This put all other events into the shade. Also, Queen Eleanor had by then borne five children in six years, and was moreover already no doubt entranced by the most recent arrival, Richard himself, staggering back and forth by then on the straw or else her Syrian carpets. She cannot have been over-pleased to know that another was already on the way. A child can sense such things early, as I remember from my own childhood, also from watching my son Arthur and, God knows, before that poor little Eleanor, whom I should never have let go to England.

Geoffrey therefore had to rely on guile rather than strength to defeat Richard, of whom he early conceived a bitter jealousy. Richard was stronger, taller, beloved of their mother and of the people of England, who hailed him as a hero and later as the Lion Heart.

Also, Richard had Aquitaine as appanage, while my husband had to be satisfied with poor ravaged Brittany, even that being trebly due for homage to France, England and Normandy in the person of its meantime duke, the Young King. The situation concerning Breton homage would have been ludicrous had it caused less suffering in war, and there seemed always to be war in Brittany.

Geoffrey's marriage to me was delayed till 1181, and only took place then because his father had promised him my full dowry-money once he had persuaded the pope to allow it. This took time, and meanwhile Geoffrey received only half. Consanguinity, among us all, was as rampant as the lion my uncle William of Scots had by then adopted as the device on his banners to describe himself. The earlier marriage of Edith Matilda to Beauclerc made matters difficult enough without the marriage of Beauclerc's bastard Matilda to Conan III as well, and the added fact that Conan's mother had been the Conqueror's own daughter Constance, my great-great-grandmother and namesake. The pope moreover had such other matters on his mind as a schism and an antipope, into whose arms he feared to drive either Curtmantle or King Louis, or perhaps both; in any case pleasing one meant displeasing the other, so wisely he did nothing.

Long before that, as I remember clearly, all three brothers, the Young King, my Geoffrey and his brother Richard, none of them being aged twenty as yet, had decamped to King Louis, having deserted their father. I missed Geoffrey thereafter less than I missed the company of Queen Eleanor, who was shortly taken prisoner while having been captured trying to follow them, dressed as a man. I was at Chinon, and I remember the Queen was brought in by night, disguised thus, her long shapely legs visible in cross-gartering and her hair cut off beneath a draped hood. She was close-lipped and did not speak to me, or to anyone. Although she was brought over afterwards on the same ship as all of us, I was not permitted to be with her. It was of course known by then that she was responsible for the defection of her sons, which hurt Curtmantle deeply.

It was at that time that he began instead to favour young John, who owing to his tender age was still with him.

It was strange, and still is so, to think of Eleanor's sons taking refuge with her divorced first husband, not to mention herself, as was planned. That last shows a certain lack of consideration for Louis' feelings. He had been loth to lose Eleanor, having they say loved her greatly. She was still beguiling, and though Louis was by then old and sick he had the son who gave him hope; it cannot be surmised what might have happened, so greatly by then did Eleanor hate Curtmantle. I do not think this hatred preserved its full force during her long years of imprisonment; once he brought her out to spend Christmas among them, and I believe sent her a gift of a scarlet gown lined with fur, and she did not disdain to wear it. In fact there was a tough alliance of body and mind between those two which would never be fully destroyed. After Curtmantle was dead the Queen wrote of him as her dear lord, and had masses said for him, but perhaps could do no less. Meantime she was to be imprisoned in Salisbury, where she remained for a considerable time.

Meantime likewise, King Louis caused Curtmantle to lose a part of the commencing war by treachery, which showed how far he had travelled since the days of taking the Cross by Eleanor's side and fighting valiantly among Syrian tree-roots on a precipice. In fact he set fire to the town of Verneuil during a truce, having learnt deviousness. Curtmantle rebuilt the walls at once, but in course of this process learned of a fresh outbreak in Brittany itself, and hastened there. I was kept in Devizes with the rest.

The leader of the rising was Ralph de Fougères. This was a man of iron, with the cunning of a fox. He had been ruined by Henry II at Dol once already, and having lost all his possessions then had no more to lose except his sword-hand and his sons. He had contrived to rebuild Dol castle, which Henry had levelled in 1158, at the same time as taking the castle of Thouars, supposed impregnable, next year in three days, thereafter lopping the lands from its seigneurs, as I know well.

Now, he summoned my Breton lords themselves to do him homage, perhaps to distract them from the thought of their young duke Geoffrey, snug as a vassal in Paris. Raoul de Fougères did not obey. Having fortified his rebuilt strongholds, he was joined by others; by Astolf de St.-Hilaire, who had shared my husband's boyhood studies and was no doubt in touch with him; also Guillaume Patry, Raoul de la Haye-Normande, with a force of twenty-four knights; and poor desolate Eudo de Porhoët, who had crept back from Wales on hearing of his enemy Curtmantle's possible discomfiture. He had never forgiven him for the seduction of Alix.

Curtmantle then sent in paid mercenaries from Brabant. In my land they are known as Rouptiers, for good reasons. They pillaged, burnt and massacred without pity, and the sufferers were not those in arms against Henry II but the common folk, who had only a patch of bare land and perhaps a cow. Raoul de Fougères, who always championed the peasantry, cornered these Brabantine brutes between Fougères itself and St. Jacques-de-Beuvron on the Norman marches, a place I was to know too well later on. He then seized the fort, also that of Tilleul, leaving many hired corpses strewn on the ground.

Curtmantle rode then in fury over Brittany. He moved rapidly as always, followed by a large force from Normandy and Anjou. Raoul fled before superior numbers, Curtmantle's troops then plundered whatever the Rouptiers might have left, and my land lay in smoking ruins.

Raoul meantime had however not been idle. He had dug, in his own forests, tunnels which debouched a long way off and whose hidden entry was at Landéan. Into these cellars, as they are called, deep underground, he invited the town-dwellers and neighbouring farmers to come. He told them to bring their possessions, their food, even their cattle; these could later be conveyed elsewhere by means of the long subterranean ways. It was a heroic stand and had been carefully planned, but Curtmantle's men trapped the convoy on its way into the woods, and seized and killed every living thing, both men and cattle.

Raoul still did not lose heart. Curtmantle however, having ridden nearly two hundred miles in two days, took charge again at Dol, set up stone-throwers, and battered the castle once more into submission. The garrison surrendered, and Henry sent Hugh, late earl of Chester, in command there meantime by Ralph's orders, to prison at Falaise, with others. The name of Chester I was to hear again, to my sorrow, but this was not yet the same man.

It may be asked what an Englishman was doing at all in the business; or why, at the same time in England, the earl of Leicester, with his amazon of a wife Peronelle, should have sailed already with a troop of hired Flemings from Wissant to betray King Henry in his absence from his kingdom. The fact is overlooked of Leicester's close relationship to my uncle the King of Scots, who was conducting his own campaign in the north, having meantime signed the alliance in secret with King Louis.

The de Varennes, Warennes or Warrens — William the Lion had no other surname but his mother's and was known by it abroad — and the Leicesters were in fact close kin from the two marriages of my great-grandmother, Isabel de Vermandois, herself a cousin of the King of France; first to Leicester, then to Warren. That is the answer, which few know, the riddle of the planned great war. William the Lion had never ceased to resent the giving away of Northumbria by his dead brother Malcolm IV in virtual exchange for the knighthood the boy coveted. Curtmantle continued to refuse the honour otherwise; and there was no other man in the two kingdoms who could knight a fellow-king. Long after the Maiden's death the blaze broke out and spread, timed for the rebellion of Curtmantle's sons to be a signal. Like a bonfire in heather it smouldered throughout Normandy, England and Brittany, with stirrings also in Aquitaine where the treatment of the hereditary duchess was much resented. Eleanor however remained in prison for the full sixteen years, and her husband never trusted her again. Otherwise, he dealt as usual with the whole matter. In Brittany there was a dreadful combat after the Rouptiers were brought back by him there a second time. My Bretons lost fifteen hundred men, and St. Hilaire, Patry and many other knights were taken prisoner. Raoul de Fougères, shut up yet again in Dol, was forced to capitulate, but they did not obtain his person; he vanished into his forests once more, joined by a knight, an abbé and Raoul de la Haye-Normande. From this impenetrable retreat, which Raoul de Fougères knew like the back of his hand, they continued to harry Curtmantle's foreign devils; but Raoul's two sons, William and Juhel, were hostages, and he must have been concerned about their fate.

However Curtmantle, again, did not prove vindictive. He forgave his own flesh and blood, and the sons were later reconciled for the time as I shall relate. Money was promised to all of them, and to Geoffrey half at once, the rest upon our marriage, as I have said by now too often; but it was often said to him and, also, to me.

Curtmantle had been everywhere at once, unexpectedly as always; no other man could have achieved as much given the time and distance. Thereafter he had the Brabantines demolish all Raoul still possessed, then rode back to Le Mans in excellent humour. Some of this induced King Louis to send his peace proposals despite the fact that all of the young princes of England except one were at his court and in his hands.

There was in those days a great elm at Gisors, on the Norman border. The kings of France and England used to meet on the edge of the disputed land to discuss affairs as and when they were on speaking terms. On the occasion I describe, Young Henry, Richard and my betrothed, then hardly more than a boy, rode in all three behind the king of France. Their father, having arrived in time to capture the favourable shade, waited beneath the elm. His freckled face no doubt beamed expectantly beneath the greying red hair: I can imagine it. Despite everything, Henry II could not but rejoice to see his strong and splendid sons ride in behind the bowed form of Louis VII. Also, he would have forgiven his own flesh anything, and did so time and again.

They parleyed. Young Henry was offered half the revenues of the royal demesnes in England, or of Normandy if he preferred to live there with Marguerite. He was also offered three castles, Richard four in Aquitaine. Geoffrey as I have said was confirmed in the lordship of Brittany on condition that he could persuade the pope that he and I were not within the forbidden degrees. It was unflattering to me, as the prospective bride, that any eagerness my betrothed might show was rather for what he might gain from the outcome than from any particular desire to have me in his bed. At the time, however, Geoffrey was only fifteen, and no doubt at eleven years old I was not at my best.

Unfortunately Curtmantle, for all his careful thinking, remained still blind to what his sons desired more than all else; power of their own. He offered them lands, but on conditions laid down by himself, and with himself still as overlord. The meeting therefore ended without satisfaction, though a saintly archbishop named Peter of Tarantais was called in to mediate at last and to advise the papal legate, who had arrived and was somewhat at a loss. The princes refused the terms. This was no doubt on the advice of old Louis, who had as I say become distinctly less unworldly since the birth of his heir.

★ ★ ★

"Greatness is vanished," said my mother. It was one of the few times we met again; for long as a child I had had a dream of our travelling in separate litters, one conveyed one way, one the other, and her lovely face looking out at me between the curtains to say farewell. She was occupied now with other matters than myself; her ageing husband, their young son Henry of whom she was proud, the affairs of the Marcher people above whom they all three lived in the great De Bohun stronghold. She had been permitted to visit her brothers while they were held prisoner before being taken to Falaise, and for that purpose had journeyed to Northampton. It had done her little good. "I was ashamed to see my brother the King of Scots brought in so, feet still tied beneath his horse," she said. "He should have been wary of a possible ambush at Alnwick; as it was, the English stumbled on him and his following taking their ease in a field, and mastered them easily. Ah, you may talk of mists and of the intervention of St. Thomas after the King had himself flogged at Canterbury, but it would not have happened in the old days my mother used to talk about, before the civil war, having heard of them from King David. Then, when he was building all the glorious abbeys, he himself used to ride down in friendship often, also his son Henry of Huntingdon my father. Now, no one can travel north or south without a paper signed with the King of England's seal."

Her face, which long ago I remembered as so beautiful, had grown discontented and uncertain, as though she was used to obeying orders from the old soldier of a husband the King had given her. It occurred to me that although Hereford had covered himself with praise over his victories in East Anglia, the massacre of Flemish mercenaries by the peasantry, and the capture of fierce Countess Peronelle in her ditch, he had after all been making war on mother's own kin, Leicester himself being as I say descended from the first marriage whose second had later on produced Countess Ada, my great-uncle Ralph and the rest. It had not been a happy union, as the second earl of Warren and Surrey their father had earlier courted in vain the Scots princess Edith who instead married Beauclerc, and the widowed Countess of Leicester made a poor replacement even though she was high kin to the King of France. I tried to reassure mother.

"My uncle William did not lack courage," I said. "He sprang to horse, but it was killed under him. He fought like the lion on his own banners, but was overpowered."

"There are too many lions," said my mother. "Princess Matilda's husband, who called himself Henry the Lion like the late empress's first, is in trouble with his overlord the Emperor Frederick, and they say will no doubt flee to his son-in-law with his English wife and child. Another, they say, is on the way."

I was less heedful of the fate of Matilda of Saxony, though later it somewhat affected Scots royalty, than of mother's expressed scorn of lions; I recalled that in Merlin's prophecies Curtmantle himself was the lion's whelp. That lion of course was King Henry Beauclerc, who had in turn called himself the Lion of Justice. I reflected how poor Edith Matilda of Scotland might well have been happier had she married my de Warenne great-grandfather after all, instead of which she washed lepers' feet while her lord and master dallied with a Welsh princess at Windsor, and others elsewhere.

"What are you thinking of, Constance?" mother asked sharply. "Little Henry is never as secretive."

Stung, I told a lie and said I had been thinking of the old story of how Beauclerc's queen had been made, on marrying him, to change her name from Edith to Matilda on the excuse that the English would not know how to pronounce the former. "I have never heard anything as deceitful," said my mother in her old downright way. "The English knew the name Edith from the Confessor's time well enough. It was to ensure that all things in England became and remained Norman, except for the serfs. There are in any case far too many Matildas also, after the Conqueror's queen, who they say was a most vengeful woman; when his eye strayed once, she had the young woman in question hamstrung and her jaws slit. Also — " and her eyes brightened at the prospect of gossip, which no doubt did not often come her way behind the stern stones of Hereford — "she imprisoned a Saxon noble who had once scorned her offer of marriage while still a young woman in Flanders, and took his lands for herself."

I wondered if it was on a par with Berthe's tales of Curtmantle long ago in Wales, gouging out the eyes of the little Welsh boys and cutting off the girls' ears and noses; and did not mention the more recent tale I had heard, and did not believe either, of my two uncles

William and David ripping open the bellies of pregnant women to disgorge their unborn young on the campaign lately in the north of England. Instead, we conversed on more tactful matters till it was time for my mother to depart. I did not see her again, and only once more heard of her: we had become strangers to one another. In fact, I was beginning to feel like a stranger to everyone except myself.

Nevertheless I reflected, in view of what she had said, that King David of Scotland, builder of glorious abbeys, had been reared at Beauclerc's court from a child. That made the difference. The closest link now was my uncle David of Huntingdon, who differed no little from his grandfather and namesake, notably in the siring of bastards. All the ladies loved him. The king of Scots, William the Lion, was however less favoured by comparison, though he had an illegitimate son in London.

The Treaty of Falaise I believe was made publicly evident again at York before King William was returned to a kingdom which never forgave him for his capitulation. The second oath was taken in the presence of the prelate there, Roger of Pont l'Evêque, an unpleasant man who in their time had been a vicious enemy of Becket. Whether because of this or by reason of the saint's evident powers as lately revealed to his own misfortune, my uncle William proceeded to build an abbey in Arbroath dedicated to St. Thomas of Canterbury and no other. It is doubtful that he did so as a gesture to Curtmantle, by then his official overlord. He and my uncle David rode off to the far north presently to subdue rebels there, gaining the wild inaccessible places Curtmantle could no more reach than had his great-grandfather the Conqueror in his day. In London, my uncle William had left behind the bastard he named Robert, but Robert of London could never inherit the throne of Scotland. Had Curtmantle had more sons, it is even possible that he would have continued to prevent the marriage of either disgruntled royal Scots vassal. However even he was forced to realise that his remaining son Lackland, who made a shiftless fool of himself on being offered the Irish crown, would not survive long among the independently minded Scots if he ventured too far north.

I must relate the romance of my uncle William here; it had its touching side. Twelve years after these events, as a middle-aged man, this big-boned Norman — he took after his mother's side — fell in love with the young daughter of Matilda of Saxony, Curtmantle's own eldest princess, who as foreseen came over to England with her exiled husband and this Richenza, as she was known, though inevitably the chroniclers have called the child Matilda. Richenza was named, of course, for the Lion Heart, whose sisters adored him.

Curtmantle played my poor uncle William like a fish, saying the whole thing should be arranged if the pope willed it, well knowing that the pope would do nothing of the kind because of consanguinity and press of affairs. He then offered the disappointed king of Scots a pleasant enough bride, kin to the Leicesters and not too young, though still fit to bear children. Her name was Ermengarde de Beaumont.

She was married at last to my sullen uncle William at Woodstock in 1186, and Curtmantle absented himself after telling the wedding-party it might hunt freely in his forests and, for him, spending a great deal on the nuptial feasting. In fact, by then it was evident that Curtmantle could not hope to control Scotland either before or after death except by favouring his Scots vassals enough to permit them to marry and breed legally for themselves. My unfortunate uncle William however had only daughters by Queen Ermengarde for a long time, something after the earlier manner of King Louis and Eleanor. However at last a son has been born to them and has been named Alexander. They say he has red hair.

My uncle David refused to marry under vassalage, but waited till he could choose a bride of his own. Meantime he joined the Lion Heart on crusade, and had a like number of adventures except that shipwreck did not, in his case, lead to imprisonment. He had already experienced enough of that at Falaise, so God is just.

I remember him well. He rules his fief of Huntingdon now in splendour, like a king. However the three sons of his marriage have either died in infancy or are, with the regard to the single one who has lived, looked on for some reason as unfit to rule. The surviving son is called John. It is a name that seems to bring with it a certain lack of qualities, if not persistent evil luck by reason of evil doings. At any rate, Prince Alexander thrives and should reign in Scotland. My mother Margaret would have been pleased.

★ ★ ★

Meantime, concerning the time which I recall from much earlier, Scotland was as much subject to Curtmantle as Normandy, Brittany, Anjou and, despite Richard and his mother, the great inheritance of the south. I myself was more greatly concerned with the affairs of my own land, which despite Geoffrey's famous Assize, for which he is remembered, was still poor, troubled and often invaded. I was aware of the existence of such men as Ralph de Fougères and the de Thouars brothers, whom I had known at once as friends that time when, a child of eight, I had emerged from Rennes cathedral by the side of my future husband. Eudo de Porhoët also had returned, an old man now, as though no other land than Brittany could be anything but strange. All of us knew, nevertheless, that the real master of us all was still Curtmantle.

4

THE niceties of homage continued to mount in Curtmantle's brain almost to the point of madness. It was a different frenzy from the one that took him in his devil's rages or his occasional wild bursts of entirely human laughter. He was determined from the beginning to make England once more as it had been in his grandfather's day and to that end, offended many including the Scots even before Falaise. Once he had rolled on the floor and chewed straw in France at mention of my royal uncle William; now, after the latter's capture and his own triumph, he was almost too benevolent, inducing a smouldering rage in my uncle which induced him for a long time to be unkind to his wife. Curtmantle had also tormented the unfortunate King Louis much earlier by blowing hot and cold over Normandy, the Vexin and Marguerite's dowry; now, there was for the time a restless peace.

It is true that Curtmantle appeared reasonable enough at first after the collapse of the great conspiracy in 1174, with Leicester and his countess taken, their hired Flemings massacred by the angry East Anglian peasantry, and everyone chiefly concerned brought in chains to Falaise. Curtmantle later called a meeting between Tours and Amboise, and again settled money and castles on his sons, though leaving them still without power. Geoffrey was as before to enjoy half my dowry-money and the whole when he married me, but it had not yet happened. John Lackland was to receive eight castles instead of the three of Young Henry's which had sparked off the original quarrel. Nottingham, Marlborough, Anjou, Touraine and Maine saw this immature and vicious creature as master, though Lackland saw no reason, as Richard did at that time with tongue in cheek, to fall at his father's feet and kiss them. Such gestures did not come naturally to the future Lion Heart, whether or not he still considered the matter of Alais.

The Young King was treated meantime

like a mouse between cat's paws. I had observed these graceful animals, brought back as mother told me from the Holy Land after the Crusades; they bred notably, and replaced genets in most households, and their habits with prey were by far more cruel, for they played with them before killing them. At first Curtmantle stated that he would not receive homage from an anointed and crowned king like himself. At Argentan at Christmas we then feasted on venison from fourscore deer from overseas, the King's abject sons seated all together with him at the same table. Even then, Young Henry was already in renewed correspondence with his father-in-law in Paris.

He refused stubbornly — Louis had no doubt advised him — to accompany Curtmantle thereafter to England; he was either fearful of the fate of St. Thomas or of that of his own mother, meantime still in prison in Salisbury. However by April, after many persuasive letters from Curtmantle, the Young King met him and, according to pattern, duly fell at his feet. Curtmantle, displaying Christian forbearance, then sent his son off to visit King Louis in order to prove that all fears had been unfounded. Meantime Geoffrey was sent back into Brittany to demolish more castles in that unfortunate land of mine. It was at this point that I was at last able to look for the lost city of Ys, whose story had always haunted me; also, Sein, Isle of the Womb.

★ ★ ★

Riding through Finistère, which was at last safe with its count Guiomarc'h and his wild wife sent off together on crusade, I thought of many things. Some of them disturbed me. I did not trust Young Henry, despite his golden looks and pervasive charm; I recalled the arrogant remark he had made long ago at his Westminster coronation, when his father had served him on bended knee at the high table afterwards. That by now was common knowledge, and was the least of it. There was no doubt that there would be further trouble. Meantime I had seen my ravaged land, talked with the poor folk when they showed themselves and did not hide for fear, and devised what I could to amend things and to promise them better days. I had spoken the Breton tongue all my life with Berthe and had never forgotten it. She was with me now, riding over the forbidden land of Cornouaille, the wind from the sea blowing our hoods back from our faces. We had stayed at the abbey of Pont de la Croix and had heard a mass said for the soul of Astolf de St. Hilaire, who had been Geoffrey's friend, and was dead outside Jerusalem.

Cornouaille had been disloyal to my father, but was quiet enough now Curtmantle's hand lay heavy on it. Few in any case lived so far west. Now and again there remained a poor hovel almost level with the ground, and once a man raised his head in its round hat from where he was hoeing away at his lopion; goats grazed nearby and we stopped for a drink of their milk. The man brought his wife, who when she received my silver called a blessing, and desired us not to go any further.

"Nobody goes to that island," she said. "It brings ill."

"Not to women, surely," I was one by then, though not yet a wife. This no doubt accounted for my restlessness and my determination to see things for myself while I could. I had gleaned certain information from Queen Eleanor over the years, from the time when she was briefly allowed governance of Brittany and elsewhere.

We came at last to Pont du Raz, an expanse of grey sea and beyond, through the mist, a flat unknown shape; the Isle of the Womb. There was a boatman who lived by the shore, and like many had hidden himself and his boat from the late destroyers; now, he was found, but was unwilling to row out.

"It brings ill fortune," he said, as the woman had done. I laughed, and gave him a coin, one of the new ones with crosses Curtmantle had lately had minted in England. He spat on it, then regarded it with interest.

"If you will go, you will go," he said, but sat with downcast eyes on the way as he rowed, and would not raise his head to look at the approaching island. I sat with my cloak wrapped about me and only Berthe with me from among my women. I forbade her to follow me on shore.

"It is not safe to go alone, little duchess. Harm may come to you."

I was tired of hearing about harm and ill fortune. "How could it?" I said sharply. "No one has lived on the island for centuries. Leave me alone. I am as virgin as the dead sibyls; their ghosts will not curse me."

I stepped on shore, accordingly, by myself. There was nothing to be seen at first except flatness and stones, over which to clamber. It did not seem as if such a place could ever have been inhabited, so lacking was it in any shelter from the wind. My hair blew before my face, half blinding me. I walked on, buffeted and uncertain, perhaps beginning to hear strange sounds above the crying of the wind. I was determined to reach the centre before the tide changed. Presently I came on what must once, long ago, have been a forest.

I felt then as if the trees, which were no longer to be seen, were growing up once more about me; fire began to blaze between the trunks, which I could make out as it had suddenly grown dark, and was no longer day. From being uninhabited, the island was again full of forms; those of women, wailing and casting up bare arms out of black garments; of strangely dressed men brandishing short swords. The grief of the women was an ancient sound, like the sea's crying I remembered but could now no longer hear, and the wind had dropped. There was death here, death by fire, by water and the sword. I could smell burnt hair and flesh, and hear the screaming, and saw for myself blood running down into the ground. A feeling of infinite desolation overcame me. I was no longer Constance, soon to be the wife of Geoffrey of Brittany, the king's son, but some woman alive God knows when. The name of God, of Christ, brought real things back; the waves of grief and death went away as they had come. I was aware then of Berthe's arms about me, her voice in my ears. How long we had been there, how long I had been left alone as I asked, I did not know. Some matter had been interrupted which would have been made known to me had I waited, and now I would never know it.

"Come back to the boat now, little duchess. We must not miss the tide."

We went: but I had seen night there and darkness, and the flames rising, and now again it was like every other day.

What had happened on that island I was not able to elicit for long from anyone, for nobody would speak of it. It remained for me to ask, when after many years she was briefly allowed on certain occasions, before being returned to her prison, to appear with Curtmantle again, Queen Eleanor. She knew, naturally; that woman of the world knew most things, and would speak of them if let.

"It was after they drove the Druids out long ago," she said. "A few priestesses remained, nine of them, under the chief, Uheldeda, and sailors would often ask them, on the island where they had taken their final stand, to pray for fine weather. It is said that they were able to assume the shapes of animals when they chose, but no doubt that is a fable. They lived there for some years before being killed."

"What harm were they doing on that uttermost island?" I said. "Could they not have been left in peace?"

"No, the Church demanded that they be baptised, and when they refused, for it is not a part of their religion, Conan Mériadech, I believe, the one who failed to marry St. Ursula as his second wife, sent his soldiers to slay them. There were nine priestesses left. Three died in the fire, three by the sword and three were drowned in the sea. It is a tidy enough tale, after all." Her strange eyes stared at me from under their heavy lids; they had not faded with the years and still had many colours in their darkness like some unknown jewel. Her spirit did not appear broken by long imprisonment. By now, since her son Richard released her, she is active in the service of her last son of all, John Lackland, who calls himself king. Had Young Henry not died when he did, and Richard, and Geoffrey himself at twenty-eight, I, Constance, might have been queen of England. As it is, Arthur my son is by rights England's king; King Arthur, as in the days of Lyonnesse.

At any rate, for centuries no one would

so much as speak of that accursed island, the Isle of Sein, Isle of the Womb, where nine sibyls had perished rather than acknowledge Christ. I myself did not speak of it again.

★ ★ ★

Geoffrey, unusually, accompanied me to look for Ys; we were seldom together, and it shows the disparity in our natures that I cannot recall by now whether or not we were even yet married to one another. At any rate his usual band of young knights had come also, but I persuaded him to leave them on shore, dicing and drinking. It was a fine day at first, but as we drew out into the Bay of Douanarnez the sea grew choppy and the wind began to rise. I leaned out over the boat's sides to try to glimpse the lost streets and the palace of King Gradlon. It was not possible; the wind whipped the sea too fiercely. Geoffrey mocked me.

"It is an old wives' tale," he said.

"It is not." I was indignant. "Fishermen know every street, and there is the tomb of Ahès also, made up of sloping rocks."

"Last time you told me she was turned into a fairy; no fairy needs a tomb." He threw back his head and laughed, briefly resembling his mother. We were staying at Pont l'Abbé. I was still restless. If indeed we were married by then, my husband paid little heed to me. He was like Richard, and preferred the company of young men.

★ ★ ★

He had been twenty when his father knighted him at Angers; I was present then at the great ceremonies, and admired the huge towers and deep moat of the castle. This was Curtmantle's homeland, his own place of Anjou. He himself, again, was the centre of attention rather than the new knight. Wherever Curtmantle might be for the time; it was impossible to notice others. He seldom paused long anywhere, but when he did so for long enough to have a word, one was instantly aware of no one else. He could talk on any subject in any place, with the wind whistling round the stalwart towers or else calm, with a mist hiding the town's clustered houses about the castle's walls. There was a market one day and we stared down together at its colourful comings and goings, while Curtmantle talked of his handsome father and how well he knew he himself was not handsome. "You have contrived without it," I told him drily, and his great laugh rang out, full of vigour. It was possible still to understand how at eighteen years old he had lured the greatest heiress in Europe from the King of France's bed to his own. I have no doubt that in those early days Eleanor, who was a merciless mimic, would divert him in it by comparing poor King Louis' erstwhile performances to his.

I think I ventured to plead for her then, and he scowled and turned away. She was still in prison, although the sons had returned for the time.

★ ★ ★

Louis VII himself did not live much longer, and the tale of his dying is a strange one. His only son Philip, got with such travail, was out with the hunt and lost himself, wandering all night in the forest and being rescued at last by a charcoal-burner. Being a sickly creature Philip fell ill of a fever, and was soon thought to be in danger of his life. His old father was in despair, and three nights in succession had visions of St. Thomas of Canterbury, who promised him that if he would only visit his shrine in England, young Philip would recover.

The old man trembled greatly, much afraid; neither he nor any former king of France had visited England, the land of his enemy. At last, in extreme fear and praying without ceasing, he set out; and was greeted by Curtmantle warmly as an honoured guest. The pair went together to the shrine, and prayed there. On return the king of France was told that his son was well, but by that time he himself was ill; the agony of the whole business had caused Louis to take a seizure from which he never recovered. Until he died, some months after, young Philip reigned as king; then smoothly, after hearing masses for his father's soul, entered into his kingdom.

★ ★ ★

Geoffrey, who was to become King Philip's great friend, had by then been sent once more to harry my poor country, having been with his father in Normandy all the previous summer. It is a tribute to the tenacity of my Bretons that there was still any fight left in them; but Geoffrey was never the warrior his brother Richard was to prove. Richard gave no quarter.

I had sewn my wedding-clothes long ago, and it seemed as if the bridal would never take place, not that I was eager for it. If my betrothed was so, it was because of the promised money. I was sixteen, and *16* growing taller; soon it would be necessary to alter the lengths of my gowns. Berthe was still with me, muttering on about Curtmantle's cruelties in the Welsh war long ago, as if nothing had happened since. For once, I turned on her.

"They fight differently in Wales, being fleet of foot and knowing their valleys," I told her. The same could be said for my Bretons, but the country is more open, with its heather and the standing stones from ancient times. Henry's blinding

263

of the two sons of Owain Gwynedd and twenty-five other hostages had taken place when he was driven mad by the mud in the flooded valleys and the impossibility of finding the enemy. In fact he avoided pitched battles himself by custom, but objected when others did the same.

His sons deserted him again at Louis's death, and fled to the new king in Paris. That last was already at war with yet another Philip, count of Flanders. There seemed always to be war.

The duke of Burgundy, the counts both of Flanders and Sancerre, and the warlike countess of Champagne, a sister soul to Peronelle held still at Falaise, rose against King Philip together; and Young Henry, Richard and my Geoffrey marched to Philip's aid. The great friendship began, and I believe delayed my marriage, as there was more money to be had meantime from France than by way of me.

They squabbled then, the brothers, my Geoffrey refusing to render homage to Young Henry for Brittany, as had been agreed earlier. Curtmantle replied by laying siege to Rennes in person. I was not present when my capital went up in flames, though later we rebuilt it. Geoffrey besieged certain English troops in his turn, they surrendered, and he then made it up in some manner with his father. In the end, after I had lost the course of events, word came that Philip of Flanders had been starved into submission at his castle of Crépigny and that at the same moment, the pope had decided that Geoffrey and I were after all not within the forbidden degrees, despite the evidence. Money speaks for itself.

We were therefore married. A great many things were going on at the same time, and Curtmantle having about then demanded eternal fealty from all his sons, Richard refused him homage. My husband went off into Brittany to collect mercenary troops, and again it was war. Curtmantle confronted his rebel sons then at Limoges and was finally greeted by a rain of arrows, one of which pierced his cloak. Next day he was saved again by his horse, which flung its head up and received a second arrow in its throat.

It was scarcely the season for a bridal, but perhaps by then it was shelved: this happened frequently, but sooner or later I became duchess of Brittany both by my right, and by Curtmantle's arrangement long since.

* * *

More money changed hands at Caen at Easter, the count of Flanders being filled with piety all of a sudden. He swore that he had already vowed to go to Jerusalem, and yielded up evidence in writing that the Young King had promised him Dover and Rochester castles in the late rebellion. In exchange for this information, Curtmantle resumed the count's former subsidy of a thousand marks a year, a sure sign that he was pleased to lay hands on the paper in question. He then accepted Young Henry's abject homage, formerly refused by him as they were both kings: by now, Curtmantle felt differently.

Thereafter I had some sympathy with Young Henry, whose sire proceeded to make a public spectacle of him as I have described. The young man was taken to England, where homage and fealty were performed once again. In addition, Curtmantle, smiling, had the letter I have mentioned read out in presence of his assembly of smug bishops. It described the young man's former sobs, his shedding of tears, his prostration at his father's feet, and his insistence on doing homage despite the respectful protests of his sire. Young Henry — his wife Marguerite had been present to witness all of it — was then taken to Canterbury to give solemn thanks for the peace.

★ ★ ★

Meantime Richard was reducing Poitou on behalf of his father. Geoffrey my husband let any prospect of marriage affect him so little that he proceeded to inflict such evil on Brittany it is a miracle that his memory is respected there: the excuse given was that certain men had held out against his father. He has been recorded as among the better of our rulers, but after the weak reign of my own father perhaps force appealed to some.

Meantime, King Henry's son by the woman Ykenai, the one I call Tacheté, was to become bishop of Lincoln. I greatly preferred this Geoffrey, as I have said, to my own, and by the end he was the only one to show loyalty to his father and was constantly in his company.

★ ★ ★

Young Henry, described by then as a most lovely palace of sin, was still being dragged about by Curtmantle over all the latter's dominions except for Poitou. This process was supposed to prepare the young man for responsibility. It is true that he had done wrong, but by this time the bear-leading had become intolerable. Like the count of Flanders, Young Henry pretended piety or perhaps really felt it, and begged to be allowed to go on pilgrimage to Compostela. This was refused. The gentleness of the paternal chastisement did not abate; but at last Young Henry and Marguerite were permitted to leave for Normandy by themselves.

They were however delayed by contrary winds till the subsequent Easter, which Curtmantle held at Winchester with all of us present, even Queen Eleanor, brought meantime again out of prison. It might have been then that I asked her about the Isle of Sein. She seemed as usual.

It was an outwardly festive occasion, even the King's bear having been brought down from Nottingham for our diversion. I watched the poor beast's caperings and thought, not for the first time, how we were all in Curtmantle's power still, as much as the bear.

★ ★ ★

Richard was presently uncertain of success in Poitou, an unusual circumstance. Still more unusually, he asked his father for help. Curtmantle, short-sightedly or else trustingly, sent the Young King to aid him, and as soon as the tide landed him and his wife on the shores of France, the latter fled with Marguerite to Paris. However he was persuaded to join Richard later on, and together the brothers besieged the castle of Chateauneuf-sur-Charente and took it within a fortnight. The Young King then absconded, having had enough of warfare.

He returned to Poitiers, leaving Richard still fighting in the Angoumois, for Richard loved war above all. Many of the Young King's former supporters joined him again, despite everything; it was feared there would be a second rebellion, or was it by then a third? A man named Adam of Churchdown, Young Henry's vice-chancellor, ventured to send Curtmantle a warning letter accordingly. It was intercepted, and Young Henry, described not long before as only a little lower than the angels, caused Adam to be whipped naked through every town they passed and to be imprisoned, at last, exhausted and bleeding, at Argentan. No doubt it relieved some of Young Henry's pent-up fury at the memory of his own humiliations.

It was Count Philip of Flanders who had introduced him, and later my husband, to tournaments. This mock warfare was less well known then in England than in France, and at first was mocked at before it became fashionable. This last was partly because it could make money for anyone who could capture a knight and hold him to ransom, as in real war. Count Philip had fitted out the Young King splendidly on one occasion when his own father's parsimony had left him poorly clad and horsed. The 'good and beautiful and courteous' Young King thereafter made mock war his particular concern. Later, it was to kill my husband, no doubt without anyone's intention.

About this time my friend young Princess Joanna went off to Sicily with her jewelled wedding dress and other gear. Her going left me lonely, for Queen Eleanor, after the feastings with the bear, had been returned grimly to her prison. There was in fact small female company left except for that of Berthe and her mutterings. The little girl Alice of Maurienne, betrothed since infancy to John Lackland, had died long since of some childish ailment, so John was betrothed shortly thereafter to the heiress of Gloucester instead. She brought him lands, but like myself and Geoffrey the two were close kin and the marriage could not be consummated. Hadwisa of Gloucester was a strange girl, said to be of the old religion of green men and forest gods, but I never knew her. Christmas that year in any case we kept at Nottingham, again diverted by the bear.

5

GEOFFREY PLANTAGENET and I became one flesh, as the scriptures put it, in the early summer of 1181. It could have happened earlier but for the reluctance in both our minds. Geoffrey, like all Curtmantle's sons except for the boy William who died and whose preferences could not have been foreseen, and John Lackland whose unamiable lusts evidently include women only, had the hidden tastes of the troubadours. One reason may have been the early instilled hatred of their father by their mother, giving them a dislike of the married state. It is true that Young Henry had an affection for his wife Marguerite, but his friendship for Philip of France was of more importance to him by far.

I myself had perhaps as little to complain of as Marguerite in that Geoffrey himself was courteous enough to me as long as we lived as brother and sister. Without doubt I was married to one of the pleasantest of the sons; I am thankful that Richard of Poitou did not fall to my lot, as he later made his Navarrese bride most unhappy and it is almost certain the marriage was never consummated any more than Lackland's. The long-drawn-out insult concerning Alais of France no doubt scarred him, Richard, as well. By the time of which I write, she was being jestingly offered as a bride instead for Lackland, who had failed to achieve the Byzantine Emperor's daughter and Alice of Maurienne. That was before he got land in England with Hadwisa.

As for my Geoffrey, he was after all handsome, hospitable and charming to his friends, agreeable to all — a trifle too agreeable — and described as an able governor of Brittany despite the harm he had done there at his father's orders or else despite them. He got himself liked by most Bretons despite being the son of the Angevin monster who had ravished Alix de Porhoët. It was no longer as evident that the real master of us all was the same man, who had sat above us in Rennes cathedral while Geoffrey received Breton allegiance at twelve years old. Geoffrey by now decided certain matters for himself, and even made a show now and again of consulting me. We were good enough companions, as I say, when it did not come to sharing a bed, when we embarrassed one another.

That was in fact never a success, as I suspected at the time and have found out for certain since. On the bridal night itself Geoffrey was inept and hurt me, getting the whole matter over too quickly. The losing of a virginity is a painful affair, as men should realise; but all Geoffrey said smugly afterwards was that at least it had been evident that his father had not got at me first, like Richard's intended bride.

"Did you suppose that I would permit him?" I asked indignantly. Geoffrey ran his fingers through his red-gold hair and smiled in the summer half-dark. He had grown what were beginning to be called machutos, the allowing of long hair on the upper lip on each side and combing, twisting and taking pride in it thereafter. This had become fashionable since the crusaders made their appearance differ from that of the smooth-faced Saracens. It was a return, in fact, to the old Saxon fashion, though of course nobody said so. Even Curtmantle later grew himself a red beard, though it was never long and he kept it firmly clipped.

"Women cannot resist him," replied Geoffrey briefly with regard to his father, and turned over to sleep. Thankfully, he did not have to share my bed often after that before I fell pregnant. It was decided by us both that if the child proved a girl, she should be called after Geoffrey's imprisoned mother. This would rebuke Curtmantle, who by then was still withholding the dowry-money; in fact, Brittany was still so greatly ravaged that there was little to be had, especially after the king's burning of Rennes.

The pangs of childbirth came in due course, and I was hardly consoled at last by the sight of the tiny silver-fair creature, with her skin, even then, like a pearl. Queen Eleanor was pleased at the naming, and somehow from her prison sent me the great Talmond gerfalcon in gift. I recovered soon enough from the birth to ride out at times and fly her.

As for my child, my daughter, I never loved her enough, perhaps less than my falcon. I can see now that many things are my fault. A child's mother should guard it, fiercely if needed; and I let them take Eleanor away to the English court, as I thought, as had after all been done for myself, the French princesses and others. They did not however keep her there, but in Bristol tower, and later in a convent at Amesbury after briefly letting her travel about with the released queen. There was a project to marry her into Austria, but it came to nothing. The cloister is no place for any Plantagenet, or for any daughter of mine. I can recall the little creature in my solar, the pale sun shining on her bright hair; and Geoffrey coming in once or twice from the hunt and picking his daughter up and kissing her; and that is all. Lackland now will never set her free. I often think of Eleanor and at times pray for her, and for myself, and constantly for my son Arthur in France.

As regards that, we both knew that Geoffrey's father would demand a son of us, and tried for a time; but I did not conceive again then. Gradually Geoffrey and I became acquaintances who saw little of one another; he had his friends, young men mostly from France, and they would dice and jest and drink together while I rode out with my women and my hawk. I would see, as I rode, the strange shapes of the dolmens, a restored stone chapel or two, a fountain or a new wayside shrine erected since the war. Occasionally the peasants would call blessings as I and my women rode by. I ceased to complain about my lot; many wives were worse off than I, and when it came to the famous Assize of Count Geoffrey I was not even resentful that it should have been in his name and not my own.

I stood with my little Eleanor by the hand to watch my husband, splendid in appearance as usual, go into the assize in procession, followed by his knights. The common people clustered outside to stare, then when everyone had gone in turned towards Eleanor, whom already they called the Pearl of Brittany. They knelt before us then, their rough heads bowed. Several of the women wished me a son soon, while the rest stared at my daughter, remembering Alix to whom they still prayed.

Meantime the arrangements made at the Assize were sensible. *Nos Geffrey, le rey Henri fiz*, had in fact less to do with its arrangements than his father, whose prudent foresight my husband lacked as a rule. It concerned the division of fiefs among heirs, differing some little from the laws of England and ensuring fair treatment of the younger brothers in a lordship, who had hitherto been subject often to the greed of the elder. From now, these young men were to be given enough to enable them to live in decency, to appear at court or to arm themselves The Geste of Constance, for war. The avid hoarding of fortunes was at an end; not that there were many left by that time in Brittany.

There was surprisingly little disagreement; bishops, counts and barons seemed in amity, and copies were later sent off to them in proper fashion, to be kept. There would henceforth be no dividing up of lands, the eldest to hold total seigneury, as in England. There were the eight shires, named likewise. Default of male heirs and marriage of vassals was dealt with; the 'odious dependence' of minors was to cease, also the refusal of landowners to accept homage from younger brothers, which hitherto had often deprived the latter of the benefits due to them. One clause allowed romance to prevail; a lord might marry an heiress who was his vassal without the agreement of her relatives. This, ironically, has happened lately in the case of Lackland, and has caused much trouble; but not all men are as vile, or all brides as young as Isabella of Angoulême.

Having dealt with the issue of younger brothers dead without immediate heirs, the conference ended and, shortly, ceased to be spoken of, as more attention was paid everywhere to the recent demand for a Third Crusade, the Second having done little except to make everything worse between infidel and Christian.

My husband, eager to go and also to persuade Philip Augustus to help him gain Anjou, which Richard then held, went off to Paris. I never saw him again, but before that we had said a particular farewell with the aid of Merlin. One other thing he did with my approval, which was to make Raoul de Fougéres, hitherto defiant in his forests, seneschal. This gained the loyalty of much of Brittany.

6

BRITTANY, my land; I love it, both for its past and for its present. Before I lost my health I used to like to ride out among my people, and they knew I did not come to take their goods but instead to ask for their welfare, bless their children and hear their troubles, which as usual were many, then do for them what I might. Nevertheless their faith sustained them, although I could perceive many things with which they comforted themselves and which were not altogether as they seemed. One was of course the famous Alix, about whose real fate I know nothing; either she died in giving birth to Curtmantle's child or else her father Eudo, remaining much mortified about the whole business, married her off shamefacedly in Wales. Berthe's version was somewhat different. "Our virgins," she would say to me reproachfully, "see in the crystal waters of our many fountains her smile, and pray to her and put flowers in the chapels to her." I myself never saw a smile in a fountain, but perhaps by then I was no longer a virgin; there were not many times before my marriage before I was left free to gaze into Breton fountains or at Breton moors.

The past of Brittany fascinates me; it used to be known as Armorica in the days of King Arthur, or as a part of Lyonnesse. The latter name is older, from the time of the Romans when their empire extended from one end to the other of the known world, and was Lugdunensis then. I had this from Curtmantle, who had studied such things; in his busy life not everyone knew he was a scholar and that reading was his favourite pastime. In Lugdunensis, Roman centurions on the banks of the Varenne in what was later Normandy were taking wives from the families who lived at the river's source and took its name which is still, as I say, the only surname of the kings of Scots. History knows few boundaries, and that Roman legacy is perhaps the reason why my ancestors were tall.

Whether the kingdom of Ys was partly

legend brought with the ancient Celts from wherever they came, there was certainly a king named Gradlon at one time in Brittany. They had later cruel kings, such as wife-eating Conamor, or Salomon who was rich enough to send a statue plated in gold leaf to the pope and was later blinded: but Gradlon looked after his people. They revered him so greatly that still, in my country, wine is poured into the mouth of his statue once a year and the drops dried with a clean linen napkin. He was married to a queen named Tigride, which sounds as if she was somewhat fierce. At any rate their daughter Ahès was very wicked, and lived in her castle of Carhaix which in our tongue is Ker-Ahès. She took many lovers. One of these was so agreeable to her that she finally promised to obtain for him the golden key which guarded the city of Ys, which her father Gradlon kept carefully on a chain round his neck. Curtmantle said this was the same as in an old Greek tale, and it was not a key but a lock of magic hair; I do not know. Ahès put her father into a drugged sleep, took the chain and key from about his neck, and gave it to her lover. He was of course the devil, which Ahès, being a fool at heart like so many wicked people, did not realise. The devil then unlocked the city's gate with the golden key, and instantly the sea flooded in. The drugged king woke; but all of that great city, which had been famous throughout the world, was drowned under water till the end of time. King Gradlon managed to escape on his horse, and being fond of bad Ahès took her up beside him to be rescued also; but the horse would not move, and the sea rose higher and higher till it reached the king's ears. A voice then told him that he would certainly drown unless he got rid of the demon on his saddle-bow. Sadly, he put Ahès from him, and escaped to govern such land as was left. Fishermen can still see the city on a clear day when the sea is calm, and know each one of its streets, deep below the Bay of Douarnenez.

"What became of Ahès?" my son Arthur used to say, though he knew the answer already for I told him the tale often. He liked to hear how

Ahés was perhaps drowned, so that her tomb can still be seen; or else that she was turned into the water-fairy Morgane, who later on beguiled King Arthur himself so that he was accursed, and lost his kingdom after fighting for it most valiantly against the Saxons. They are the white dragon while Arthur is the red. That is a prophecy of Merlin also. Both are said to have lived in a cave beneath a lake in Wales for a thousand years, till Merlin himself caused them to rush out, confounding everyone as I shall relate.

"You are the second Arthur," I would say meantime to my son. "You must not be beguiled by the fairy Morgane. You are to marry a princess from Sicily."

At that time, his uncle Richard had arranged it, on the way to his crusade. We have heard no more since John Lackland claimed the crown.

Arthur, his fair hair shining, used to promise not to be beguiled. What a king he will make when he overcomes Lackland! I am glad he has the protection, while he is still so young, of France.

King Philip they say loves him greatly. So do I; enough to have parted with him for his own safety. How I wish this birth was over! However after it, I will soon die.

7

ERLIN, who has been trapped in his tomb for several centuries, was responsible for the conception of my son Arthur of Brittany. Of that there is no question.

There is an ancient forest which used to be called Brocéliande and in its day, extended over half Brittany. We had ridden out, all of us, there one day from Rennes for Geoffrey to hunt with his French following, with whom he would shortly ride to Paris. I left them as they turned into a clearing, and heard the horns wind as they made off. I do not like watching the stubborn brave wild boars stuck; they have no chance against the nets and staves. Also I was anxious to find, by myself, Merlin's tomb.

I had been nourished on tales of him from childhood, both by way of Berthe, who of course knew many of them, and also Queen Eleanor. In the latter's brief regency of Brittany she had learned much ancient lore, no doubt being interested in Merlin since he had called her the double eagle; this had not happened in the land of the troubadours. As I rode, hearing my mount's hooves soft on the forest moss while the sounds of the hunt grew ever fainter in the distance, I remembered what I had heard, moving among green shadows.

Merlin's name was Merlin Ambrosius. He was the son of a king's daughter who swore she had never lain with any man. After his birth she became a votaress in a church said to be dedicated to St. Peter. Merlin himself, playing as a boy with others in the town's streets, was mocked by the others as a moon-calf, something which has no father. The emissaries of King Vortigern, who like many ruled by murder, then rode by. They were looking for a male child born of a virgin, that they might have his blood. This was to be soaked into the stones on a castle the king was trying in vain to build in Wales. However the stones kept disappearing into the hill, and a voice told them in the end that only by this means of blood could the castle be completed.

They had set out over the length and breadth of England to find such a one, without much hope. However seeing Merlin, they brought him instantly to the king. Vortigern, for once, decided not to spill blood; the young Merlin was handsome as an eagle, with a quick bright eye.

"Take me to the mountain," he told them. When they reached it he made a prophecy there, the first of many. The stones would not settle, he informed them, because under the mountain lay a great lake. The stones continued to fall into it and would do so until the lake was drained dry. "If the king's men dig into the base of the mountain and let the water out they will find, when it is drained, two caves in which live two dragons, a red and a white." These are the dragons I have already mentioned; and then, Merlin promised, the castle could be built.

All this was done, but the dragons, when unearthed, made so terrifying a din and smoke, and battled with one another so fiercely, that the king and his men were struck with terror. Merlin accordingly prophesied again. "The white dragon will tread on the neck of the red at last, until one Arthur, *Aper Cornubiae*, comes out of Cornwall." These words mean the Cornish boar, and so the first Arthur was known when he came, and trod on the white dragon, the Saxon race. I myself, having blood both red and white, take great heed of this story.

Now, riding for a little while, I found the tomb. It was a flat stone overgrown with holly, a sacred plant to the Druids as well as their mistletoe, which they said was frozen lightning. I dismounted and knelt by the stone. Merlin in the end had been beguiled by the wicked Viviane, his paramour, and caused to tell her his inmost secret. To keep the power to herself she used his spell to immure him under the stone, as she thought forever; but it is known that he will come again, as will the hero Arthur.

As I knelt there, I heard again the words *Aper Cornubiae* spoken by a voice. It came to me that Brittany is Little Britain, and that Cornwall and Cornouaille come from the same root, said to be the name of Cornutius, a Trojan prince descended from Aeneas. All things go back to the beginning; Aeneas' mother was a Greek divinity named Thetis. Then I heard more words, as if a voice spoke from the tomb and yet was at the same time within me; and I recalled the legend of Merlin's mother who said a most beautiful young man came to her, then vanished when the other virgins appeared. Some said he was an incubus, sent from the devil; others from God. At any rate, their son Merlin spoke then to me.

"Go now to the Valley of No Return, to the high rock there, and wait for your husband. You will conceive a son together, and call him Arthur."

I felt my senses swim, and presently rose. I then mounted my horse slowly, and slowly rode on to where the valley lay. It was shaded by trees and a light wind started up, which as I dismounted and climbed the rock, grew stronger. I waited, warmed by the sun and buffeted by the wind. I knew that Geoffrey would be caused to come here alone, and knew also what I must say to him.

He came in the end, saying he had seen my palfrey tied to a tree. He was hot with the hunt, perturbed and somewhat cross at having to search for me. He seldom left his friends.

"Why did you go off like that?" he said. "You should have stayed with the hunt. We brought down a fine boar. The rest have gone back." He stood there frowning, the sun shining on his bright hair and the cherished whiskers, which drooped.

I said "You came because I knew you would come. You must lie with me here, now, on this rock. We will make a son together."

"Are you mad?" he said. I heard his hard Plantagenet laughter. It was different from the bonhomie he showed to others. I knew he and I would never be one in spirit, but I made him lie down, and be a husband to me, as had not taken place for long. I felt my body yield itself in a way that had never before happened from the beginning. The wind still blew among the trees and about the rock. I shut my eyes, thinking of our son.

Geoffrey rose presently, flushed a little with more than hunting. "You were always strange, Constance," was all he said, but took my hand to raise me, and we went back together down the slope. Next day, he left for France. Within the month, I heard that he was dead. He was twenty-eight years old.

8

THE reason given out for my husband's death in Paris was that he had taken a fever; that is not the truth. I heard later that what occurred was that during a tourney, which the young king Philip in any case disliked and preferred real warfare, my husband quarrelled with some knight, was dragged from his horse and trampled on by others to the injury of his intestines, so that he died soon after. Philip Augustus was in great grief, and at the requiem in Nôtre Dame, made show to leap into the grave. I do not think it was entirely sorrow over the loss of Geoffrey — they had however been friends — so much as the receding of the prospect of homage both for Brittany and Normandy, both of which my husband had lately performed, betraying his father.

The requiem itself I believe was a stately one. Marguerite was still there, present in Nôtre Dame to hear

Maurice, bishop of Paris, pronounce the funeral oration. The king founded four chaplaincies to say perpetual masses for Geoffrey Plantagenet, *un jeune prince devenu breton de coeur et d'affection*, or so it was said. There had been a poem written about his brother Young Henry, the latter's arrogance and folly forgotten;

> *The sum of tears that this sad*
> *century has shed*
> *Seem light against the death of the*
> *young king.*

There had however been an earlier verse still written to my husband, in the days before the Young King himself became a miracle-working saint. It inveighed against the latter and Richard, and said

> *If only Geoffrey, noble duke of*
> *Brittany,*
> *Had been the eldest of the English*
> *princes;*
> *For he's a better ruler than you*
> *both!*

That being as it may, Geoffrey had done the part God demanded of him; at our coupling on the high rock he had fathered a son born eight months after his death. Perhaps I should have grieved for my son's father more. As it was, when the news came, I still lay on in my solar, cool as it was out of the August sun. I knew I could govern Brittany alone better than any man, for Queen Eleanor had taught me out of her experience there. My child was new within me, and meantime I told no one.

★ ★ ★

There was a further requiem mass for Geoffrey held in Rennes cathedral, when the trees were already dulling their leaves beyond in the forest. After it was ended Archbishop de Fougères came, and Du Hommet, now bishop of Dol; Roland de Pise of Avranches, and William de Lanvallay the seneschal, to me. All were Curtmantle's men. They regarded me gravely. I knew why they had come.

"Madame." The archbishop wasted no time. "Your daughter is the heir to

Brittany now, with our sad loss of her father, whose soul God rest. It is possible that the king of France may seize her for his own purposes, as he did the heir of Chateauroux and the heiress of Issoudun. He could then marry her where he will. It is best that she is conveyed, instead, safe to England."

"That is what our lord king would have us say," put in Du Hommet; he knew me a little and had always defended my uncle the king of Scots. "You would be wise to heed him, duchess; the child will be reared as befits her station. You yourself were so at Woodstock, under the queen's own care."

They were talking too much, trying to persuade me against my will, forgetting that the same queen was in prison. No mother wants to part with her child, despite the custom of courts in which I had myself been reared in England; but I was prepared. I had revealed to nobody the secret in my womb; the Pearl of Brittany was no longer Brittany's heiress, and nobody knew it except myself. The knowledge gave me power. I lowered my lids and appeared to be considering, a sorrowing widow about to be bereft of her only child.

I knew that they had taken what they thought to be my state into their considerings among themselves and earlier with Curtmantle; and had decided that I could do no harm to Angevin interests in Brittany, left to rule her alone. No remarriage I might make would give future children of mine any prior right over the heiress of the Plantagenets. She would be safe enough in their hands.

Eleanor clung to me, crying; she knew something had been decided concerning her. "You are to go to the English court to be made a great lady," I whispered, and kissed her. Her hair was already long enough to reach her shoulders, in shining ringlets. I waved her farewell presently where she sat perched on the crupper with one of their knights, hooded ready to ride. Then I set myself to wait, discreetly, till it was time to give out news, to my Bretons, of the pending birth of my son. I almost smiled as I thought how Merlin and I had outwitted Curtmantle together. The latter might well chew straw again in his wrath; and nothing would induce me to part with my heir, or to name him other than Arthur, the name of the hero of Lyonnesse, of Breton legend and the Round Table.

★ ★ ★

On Easter morning of 1187 I gave birth to my magnificent son. He had hair of true gold, eyes blue as the sea when they opened, and next day he sucked valiantly. I had borne him from the beginning with as little pain as Our Lady at Bethlehem. I insisted on feeding him myself; no nurse should have him. My Bretons guarded Rennes by then as if it had been a fortress; Curtmantle, on hearing of my pregnancy at last, had sent word that the child, if a son, was to be christened Henry. We laughed, and christened him Arthur. I had never been as happy. I knew by then why I myself had been born.

9

I MUST now return to earlier matters. The Young King Henry Plantagenet, my husband's eldest brother, had died of fever at Martel three years before after plundering the shrine of Our Lady of Rocamadour, and others, to try to pay his mercenaries. He had betrayed his father so often by then that when word was brought to Curtmantle that the young man might be dying he refused to come himself, lest it be a trick. Instead he sent, by Count Rotrou of Perche and Bishop Bertrand of Agen, one of the three precious rings he himself always wore and which had belonged to his grandfather, King Henry Beauclerc. Young Henry used it as a seal to send a last letter to his father. When he was certain that he was dying, he made amends to the latter, to his friends and to God. He had himself wrapped for a few moments in the crusader's cloak he had accepted but never worn, then had this taken off him and given to his faithful friend William Marshal, begging that last to take it to Jerusalem. Not long before, the friends had fallen out over a malicious rumour that Marshal was Queen Marguerite's lover.

Young Henry died on a bed of ashes, with a stone beneath his head and another at his feet. He was wearing a hair shirt like Becket. They took out his eyes and entrails, filled the body with salt and spices, and sewed him up in leather like Beauclerc. The ring could not be pulled from his finger. All of this was related to me by Berthe with relish. "Anyone would think the Young King was a saint himself," she said. "The people of Le Mans would not permit his burial at Rouen as he had asked. They kept the body to themselves, and miracles are said to be happening at his tomb." To me, the miracle would be if this was true, but people can persuade themselves into a state of recovery if they determine hard enough. "One of his servants would neither eat nor drink for grief, and died like a dog faithful to its master," Berthe finished. She added that

Curtmantle had been told at last of the death where he was sheltering from the summer heat in a peasant's cottage. His cries of anguish could be heard far beyond it. This after all was the son on whom he had set his early hopes, who should have been the heir to England. No doubt the treacheries were forgotten, while he remembered only a golden-haired boy in a golden crown, who could charm a bird off a tree. Now instead there was Richard, whom his father did not love.

The people of Rouen vowed that they would make war on the people of Le Mans if the Young King's corpse was not delivered up to them for burial. It was less an acknowledgment of the sudden sanctity of Young Henry than a matter of local pride; most of the early dukes and, still earlier, patricians, of Normandy were buried in Rouen cathedral, from old Rollo on. In the end the body was disinterred, and taken with pomp to lie beside the old pirate ancestors, Longsword and the rest.

Meantime my husband Geoffrey, still alive then, was forced to humble himself rather than rising higher in his place as the next heir but one. It was suspected, and I knew no more then than anyone, that this time it was he who, out of jealousy, had led away Young Henry, rapidly by then assuming the aureole of a saint, against Richard, still distinctly of this earth. Certain Breton castles were taken away. Our lives again grew uncertain.

Curtmantle could persist in a kind of blindness despite his cunning, and he did so then: certain things he would not or could not see, and one was that Richard would never part with Aquitaine. He was steeped in its suns, its wine and its troubadours' songs; it was his gift from his mother who loved him, not his father whom he hated. Cruel he might be to the people of Poitou, but they were his people. To try to give the domain to John Lackland instead, as Henry II tried then, was to worsen things irrevocably. Richard, grown wiser with the years, temporised instead of blazing forth defiance; he pretended that he wanted to ask the advice of his friends. Given time to do so, he took horse and rode off as fast as it would carry him, sending word then that nothing in this world or the next would cause him to deliver up his mother's own inheritance of Aquitaine, her duchy.

Curtmantle then met King Philip under the old elm at Gisors. The question of Alais, whom Philip Augustus hardly knew or remembered any more than Richard himself did by now, was raised, and the suggestion made that she might be married to one of Henry's remaining sons, which meant nothing except, again, Richard or John, and John was betrothed. The Vexin was relinquished by France, however, and money, or the promise of it, changed hands regarding poor Marguerite's jointure. I rather think it can have been only the promise; Curtmantle did his utmost soon to marry her again into Hungary to avoid further payment, and succeeded.

Geoffrey and I had held our Christmas that year at Rennes, whose new houses were rising in discreet fashion. Surveying my husband's amiable, self-satisfied face, I reflected how he had probably wrought the harm between the living brother and the dead. Curtmantle and Lackland were meantime together at Le Mans, hearing mass nearby Young Henry's first tomb and that of his long-dead grandfather Geoffrey Le Bel of Anjou. They made no effort to join us. No doubt Lackland made the most of his opportunity with his father to win favour; but as for Geoffrey, his next act was to turn Lackland himself against the remaining elder brother.

Another part might have been Lackland's to play, and might have saved his soul. While my husband Geoffrey lived, the youngest brother hoped to be allowed to go off to Jerusalem to be crowned king there. The patriarch of the holy city had been sent by the dying leper, Baldwin IV. Time was running out for the Christian kingdom established after the first crusade, and no one knew it better than he. He was only twenty-four; he and I were born in the same year. His disease — how well I have come to understand it! — had prevented his marrying, or fathering heirs: few dared enter his presence except his unafraid Franciscans who cared for him. By now, the Leper King was more troubled in his mind even than in his rotting young body; his heir was a sickly infant, son of his sister Sibylla's first marriage. Should the child die, who would accept the crown of Jerusalem and guard the Holy Places? Sibylla refused, being too greatly enamoured of her new husband Guy de Lusignan. This was a knight who, with a certain thoughtless compassion, had lifted the leper in his armour from the ground when no one else would, after Baldwin had slid helpless from the saddle, having won by his own amazing courage the last Christian victory of all at Montgisard. *Christus vincit, Christus vincit, Christus imperat*, he had cried aloud at the head of his army, careless of whether or not he himself was killed in the charge, knowing it was the last time he would mount a horse or make his failing voice heard. He had not been killed in the battle, but the astonished infidel had fled for the time. Nevertheless with death at last approaching, Baldwin IV took thought for his kingdom, knowing Saladin would return. He had a younger sister Isabella, who, however also refused to inherit; she likewise was in love with her young husband, Humphrey of Toron. They had no heirs as yet, and not long afterwards

Humphrey was cruelly beaten and chased off by the Christian knights because they said he was impotent, and had the marriage annulled. The unfortunate Isabella was forced to marry one disliked husband after another, in vain; but that was later, when Jerusalem was in Saracen hands. This in itself had not happened yet; but I remember the fate of that unhappy young woman, which in a manner resembles my own. Meantime Henry Curtmantle knelt with the rest and vowed to take the Cross. So did the duke of Burgundy, the counts of Flanders and of Blois, and the king of France himself. Few reached Jerusalem, despite the vow.

It might have been foreseen that Curtmantle, never one to be swayed by his emotions, would think of a way out of this. He was not craven, merely prudent; to leave his lands would invite disaster. First he suggested that he and King Philip should set out the next Easter but one. Meantime, a tenth of all men's incomes, to be called the Saladin Tithe, must be levelled in France and England to pay for the intended crusade. This tithe proved most unpopular.

At the same time Richard himself, burning to go, was kept waiting by his father a full year. Richard asked for the fealty, saying that they owed it to his father, of the barons of England and Normandy before he went. This was reasonable in view of the evident preference of the king for Lackland, who otherwise might seize everything in the event of Curtmantle's death. However that schemer, his father, made an evasive reply.

"Together, my dearest son, together, not separately, we will set out on the road, and we will have not money alone, but all things necessary for our journey in common, as is fitting." He added that nothing but death itself would separate them.

Richard was not deceived by this speech. They were to say afterwards that he left his father then both in body and heart. He returned alone to Poitou to prepare for his own journey to the Holy Land, and Curtmantle sailed once again for England. Once there, he called a council to enforce the unwelcome Saladin Tithe. It was never fully collected.

Lackland had by then flung himself at his father's feet, a habit of all the sons when they wanted favours or forgiveness. He begged to be allowed to go to the Holy Land and I believe genuinely saw himself as the saviour of Jerusalem. However Curtmantle, who had himself evaded the necessity of crusading on several occasions and had just refused the abovementioned crown of thorns for himself, curtly refused.

The Patriarch Heraclius, kneeling at first, then spoke out to Henry Curtmantle as few men had dared to do since the dead Archbishop Becket. Henry had been offered, he told him, the keys of the kingdom, the way to Jerusalem and the Holy Sepulchre itself. "In you alone, after God, do they have faith and hope for their salvation," he said, adding what everyone knew, namely that Saladin's hordes were already at the gates. Curtmantle took the holy man and raised him to his feet.

"God is your best helper. I myself will do what I may." He did not however intend leaving his kingdoms to be torn asunder by rebellious sons and recently subjugated barons. He was not easily swayed by sentiment, although he was not without his own religion.

He temporised by summoning a council. It met in Lent. Curtmantle spent the waiting time in hunting alongside Princess Matilda's husband, the exiled duke of Saxony, then at odds with the emperor and meantime Henry's visitor. They drank beer together, undisturbed by the many blinded and castrated peasants in the recesses of the forest who at one time or another, to provide food for their family's stewpot in hard days, had transgressed the harsh laws laid down by the Conqueror. A monk came up at this point to urge the king to go to the Holy Land, saying what an honour it was for the patriarch to have come.

"If the patriarch or others come to us, they are seeking their own advantage more than ours," observed Curtmantle truly, while his son-in-law downed his remaining beer. The monk however persisted, and Curtmantle lost patience.

"Boldly indeed can clerks urge us on

to arms and perils, for they will receive no blows in the fight, nor will they bear any burden they can avoid." He wiped his mouth free of froth from his own beer, while the monk turned away.

By the time the council met, Henry had already instructed them to vote firmly against his leaving his dominions to fight in a foreign land. Instead, he offered Heraclius fifty thousand marks for the defence of the Holy City.

"Not in this way, king, will you save your soul. We came to seek a prince, not pelf." The patriarch raised his dignified head and stared into the pebble-hard Plantagenet eyes. "Almost every part of the world sends us pelf, but not a prince," he said quietly. "We want a man who lacks money, not money that lacks a man."

It was at this point that young Lackland was suggested; he was after all equally a descendant of Black Fulk of Anjou, onetime king of Jerusalem. The young man himself as I say was burning to go, but was forbidden. After that he gave himself more than ever to the devil.

Meantime, Richard of Poitou, to be avenged on my husband, had invaded Brittany. I and my little Eleanor from our solar had heard the sounds of attack and of shouting, and saw walls crumble and stone-dust rise. The cries of battle and fear came from all directions; beyond, around, below. I was sick of war. When there was a respite from the fighting, I would go out among my sad people and give them such food as might somehow be got; we ourselves were hungry. Each poor field had so frequently been ravaged and burned that there was no heart for coming harvest any more, though it was spring. Their faces were gaunt with starvation, their patient eyes devoid of hope. I think that by then, despite the fact that I was Conan's daughter and married to the son of the Angevin monster himself, they had begun to love me for my own sake, and my little daughter, the Pearl of Brittany, for hers. I wish I could have done more for them, and for her; but that is too late. My mother sent me her pearls on my marriage; they are said to mean tears.

Curtmantle meantime made ready to sail across to Normandy to make peace between the brothers. In mid-April there occurred a great earthquake in England, which was taken as a sign of the wrath of God; the tower of Lincoln fell down. Next day, Curtmantle and the patriarch rode in company together to sail across the Channel. Heraclius, having meantime no doubt prayed copiously, made a final appeal for a change of heart in the king.

"God has given you honours, wide lands, a long reign, glory, success and victory. How have you shown your gratitude? By breaking faith time and again; breaking it with your lord King Louis, whose soul God rest; taking his lands, stealing his wife." The patriarch's eyes were stern. He did not mention Alais, of whose fate he was probably too innocent to be aware. He turned on the king then and told him roundly that he was guilty of the murder of St. Thomas Becket. "You sent your executioners to do the deed for you. It is as if you had done it with your own hand."

Curtmantle turned on him then, his

own eyes blazing. The patriarch bent his head and exposed his neck.

"Do to me what you did to the blessed Thomas," he said. "I would as lief have my head cut off by you here in England as by the infidel in Palestine, for you are worse than any infidel." Henry gave vent to an oath.

"By God's eyes! If all the men of my land were gathered in one body and spoke with one mouth, they would not dare to say such things to me."

"Do you think then that they love you, when they look only to your wealth and not to your works? The crowd follows the booty, not the man; power, not the person, is venerated everywhere."

Curtmantle, containing himself admirably, then explained once more the matter of his warring sons and that these were the chief reason why he could not leave his dominions.

"No wonder. They came from the devil and to the devil they will go." These were the very words, uttered long since, of Abbot Bernard of Clairvaux to King Louis himself concerning the same Henry of Anjou, duke of Normandy. It was evident that the saying had spread throughout Christendom, no doubt borne by travelling pilgrims or crusaders.

It was thereafter that Lackland was sent, not to Jerusalem but, blindly, to Ireland. His father would have been better to let him follow his desire; what befell among the Irish, the pulling of friendly chieftains' beards and the rest, is well known. It was two years before the pope sent a diadem of peacock feathers to crown John king of that unhappy land, and by then it was too late. As I have said, by then many things were so.

It may be asked how I knew all of this, word for word; Berthe would not have heard it. The answer is that Curtmantle told me himself, when we had later dealings. However I will leave those until I am compelled to remember them.

★ ★ ★

Meantime, he played another trick. Allowing that it had been a mistake to crown the Young King during his own lifetime, Curtmantle had no such affection for Richard in any case as to repeat such a ceremony. Instead, behaving like the weather-vane his own sons resembled, he decided to deprive Richard of what he loved best, namely Poitou. He called for Queen Eleanor out of her prison, brought her across the Channel under the escort of Matilda's beer-drinking Lion of Saxony, and ordered Richard to return Poitou and Aquitaine to his mother, their rightful duchess. This was an act of deep cunning and unkindness. Richard, as his father had known would happen, surrendered his mother's possessions to her without a blow.

Richard must have been bitter. For once, despite the harm he had wrought in my country, I was in sympathy with him. He had after all fought with Curtmantle under the walls of Limoges while they rained down arrows on them both. It was unlikely that he would fight by his side again. He returned, like the Prodigal Son, to his father now, but did not kneel at his feet.

10

HAVING used her presence to gain control of Aquitaine and Poitou, Curtmantle took his queen under guard back again to England, leaving Richard with a large sum of money in order to control, without title, the rebellion that had broken out in Poitou itself during his year's absence in Normandy. There was no doubt that Richard and no other was the man to control the turbulent southern inheritance.

His father however had made plans of some other kind. I think that he had, some time since, made the discovery, which any other father would have noted long before, that Richard had no interest in women and would be unlikely to father an heir willingly on Alais of France or anyone else, though rumour gave him a bastard son Philip whom he maintained responsibly. Tales had of course been spread about him

318

in Poitou as ravishing noble virgins nightly and then turning them over to his troops as whores. These tales I believe to have been spread by Count Raymond of Toulouse, Eleanor's rival of long ago, who had meantime, during Richard's absence, seized Quercy and no doubt renewed his ambitions about the rest of the duchy. The tales of ravishing were however on a par with Berthe's tales much earlier about Curtmantle in Wales, and the others about the savage conduct of my Scots uncles when harrying the north of England.

* * *

All aspects of Curtmantle were not in fact without their human side. My uncle Ralph de Warenne was dead by then. I missed his gossip, and I forget how I heard this tale of Curtmantle's relations with yet another saintly personage, Hugh of Witham, later bishop of Lincoln.

The king's displeasure was aroused by Hugh's excommunication of a forester. These officials are regarded as of greater importance than the wretches they are entitled savagely to punish. Hugh had courage in his lack of accustomed reverence.

He was in fact a person of great sanctity and humour. He had been summoned from his mysterious mountain mother-house at the course of the Seine, Chartreuse, to succour the unfortunate monks Henry himself had invited to found a Carthusian community at Witham in England. He had promised them a manor and money, but when they got there it was to find no roof for their heads, as the peasantry had moved into the manor and would not move out. The luckless monks built themselves huts and survived somehow in a strange land full of marsh and forest; but the king still sent them no money, and in the end they were so discouraged that they were on the point of returning to the Grande Chartreuse. At this news Henry, alerted at last, sent a bishop overseas to persuade Hugh, already famous for his ascetic life, to come to England and mend matters at Witham. He did so, and turned out the peasants from their manor, but did not leave them comfortless. He forced

Curtmantle — and it was hard to force that man to do anything of the kind — to give them money in recompense. Hugh knew how to treat the king. He never took Henry's rages seriously, but continued, in a manner, to treat him as a boy, which in a way all men are. After the business of the excommunicated forester Henry was however so greatly enraged that he would not even speak to Hugh, and remembering the fate of an earlier churchman none of the court dared do so. As the holy man approached, Curtmantle took horse and rode off with his following into the forest. Hugh came after the scowling monarch on foot, and found the king at last seated on the ground busied with a needle and thread, for he hated to be idle, and had meantime injured his finger and was stitching up a leather stall. Hugh of Witham laid his hand on the nearest courtier's shoulder, but the man would not respond, and all the others averted their eyes. Hugh then sat down beside the king. "How like your cousins of Falaise you look!" he remarked cheerfully. Curtmantle rolled on the ground with laughter. Nobody else would have dared make a jest to him of his ancestor the Conqueror's origins, the latter's mother having been the daughter of a tanner of Falaise whom they say Duke Robert the Devil first caught sight of paddling in the river. In any case all was well; the forester ended with a flogging and continued great friends with Hugh.

Later I liked Hugh less from a second story I heard; he had visited Godstow convent and had asked whose coffin stood before the high altar, covered with silk and surrounded by candles and flowers. When he heard that it was Fair Rosamund's, he ordered it out of the chapel beyond the wall, saying a harlot must not lie in consecrated ground. The nuns obeyed, but secretly brought back Rosamund's coffin afterwards, as they had loved her. Still later, I heard that Lackland had had the jeering rhyme inscribed on her tomb everyone knows of. We all come to it, and so will he.

11

I SAT in my solar at Rennes, suckling Arthur nearby the brazier, because the winds of late spring were still cold. The flames flickered blue from the sea-coals and a pleasant warmth came out. I stared happily across Arthur's head, covered as it was by now with a straight stubble of fine hair, the colour of new-minted gold. His blue eyes were thoughtful, seeing nothing but my breast. He sucked at it without let, and grew almost as I watched him.

I was as full of my own achievements as my breast was full of milk. For eight months, since news had come of Geoffrey's death in France, I had governed alone. I had listened to pleas from priests and peasants as well as from my nobility. As my pregnancy continued I had had myself borne out daily in my litter to see for myself how the ordinary folk fared, and if any of them had had the heart to sow crops over the past weeks;

telling them that if not, it was perhaps still not too late; there was no more war. They had brought me fish caught fresh from the sea, baking it for me in fires lit by the wayside as I passed. They had called blessings on my growing girth, all knowing that I bore in my body the heir to Brittany. It was never doubted by any of us that God would make him a son. Now, he lay in my arms and I asked no more. After he had done feeding I set him aside to sleep, watching his face always. He would be a handsome man, a strong ruler, the saviour of Lyonnesse.

There was the sound of a party of horsemen arriving below soon, but I did not concern myself greatly; any news would be brought up to me in the solar. How my life had centred itself meantime on this small room, where all my world now lay! I hardly took note when Berthe came to the curtain: she had after all been there all my life.

"Duchess, it is the king of England, with only a small following. He asks to see his grandson."

I drew closer to the sleeping Arthur; they should not take him from me as they had taken Eleanor. I gave discreet orders that the Breton guard was to be doubled, then that the English party were to be given meat and drink. "They will have travelled some distance, no doubt," I said drily. I did not know, on this occasion, whence Henry Curtmantle might have come; it could have been from anywhere at all, including Normandy. I knew that he was in the midst of fresh quarrels with his two remaining sons, but I had lost interest; there had been too many, and it no longer, thank God, concerned me. I waited, having drawn my robe close after the feeding. The thought occurred to me that, facing Curtmantle presently as I must after he had refreshed himself, I would look well enough: Berthe assured me everyone was saying I had never been in greater beauty. The thought pleased me. Apart from all else I, Constance, had succeeded where Marguerite, Alais and all of them had failed: none had bred a living son from any of his, except for myself. I had Brittany's heir, and by now the heir to England and Normandy, safe by me, and safe he should stay. The devil's descent had come to this; one

325

small child with golden hair, kicking in his cradle.

I heard Curtmantle's footsteps then on the stairs, hasty as usual. He had come up alone.

When I saw him, I noted how greatly he had aged. He had thickened, and was more than ever corpulent: his hair, once red as a fox's brush, had turned grey. Nevertheless the pebble-hard gaze was unchanged, and his movements were still quick as those of a young man. He strode over in the old way, and kissed my hand.

"Constance," he said: no more than that. He turned then to the cradle, poked a thick finger at Arthur and woke him; the baby's grasp curled at once about his. "He seems a fine knave," said Curtmantle. I recalled how long ago, when I was in England and he had come striding in, he had picked me up and held me close against him; he did not do so with Arthur now. It came to me that he was envious of the child in some way, perhaps resentful because he had not been named for himself. As if he had read my thoughts, Curtmantle said then

"We found the graves of the real Arthur and his queen Guenever, at Glastonbury. He had the bones of a giant. Her face was still to be seen when we opened the grave, and her long plaits of hair, white in colour. She crumbled away in moments, on the entry of the air."

I shivered; there seemed more sinister intent in the way he spoke. I made myself ask how my Eleanor fared. He answered absently that she did well enough, and would be a beauty like myself. He turned then to face me. The room as I say was small.

"Send the child to his nurses," he said. "I would talk with you here, alone by your fire."

He stretched out his large chapped hands to the brazier, warming them. I sent for Berthe and she took Arthur away, with a grim look cast at my guest.

I asked if they had fed him well enough below stairs. He did not reply, but instead unhooked a flask from his belt. "Drink with me," he said pleasantly. "This is made out of good Norman apples. There's nothing like it for a cold day; I carry it always."

I had a great cup with a silver rim in the solar. He poured some of the golden liquid into it and we drank it in turns, sipping fire together. It was unlike anything I had ever drunk before in my life. "It will taint my milk," I said "and make Arthur tipsy." I had begun to feel that way a little myself. I saw him look at me in John Lackland's remembered fashion, as if he saw me naked.

"You should not spoil your pretty breasts by feeding him," I heard Curtmantle say. "Get him a wet-nurse; any peasant will be glad of silver."

I felt pride rise in me, and spoke incautiously then; it was the drink I had taken, no doubt. "He is the heir to England, is he not?" I said. "There is none better able to nourish him with royal milk than myself."

For reply he reached out, setting the cup aside, and slid his hand beneath my robe, grasping my breast. I felt the milk ooze out on to his palm, and the palm's hardness.

I cannot explain what happened then. What had I told him but the truth as he must already know it? Yet I felt his eyes upon me, pitiless as stones; and in the old way felt my knees turn to water. The charm of the man, his warmth, were close to me; and I had drunk with him from his flask. He had after all sprung from the devil; it was the devil's drink. He had not withdrawn his hand. "Constance," he said again, as he had said when he came in. "Constance." His voice as always was hoarse, and still held the accents of Anjou, of his youth.

I could have called for aid, and did not. The fault, I know, was mine as well as his; this man the like of whom there was not another in the world. Old he might be, while I myself was still young; ageing, thickened, balding: it mattered nothing; this was the lover of Eleanor of Aquitaine, of Alais of France with her trembling lily garter; of Rosamund Clifford and Alix de Porhoët; of the whore Ykenai; of all women on whom his desire briefly rested. I cannot but recall our coupling at last, god and goddess together; and became aware that never before in my life had I bedded with a full man. Even that day with Geoffrey in the Valley of No Return, on the high rock, I had not known such fulfilment. I do not know how long we lay together, only that nobody had come in to light the candles; order must have been given that we were not to be disturbed. I remember babbling of the fairy Melusine, then that after he had left me it had grown increasingly dark. I had not heard them ride away, him and his following.

* * *

My milk dried up. After Curtmantle's second or third visit they had to find Arthur a wet-nurse, which was of course a matter of no difficulty; but I was chagrined. I knew well enough that I was bewitched, a fool like any other woman; yet still felt my knees betray me as soon as I heard horse's hooves. They say a sow that has lately littered is ready again for mating. By now, I had no doubt become such. I often gazed at my reflection, amazed that it looked as usual. I had lain with the devil, knew it, and cared nothing.

Once Berthe said to me, in reproach, "You should not permit him, little duchess. Remember the poor princess Alix, and what befell."

I should have heeded her warning, but by then I had half forgotten who Alix was. Afterwards, I had time to remember.

12

WHEN Curtmantle next rode into Brittany he came from the north-west. I had relaxed my guard, and as they said clerics were with the king I thought no harm and let them in. Henry did not come up to my solar, but instead desired me to go down to him in my hall. I assumed that it was the clerics' presence which prevented his coming up; I had been otherwise anxious to run to him, to be clasped once again in his hard, demanding arms.

When I came down, he was seated gravely among them all, in the carved wooden chair that had belonged to my great-grandfather, Conan III: it had survived the burnings. It was unusual to behold the second Henry seated at all. He occupied it, however, no doubt as yet another descendant of Beauclerc and the Conqueror. His short cloak was flung back to reveal his thickening body: for instants I wondered what had made me lie with him so willingly and often. When he spoke, his voice was that of a stranger.

"It is essential, in view of the danger to your duchy from France, madam, that you marry a man who will guard it on my behalf. Here is such a man, ready and willing to be your husband."

A knight stood by him, one I did not yet know and was to know too well. Ranulf de Blundeville had come from the north, and was by now earl of Chester, the earlier one, Hugh, having died after Falaise. This seemed a brutal creature from his face. When he spoke, which happened seldom, his accents were those of Richmond I remembered, but this did not rouse liking in me. I protested that I had no need of any husband. Curtmantle gave his grim smile.

"All women need a husband, widows more than most. For your son's sake, born as he was eight months after the death of his father, it is best to ensure his admitted legitimacy. Were you, for instance, to bear a second child out of wedlock, women being weak, there might well be doubts about duke Arthur himself. The same thing befell your great-uncle Hoël in his time, and he forfeited his inheritance."

I flushed deeply, before them all. I was full of his seed, and both of us knew it. I saw now how I had been duped, but it was too late; if I bore a child as a result of our couplings, without this marriage, Arthur would suffer. At least I must make certain he was not taken from me. I spoke of this, firmly.

"Your son will remain in your care if you agree to marry a man of my choice." The voice might have been a merchant's, bargaining. How much de Blundeville, lately of Chester, knew, I cared nothing one way or the other, except that the prospect of marrying him was unwelcome. To plead with such as Henry of Anjour was however useless; I made no such attempt. It was clear that, if I did not agree to this marriage, Arthur would be taken from me or else ruined by rumour: and my carelessness had permitted them to bring, this time and the others, enough men to overcome my own. There was only the nurse, and Berthe upstairs, to guard the heir of Brittany. I thought of my son; and gained strength; after all I myself by now was nothing.

I went into the chapel and took the vows with De Blundeville: the formalities had already been arranged, must in fact have been so before Henry's recent visits to me. He himself left, as he had left after my Scots uncle's nuptials at Woodstock; having manned my castle meantime with Chester's men. It was evident that I was to be permitted to play no tricks on anyone.

I was however determined that the marriage, as it had had to be, should be one in name only. In my chamber that night I awaited de Blundeville with my robe still close about me and my hair not yet plaited for the night. I know I am more queenly so. He came striding into the chamber, took one glance and laughed. Outside, there was the half-seen glimmer of mail. His guards, several of them, stood beyond the curtain.

"The place for a proud woman is on her back. That is a saying of our lord the king, and by God's death I will lay you there. Constance of Brittany."

He advanced; his breath smelt of wine, for they had been drinking below to celebrate the marriage. "You will not touch me," I told him clearly, and called for Berthe to instruct her to come and sleep on my pallet. I did her no service thereby: she tried to reach me, and I heard the men-at-arms seize her. Chester laughed. "It is later for her than for yourself," he said, "but never too late." He grinned while they began to ravish Berthe, meantime fetching me a clout across the mouth. I staggered, and Chester seized my long hair, twisting it about his hand. By this means he cast me to the floor, where I lay half stunned, my face stinging. I saw him unbuckle the leather sword-belt from his waist, at the same time hearing poor Berthe's whimperings as one after the other man took her body though she was no longer young.

I had never been beaten before. I kept my fists in my mouth as the blows rained down, hearing the vicious thwack of leather on flesh, and the flesh my own. There followed rape, as was still continuing beyond the curtain; brutal and most loathsome rape, which despite its very nature brings in the end in some way a kind of pleasure. I heard de Blundeville's mocking laughter at that, and the worst thing of all he said, which was about my mother.

"The king had Margaret of Scotland long ago, as he had yourself lately; how else did you suppose she married Hereford so soon without protest? It is his way; and now, again, bitch, whore, duchess . . . your great-grandsire filched Carlisle from my kin; I will take payment now." He took it, time and again.

Through my anguish I made myself think of my son, and of how it was, after all, worth even this to keep Arthur with me. I would live, despite these devils, for his sake.

I still heard poor Berthe's useless cries through the curtain. They had her all night, one after the other.

★ ★ ★

I may add that the news of my forced marriage caused most of my seigneury to declare, then or later, for the king of France. The devil can deceive himself.

I thank God and all the saints that I had conceived neither by Curtmantle nor, in the nine years of our appalling marriage, did I do so by the new-made earl of Chester. The latter had lands in the Avranchin, one reason for Henry's choice of him for my husband; that region formerly belonged to Brittany and adjoins it. At first Chester, suspicious of leaving me to my own devices, would take me there under guard; but I soon deceived him as to my meekness, and was at last left in the company of my son. To allow both men to think that they had defeated me between them was the only choice while Curtmantle lived; otherwise Arthur would be taken away or declared bastard.

Berthe had proved less fortunate than I. She had conceived at her age, being over fifty; but that is the age at which Queen Eleanor gave birth to Lackland. Berthe, unable in nature to say which of the soldiery had been her child's father, gave birth in time to an innocent, that is to say a child which lacks its wits, has tight eyelids and strange thumbs. Such little creatures are harmless and remain without sin after they are christened. Berthe transferred much of her devotion from me to this child, whom she named Havoise and kept always with her. She did not blame me for what had happened, though I blamed myself.

* * *

It is just possible that Curtmantle knew, that time he arranged my Chester marriage, that he himself had not long to live. I do not think so, as few men think of themselves as mortal. As for some others, I recall a description from a chronicle of the days of the Empress Matilda, his mother, in her wars long-ago with King Stephen; she had lacked good advisers apart from her half-brother Robert of Gloucester. The rest were 'haughty, but withal foolhardy, constant in nothing, and conscious in nothing, and conscious only of conspiracies ... who propose great enterprises, but never bring any to good effect; and with such leaders, the more they be in company, the sooner they be overcome.'

Curtmantle in the end had little company at the time of his death, except for his son Geoffrey by the whore Ykenai. I must recall that death now, and the manner of it.

13

MY husband Geoffrey's death had put paid to King Philip's plans to use him to stir up trouble in Normandy and Brittany against his father. It had begun to be spoken of in secret before the fatal tournament: if Philip had disliked these earlier, he liked them less after the event. Having refrained from throwing himself into Geoffrey's grave, he now resurrected a worn and sorry farce; the demand for the marriage of Richard and Alais of France, his sister. I may say here that Alais ended, later on, as the wife of Count William of Ponthieu, who had little respect for her. She was by then in her late thirties, and well used.

Philip had already demanded, as expected, the custody of my daughter Eleanor and her wardship till her marriage. He had not obtained either. Eleanor's grandmother and namesake, much later, when she herself was free, took the little Pearl with her on certain journeyings;

after that no more as I say was heard. The fate of my daughter troubles me. I should have paid more heed.

King Philip's third demand led to war once again. Richard meantime, with his customary despatch, had driven Count Raymond of Toulouse out of Quercy; few others could have achieved it. Philip however demanded that Richard cease making war on Count Raymond, who was his own vassal, and that if he refused he, Philip, would invade Normandy. One excuse was as good as the next, after all.

Curtmantle, alerted and alarmed, then sent an embassy. This obtained a truce until Hilary-tide, but not for longer; yet in a bitter January it was unlikely that there would be movements of troops across a starved country, as they would be starved themselves.

It was at this point that the crown of peacock feathers I have already mentioned arrived from the pope for John Lackland, king of Ireland. Seen at a distance in time, such matters can divert one. It was delivered in solemn procession at Westminster Abbey on New

Year's Day, but never put on Lackland's head, then or later. The situation in Normandy was too grave to consider such matters then, and since then he has acquired, to my sorrow and anger, a more solid crown.

He crossed seas then to Normandy, followed by his father. It was in the midst of their preparations for war that I gave birth to my son, as I have related, and Curtmantle thereafter made his visits to me and arranged my second marriage. He was still adept in all such contrivings.

★ ★ ★

The kings of France and England meantime faced one another, preparing for the pitched battle that is rare in war. Curtmantle all his life had avoided them when he could. I have since heard that under cover of night, the count of Flanders came to Richard and persuaded him to change sides and to support the king of France. By then, Richard hardly needed persuading. "King Philip is young in years, but prudent in wisdom," he was told; the count of Flanders was a dangerous makeweight in any alliance. Being assured that Philip was never forgetful of benefits done to him, Richard replied, probably with truth, that if he might have France's favour, he would be willing to go barefoot to Jerusalem. To get there, by whatever means, was after all his chief desire.

He was however advised to confront King Philip not as a suppliant, but fully armed and accoutred. Few men could look more splendid so, and the appearance of dead Count Geoffrey's even more handsome brother won Philip Augustus' cautious young heart. Richard passed through the enemy lines, conferred with the French king, and returned for the time.

Curtmantle, whether or not informed of all this, then made the promise he had made already too many times to be believed; namely, that if the king of France would grant a truce that lasted two years, he, Henry, would take the cross and go to Jerusalem. "I acknowledge that up till now I have led an evil life in many respects," he admitted. He said he wanted to make amends and to be reconciled with God.

It is possible that he had pictured himself as addressing the late King Louis VII. After his admissions about himself he burst into tears; the young French king, regrettably, burst out laughing. Whether or not this was the reason for a change of heart, by the time the delegation arrived Henry stated that he would not, after all, accept the truce. He had become like a portly eel, writhing this way and that. He had been both lion and fox in his time; now, this was almost over.

The king of France drew up his forces for battle, and Henry sent for his son Richard. "What shall we do?" he asked, like a child. He was in fact no warrior born, being rather schemer, governor and lawyer. As I have related, he could also be other things. Richard, his tall height kneeling, looked up at his father, his blue eyes cold.

"Although it is a shameful thing," he said, "I will if you order it go to my lord the king of France, and ask that he again allow the truce you refused yesterday."

He then crossed the French lines, offered Philip his sword, kneeling then bareheaded, and asked for the truce as before. "If my father breaks it in any way I offer my own body to the king's court of judgment in Paris."

Philip Augustus looked down at the great warrior's body and saw that it was fair. The army was withdrawn, and Richard rode into Paris at the king's side as friend rather than hostage.

I heard later on that it was like David and Jonathan between them; they ate at the same table and out of the same dish, and shared a bed. "The king of France loved him as his own soul, and they loved each other so much that because of the vehemence of the love that was between them the lord king of England, seized with a great astonishment, wondered what this was." I doubt if, by that time, Curtmantle did not know.

14

THAT news from Jerusalem should have given pause to all war between kings, and for a time did so. However it is probable that Curtmantle had already sent money to certain malcontents in Poitou in order to delay Richard's departure for the Holy Land, as by his oath it would also mean his own. Richard replied by capturing a castle and sixty knights, setting them free only on their vow that they would come with him to the East. His heart's dream was nearing. Count Raymond, the old enemy, however chose this time to blind and castrate certain harmless merchants passing through the country, and Richard in revenge invaded, and shortly took, Toulouse itself. This was the gateway to the Mediterranean; and Count Raymond, infuriated, seized in turn two knights who were returning from pilgrimage to Compostela, thereby breaking the accepted custom that pilgrims are to be left free of attack. King Philip himself came south to avenge this outrage, but failed to make peace and returned in anger to France.

Richard by then had taken seventeen castles, and swore that King Philip had given him leave to make war on so unnatural a vassal. Count Raymond then appealed to Philip for help. Richard's erstwhile Jonathan replied by sending messengers to Richard's father, who merely replied in bland fashion that he could not condone his son's behaviour. Philip thereupon proved himself a warrior, struck behind Richard's back and captured most of Bern itself except for Loches.

Curtmantle knew then that he would have to return in person to Normandy. He sent Lackland, whom he always trusted, ahead of him, and foraged meantime in Wales for mercenaries. When they reached Portsmouth ready to embark, my own mother Margaret, widowed by then of De Bohun, came to him and warned him that his people were turning against him because of the Saladin Tithe. She had never been afraid of speaking out, and had come herself with the men from Hereford.

"My lord, I have never had such fear concerning your state as I do now," she said. Their eyes met for the first time in many years. "In the past," said my mother, "when adversity came upon you, the blessings of the people followed you in your doings, but now, I grieve to say the contrary." The exaction of the tithe had brought curses on his head from all ranks of men in England, she assured him. Curtmantle replied by falling into a rage.

"These vile people have no cause to curse me," he shouted. "In the future, if I live and am able to return, they will indeed curse me, and not without cause." It was like Solomon's son threatening to chastise Israel with scorpions; but far worse were the words Curtmantle uttered then to Archbishop Baldwin, who had brought bad news out of France, and the king's own friend the saintly Hugh of Lincoln, the same who had once made him roll on the ground with laughter in the forest.

"Why should I worship Christ?" he snarled now in their shocked faces. "Why should I deign to honour him who takes away my earthly honour and allows me ignominiously thus to be confounded by a mere boy?" He then spurred his horse, and rode off blaspheming; some recalled the days when he had said a similar thing at Bures, about a jumped-up clerk by then archbishop of Canterbury.

He sailed with the tide after that, and went to Alençon, the men of Shropshire, Hereford and Gloucester following in great ships. There were, they say, almost two thousand foot-soldiers and almost a hundred cavalry.

Meantime the cautious Philip had withdrawn from Bern, leaving one of his captains in charge. He did not desire to be trapped between Richard from the south and Henry of England from the north-east. As had already been noted, although young, he was wise.

* * *

There came to the king of England then the faithful friend of his dead son Young Henry. Now that his widow Marguerite had gone to Hungary as its queen, the slur that William Marshal had been her lover was forgotten. In any case he was always loyal to the king. He had returned from the Holy Land, having made his way there while others fought at home, and had many tales to tell. It was from such sources, nowadays, that I obtained such gossip as I might; and one of the knights who had returned was Aimery de Thouars. His brother Guy, who was quietly about my court, used to ride out hawking with me after my son's birth and before my second marriage, and it was he who told me of the fall of Jerusalem, as his brother had told it to him. I listened to the stories of the Holy Places, the hill of the Visitation and the Pillar of the Scourging, placed for a time for safety on Mount Sion; and the Sepulchre itself, wherein the emperor Constantine had placed a small marble pillar. "None of them are ours now," said Guy de Thouars, who had nothing of his own left in any case; as I have said before, Curtmantle had taken his family's lands and levelled their castles three years before my own birth.

I stared at the sky. There were few

wild birds left in Brittany. All of them had been shot down with arrows or else snared by my hungry people for food. My great royal gerfalcon stretched her white wings in the air, wheeled aimlessly, and presently brought down a fat buzzard, all there was. I cast it on the way to a poor family for their stewpot. Guy de Thouars served me then and with constant devotion at all times; he was a quiet and gentle knight, never one to assert himself.

We would talk together as friends. Guy told me once that when he was a child with his brother, they had had a rare young hobby-hawk hooded to train. "She was flat-headed, with wings the colour of blue slate; a pattern on the chest like ermine, and yellow thighs feathered thickly. There was a dark streak down from either ear-mark, like the muchatos they wear now. I have never seen it on any other bird." He smiled, remembering. "She could twist and glide most remarkably," he said. "I had almost trained her to return free."

His face fell, and I asked what had become of the hawk, though I knew.

"In the taking of Thouars she was lost, no doubt burned with much else. That castle was said to be so strong no man could take it, but Henry of Anjou took it in three days." He would never speak of Curtmantle as king of England. I understood, not for the first time, what it must mean to lose all one's possessions. I decided to keep Guy de Thouars about me, also, when I could, Raoul de Fougères, who however had continued again defiant. Such men resent foreign authority. Raoul was a true Breton.

★ ★ ★

"I will henceforth bear no fealty to him as his mortal enemy, but will harm him in all ways as his foe, and inflict all the damage I may on him and on his land." These were the words sent by the devil's descendant, Henry II, to the king of France, who in turn replied that he would not cease what he had begun until not only Berri, but the Norman Vexin, lay again in his power. Richard, having promised faithful service to both sides, prudently retired to Poitou.

The last meeting of them all under the great elm at Gisors took place for three days in mid-August. It was the vintage, and the men wanted to go home. The hoped-for saving of Jerusalem was long in the past. The heat was intense; neither king, the young or the old, would reach agreement, and it was then, after Curtmantle had departed, having earlier as usual assured himself the benefit of its shade, that Philip in a boy's rage ordered the famous elm to be cut down. The thudding of the great branches, still heavy in leaf, sounded to the riding off of many of France's noblemen. They thought it folly to continue the war and were disgusted by the sacrilegious sight of two crusaders determined on fighting one another instead of the infidel. The scandal, they said, resounded throughout Europe. "We will never bear arms for you again till you have returned from the Holy Land," Theobald of Blois, who had himself taken no vow to go there, swore. Count Philip of Flanders and the rest so inclined did likewise. Philip Augustus, troubled by these desertions, asked for another conference elsewhere. He may already have regretted the lost elm.

This time the warring monarchs met again between Bern and Touraine. It was by then October. The knowledge that all the world regarded them with disgust — it was said that this contempt was even echoed by Saladin — caused the two to agree better than had formerly been the case. Philip agreed to part with his recent conquest of Bern if Richard would give up Count Raymond's southern castles. What would have been the result was never known, because King Philip foolishly — his wisdom occasionally succumbed, even by then, to his youth — cast in a clause at the last moment to the effect that Curtmantle must make over to him a castle named Paçy, on the Norman border. Curtmantle furiously declined.

Both sides were by now short of money with which to pay their men. King Philip resorted to a ruse. He promised to pay all his mercenary soldiers in full when they reached Bourges, but when that town was reached, being full of Philip's own supporters as he had foreseen, he had the poor devils stripped naked and driven off, lacking either horses, money or armour. Had Curtmantle been a soldier at heart he would have attacked then; but instead he copied Philip and got rid of his Welshmen, without however stripping them: perhaps they had less to lose.

Richard, still fuming at the delay in setting off for his crusade, then offered to stand trial in Paris for his behaviour regarding Count Raymond. When Curtmantle heard of this his anger was extreme. He refused to give his consent, which still counted, and the plan was abandoned.

Richard then bared his soul in private to Philip Augustus. He explained that what troubled him was the likelihood of his father's conveying of the whole inheritance to Lackland if he himself were to depart to the Holy Land. "If *he* should die, this may well happen."

Yet another conference was proposed; conferences were meat and drink to the young king of France, as they enabled him to use his wits without fighting. This time the conference was at the evident suggestion of John Lackland himself, about then having been made count of Mortain. John had inherited a certain amount of the hard common sense his father had shown in younger days and lately seemed to have lost, being however not yet in his dotage. Meantime Philip Augustus smoothly proposed that both sides give back what they had taken since the swearing of crusading vows in the previous January. Curtmantle, who had taken nothing, was of course ready to agree. Richard, who by his own efforts had taken a great deal, was not. He said it meant giving up a thousand marks a year, which he needed to provision his crusade.

Philip, innocently or not, then suggested that Richard marry Alais forthwith and that Curtmantle allow his barons to swear fealty to Richard as his heir. Curtmantle rejected both notions. Richard then asked him, in the hearing of all, to name him as his heir, in any case. Henry II refused. The air was full of hate.

"Now at last I believe what seemed unbelievable," Richard said aloud. He unfastened his sword, and stood facing the king of France. Then he knelt, with hands outstretched and joined palm to palm, in the ancient aspect of feudal homage. Philip took Richard's hands between his, and Richard then did homage "for Normandy and Poitou and Anjou, Maine and Bern and Toulouse, and all other fiefs this side the sea" and swore fealty to France against all men, saving what he owed to his father the king of England.

The silence was like brooding thunder. Curtmantle did not move or speak. King Philip calmly restored certain castles to his friend Richard including those in Berri, and the pair rode off together, leaving an old man staring after them from his appointed place. It was beginning to be cold, being already November.

15

CURTMANTLE spent his last Christmas in Anjou, the cradle of his youth: the place where his young father had taught him the cunning of governance, of survival, of the means to achieve his ends. Now, only the aim to survive seemed to be left.

With the king was his son Lackland, by now as stated count of Mortain. This young serpent had remained in Normandy, his marriage to his cousin Hadwisa of Gloucester remaining unsavoury and mysterious. The pope had forbidden the pair to live together because of their close kinship; nevertheless Hadwisa's elder sisters had been deprived of their lands by the king and recompensed by him with money, while the lands had gone to Lackland. Hadwisa herself was an unchancy girl who, as Berthe swore and as I believe, practised the old religion like King Rufus, himself a willing victim to the expected arrow long since in the New

359

Forest; he was the chosen green man, the new century's sacrifice. I had never forgotten the sight of Richard, kneeling long ago at the black slab which hid Rufus's tomb.

Be all that as it may, the count of Mortain deemed it politic to stay near his father. I have said before that Curtmantle, for all his cunning, could be blind. After John's lamentable behaviour in Ireland he should at least have guessed that his youngest son was a fool. However Lackland — he was forever known by that name in my own country — had since persuaded his father that the fault lay not with him but with Hugh de Lacy, since murdered in Meath. All that was long past, and what they planned together at Saumur, at least in Henry's estimation, was how best to act with regard to those loving friends once more, Richard and the king of France.

Also present at that sad Christmas was Geoffrey of Lincoln, the whore Ykenai's son. Few others of any note remained; many of Curtmantle's lords had ridden off to join Richard, seeing in him the rising sun. Many of my Bretons joined them also; they loathed Curtmantle and missed no chance to show it. The truce had expired in mid-January of the former year, and despite the cold and lack of provender, Philip and Richard had invaded Curtmantle's lands, including my own, and had wrought as much damage as they might. Brittany was once again made smoking ruins, filled with starving people, barren for the year.

Curtmantle himself was by then ill and could make no reply. He had an anal fistula which pained him greatly and which was not improved by riding. He took shelter at Le Mans, almost thereby returning to the womb; but it was his father's tomb at which he knelt, nearby the relics of St. Julian. Both had escaped the earlier burnings.

I myself once saw the effigy of Geoffrey Le Bel. Even that was handsome: the empress was not so unfortunate, after all. He wore a black surcoat painted with golden leopards, and a peaked black helm. Beneath it, his eyes were light, aware and sharp, as though he still lived. They say he was Queen Eleanor's lover. Meantime his son postponed a further meeting with the king of France, saying truly that he was not in health to come. He put off such an encounter till Candlemas, then Easter. It was no longer prevarication, but his true state; he knew he would never see Jerusalem. He sent Archbishop Baldwin, who still remained with him despite the earlier blasphemous words in England, to Richard to try to persuade the latter to return to his duty. However Richard by then would trust no messenger of his father's and refused the archbishop audience.

At last Curtmantle forced himself to encounter his two enemies between Easter and Whitsun, as the papal legate had meantime arrived. The conduct of the three warring crusaders was, he told them roundly, a scandal through Christendom, and he threatened excommunication for them all if they did not make their peace and start their journey. That Curtmantle was already beyond it the pope could not know.

Perhaps on seeing him, the legate temporised by excommunicating all, except for the two kings, involved in the late disturbing of the peace. One of the candles to be snuffed out was in the name of Richard, the most dedicated crusader of them all.

A stormy meeting was held at last in early summer at La Ferté, north-east of Le Mans. The legate, four archbishops, and a pressing crowd of barons and earls were present, concerned for their immortal souls and fortunes. Alais was again demanded as Richard's wife, but not by Richard. He himself, it was stated, must be assured of being his father's heir, and Lackland — this was a new thing — was to take the cross and go to Jerusalem with his brother. As this was an obvious move to ensure that the young man did not seize everything in Richard's absence, Curtmantle refused. The old lion still had teeth. He proposed, not for the first time, that John marry Alais instead. No one considered the state of the Gloucester marriage, which presumably could be dissolved. The whole endeavour was intended to state clearly that Henry II intended making his youngest son his heir. In addition, it mocked Richard regarding the bride now promised to him for more than twenty years, having spent a fair amount of that time in bed with Henry himself.

However Alais remained a Child of France. One of the cardinals turned on France's king. The whole thing was Philip's doing, the eminence swore, and he would have Philip's kingdom placed under interdict unless he made peace with the king of England. "I do not fear your sentence," replied young Philip coldly. "It does not concern the Roman Church if the king of France, to avenge his injuries and the insults to his crown, puts down his unworthy and rebellious vassals." He added as a rider, no doubt with truth, that the cardinal in question stank of Henry's sterling.

The conference dispelled, Curtmantle returned once more to his beloved Le Mans and assured its citizens that he would never abandon them. It is possible that he hoped shortly, by then, to leave his bones there. He loved the place more than any other, and told them so; reminding them that his father was buried there, that he himself had been born there. While King Philip marched through Maine, Curtmantle lingered in his birthplace day after day, letting Philip, ever nearing, take one castle after another. It was as though the king of England lay under some spell; in his youth he would have had enough resolve to dispel twenty such enemies.

It was a Sunday, with everyone at church, when Richard and Philip appeared with their army outside the walls of Le Mans. Curtmantle made no move, having meantime blocked the fords. However his safety was a dream; the French found a hidden ford, and crossed that way over the river. Henry, hearing, started a fire to drive them off; and therein lay his worst fortune, for the wind changed. The fire was driven back into the city itself, and all of Le Mans went up in a blaze, the wooden houses catching instantly. The terrified citizens opened the gates to escape into the countryside, and the French shouldered their way in past them. King Henry and seven hundred of his knights rode off in flight, looking back at last on the pall of black smoke hanging over the ruined town. "O God," cried Curtmantle, "since you have so vilely taken away from me today the city that I loved most on earth in order to heap up confusion on me and increase my shame; the city where I was born and bred, where my father lies buried and St. Julian is enshrined, I will pay you back as best I can: I will take away what you love best in me; my heart."

How long he had in truth deserted God he alone knew. Meantime a great broad-shouldered figure, horsed, but clad in a quilted doublet only and a plain helm, was galloping up at the rear; Richard, lance poised. William Marshal turned, levelled his own lance, and faced the devil's son.

"By God's legs, Marshal, do not kill me! That would be an evil thing to do; I am unarmed."

"No, let the devil kill you, for so will not I." The good knight thrust his spear into Richard's horse, which fell dead at once. Richard was thrown to the ground, and lay with an ugly look again on his face till he was mounted by his following. The pursuit by then was abandoned.

★ ★ ★

There was by this time no sign of John, count of Mortain. He had slipped away at some point best known to himself. With the king were left only Marshal, the earl of Essex, and Geoffrey of Lincoln, Henry's faithful son Tacheté, who stayed with him till the end. Many of the seven hundred knights lay dead by the roadside, roasted to death in their armour in the summer heat. The rest rode twenty miles, and then the sick king flung himself down on a bed at Fresnay-le-Vicomte, without undressing. Geoffrey of Lincoln covered him with his cloak.

"Press forward to Normandy," Henry's advisers told him next day. "It is no more than ten miles from here to Alençon, and from there, you may send for help to England." But Curtmantle refused. He said again "I will go to Anjou."

★ ★ ★

The devil's country saw him once more, and he gave instructions that the keys of certain castles were to be delivered up to nobody except the count of Mortain. He put Geoffrey of Lincoln in command of what remained of his army and sent them off to Alençon. He himself was by then in great pain.

Geoffrey Tacheté carried out his duty at Alençon and then rode back to rejoin his father on the seldom-used forest paths, with a hundred picked knights alongside. Philip's forces manned the known roads; it was necessary to ride almost two hundred miles, by devious ways, before they reached Chinon. "Bring me William Marshal," ordered Henry then, with what was to be almost his last authority. Only the men who followed the Marshal's banner had been allowed to accompany him. He must perhaps have known that even he would soon die.

King Philip meantime, after levelling and securing Le Mans, had taken all the castles on the way to Tours and was about to lay siege to that city itself. He arrived there with Richard on the last day of June. They sent Henry a message which was in fact an order; to meet them without fail at Azay-le-Rideau, a small fortress reflected pleasantly in a smooth lake; but Henry had a fever from his inflamed fistula, and did not reach Azay except to go to bed. "It is one more ruse," they said, and rode on instead to attack Tours.

On the Sunday, three men who of them all had least cause to speak, the counts Theobald of Blois and Philip of Flanders, with the archbishop of Rheims, came to try to persuade Curtmantle that his position held no hope. He would listen to nothing they said; he was suddenly like an obstinate old woman who has been told her house is in danger of flooding, but will not leave it because she has always lived there and cannot believe that it will happen.

Tours fell in a day, eighty knights and a hundred soldiers being made captive by King Philip. Once again he forced the dying king of England to ride to a conference nearby; and this time the loyal Geoffrey, distressed beyond measure, asked leave not to accompany his father, that he might not witness the latter's humiliation. It is curious that a whore's son should be a finer man than princes.

Curtmantle in some manner reached a place named Ballan, which is five miles south-west of Tours. He dismounted before a house which belonged to the order of Knights Templars. By now he was in cruel pain all over, this having begun, he said, on his feet, rising at last to grip his heart. "I have neither body, heart nor limbs," he said to William Marshal, who never left him. The latter saw his face blacken and persuaded him to go to bed.

Richard and Philip meantime, having reached the place of conference, asked where the king of England might be. They were told that he was so sick he could neither sit nor stand. Richard laughed. His father was feigning illness, he said; he knew him of old. Hearing this saying related, Curtmantle had himself placed in the saddle and rode, held there by two men, to meet the son who was his enemy.

As he came up, even the king of France perceived his state and pitied him. He ordered a cloak to be folded and placed on the ground, for so grievously sick a man to sit down. Henry, held still in the saddle, replied "I have not come here to sit with you, but to hear what you demand of me and to ask why you have taken away my lands from me."

A thunderclap then rent the sky, and presently another. It was as if heaven had opened to hear the last humiliation — of Henry FitzEmpress, king of England. Terms of abject surrender, far worse than he had inflicted long ago on my uncle of Scotland, were read aloud through the thunder and the beating rain. The vanquished man, with a face like stone, sat still in the saddle, hearing.

. . . *whatever the king of France may devise and ordain, that the king of England will do with all his might and without gainsaying.* Alais — how they clung to wretched Alais! — was to be given up to the guardianship of five men to be named by Richard, who would marry her, or said so, when he returned from Jerusalem. Richard meantime was to receive fealty of all his father's subjects on both sides of the sea, as lawful heir to all his father's lands. No baron who had left Henry to join Richard was to undergo punishment. The two kings, with Richard, were to meet by mid-Lent at Vézelay, where Abbot

Bernard of Clairvaux had preached, in the market-place to thronged crowds long ago, the Second Crusade. To repay France's costs for all of this, Henry was to give Philip twenty thousand marks. All Henry's barons were to swear that if he failed in his word, they would join Richard and Philip and "with all their strength, help him to keep it". Le Mans, Tours and two castles in Anjou were to be given up to France, or else Gisors, Paçy and Nonancourt on the borders of Normandy.

Finally, Henry was to give his son Richard the kiss of peace. This meant, above all, that promises were irrevocably binding. As this was shamefully achieved the old lion whispered fiercely to his cub "God grant that I may not die till I have had a fitting revenge on you!" Richard told the story later on, still laughing, over dinner.

Curtmantle was carried back to Chinon then, lying in a litter, possibly the first time he had ever occupied one. Not yet silenced, he sent a servant of his household, a man of the name of Roger Malchael, back to Tours to obtain from

King Philip a written list of the names of those who had left him to join the enemy. By the time Roger returned to Chinon with the list, his master was *in extremis*. "Read it aloud," commanded Henry Curtmantle.

"Sire, may Jesu Christ help me! The first name written here is that of Count John, your son."

This was the news that killed him, at last; though Berthe had another version.

★ ★ ★

She had grown fat since the birth of her innocent, and came waddling in with Havoise by the hand. She was of course jubilant at news of the death. I was, for my own reasons, in tears; my husband had ridden off to secure Avranches, which was fortunate. Berthe told me that Geoffrey of Lincoln, Tacheté, who was with his father to the last, holding him meantime in his arms while he cried out with incurable pain and grief, had left him for an instant, perhaps to relieve himself, or else to make secure a sapphire ring he had been given, third of the ones

373

Curtmantle always wore. The dying man had promised to make him a bishop; later it happened. Meantime Berthe insisted that when Curtmantle was not yet dead, two servants whose wives he had ravished came in and strangled him with a bad mule's halter. This ugliness may not be the truth, but it gained credence in Brittany. In any case, once he was dead they stripped the body naked and left it lying on the floor. A knight named William Trihan later came and covered it with his cloak. It was a short one, like his own.

"He had none present to give him the last sacraments," gloated Berthe. "He will have gone to the devil, his ancestor. It could have been foreseen."

I was still in desolate tears. A living force had gone from all our lives; for good or evil, there would never be such a man again. However I knew what I myself had to do.

★ ★ ★

Somehow enough state was scratched together to bury Henry Curtmantle as a king. Richard having taken all the treasure already out of Chinon, there was no circlet to be found to put on his dead father's head. They found instead a lady's petticoat, mine from long ago, and cut off a part of its tarnished gold fringe. This made Henry II a mock crown for his burial at Fontevrault, to which they carried him then in procession from Chinon. I remembered the dead man I had seen lying long ago, crowned with a paltry fringe of gold; now it had happened. My mind was half full of my own plans, and I hardly heard the rest of what Berthe had to say; how there were no alms as were given, by custom, to the poor when the body of a king passed by. The seneschal of Anjou had refused to part with any money. "He made you rich enough," said William Marshal bitterly. At Fontevrault, the nuns there made a procession as best they might, and took the body to lay it before the high altar until the entombment. "They chanted the Office for the Dead then, and prayed God for mercy on his soul, though he denied God with his own words, twice over," Berthe continued. "God will deny him in turn, to be sure."

I could hear the echoing of the great vault to the nuns chanting. Berthe, merciless, went on to describe that she had heard Duke Richard — "he will be king now" — had come, and as he was his father's murderer the body had bled from its nose and ears as long as he remained, which was not longer than it took to say a paternoster. If this horrible story is true, it was no doubt the putrefying brains turning to liquid as they will; there had been no surgeon present to remove them, as is the custom.

Richard was in any case less the murderer than John Lackland. As Berthe had said, Richard was now king. One of his first orders as ruler of England was to free his mother, Eleanor of Aquitaine.

★ ★ ★

As soon as Berthe had taken herself and her mumbling off I sent for Guy de Thouars. "Take my gerfalcon and ride round my lords, as many as are left in Brittany," I told him. "Tell them I want them here in Rennes at King

Henry's requiem, as I have word for them." I knew that with the sight of the great falcon, and a ring I gave Guy to show them, they would know it was no ruse. Meantime I went to my chapel, taking my three-year-old son by the hand, and told him he must pray for his grandfather's soul. I was thankful that the earl of Chester was himself absent in Avranches.

16

BEING uncertain of the time and nature of Chester my husband's return, I had four knights, the de Thouars brothers, the Sieur de Vitré and Raoul de Fougères stand near me at the requiem, with the bishop of Rennes already informed that I would speak, when permitted, to my assembled baronage. There was as yet no sign of Chester, however, as the mass for the dead proceeded, and despite the firm decision I had taken, my thoughts in course of the chanting were with the soul of Henry II, wherever it journeyed. At the end, I rose, with my son by me: and standing before the altar where lately the Host had been raised, I spoke clearly.

"I would have all my lords of Brittany hear this. I am your duchess, and I have by my side my son your duke Arthur, to whom by right you owe fealty." There was a murmuring among them at sight of the bright-haired child with a hero's name: I held him up, so that they might see him.

"Listen, all of you," I continued. "I would not have given my hand in marriage to the earl of Chester except under force. I was constrained to it. He has taken the title of duke upon himself and rules Brittany without right in the name of the king of England, both the one now dead and the one living." I knew this would anger them; Richard himself had done more harm in the land than Curtmantle. "You loathe the English invaders as I do," I assured them, for they knew I had been brought up at the English court and perhaps thought otherwise. "My late husband Geoffrey was liked among you, and made himself a Breton. He is this child's father. I rely on your aid against the man I must now call husband. If you will rid me of him by merciful means, for I would not have his blood shed, I will govern you fairly till my son is of age."

The bishop came down then from the altar, his robes making a hushing sound. All those in church clustered about me and my son, ready to defend us. At that moment Chester himself appeared in the doorway, not followed by his men; he had returned late from his ride to Avranches, divested himself of his armour, and no doubt expected that, having put in some appearance in church, he would then be free to eat his dinner of mortrews and, some time thereafter, enjoy me in bed when he had drunk enough wine. All turned to face him, however, and hands were on swords; my four knights stood firm between him and my son.

"There he stands," I said; I, Chester's meek and silent wife he had thought it safe enough to leave meantime. "Do not draw your swords here; take him outside, and put him in the saddle again to ride off to his own place." He would be hungry, no doubt; that was the least of it, and I cared nothing.

There was silence like a rearing wave; then the wave broke. With an angry roar, they turned on De Blundeville of Chester and hustled him out of Rennes cathedral; I heard their shouts as they drove him off and the sound of hoofbeats at last. Guy de Thouars came to me afterwards, his gentle face stern for once.

"They have whipped him out of Rennes, and out of Brittany," he said. "He will not dare draw rein till he is once more in Avranches, and will maybe go further yet."

"Wherever he goes, you are safe, and the little duke also." Aimery had joined him; the pair were devoted like twins, though they had two years' difference in their ages. Aimery was a devout man; he spent much time in monasteries, though he had not taken vows. Raoul de Fougerès came back then also, sheathing the sword he was always quick to draw.

"The royal falcon was a sure sign," he said, "and your ring, duchess. Without them, I would have thought it one more trick."

"There will be no more tricks played among us now," I promised, and meant it.

Arthur had been watching and listening, and had conducted himself well. He had not been afraid at the growing roar of anger, or at the threat of drawn swords. Presently, with Chester hard on his way across the border, many of my lords came to offer Arthur fealty, kneeling with their hands placed between his small ones. I had instructed him in what to do; again, he contrived very well, accepting the homage seated in Conan III's carved chair, his legs too short as yet to touch the floor.

★ ★ ★

Later it was decided, and duly sent to the pope, that Chester and I were within the prohibited degrees and that the marriage was null. I forget what excuse there was for this; it may have been the like marriage of my uncle David of Huntingdon, which took place to Maud of Chester about then. It would take some time to disentangle at the Lateran, but meantime I was not troubled again by De Blundeville. I took up the business of governing my land again, and watched my son grow.

I spared time to send a letter to King Richard with the relation of events. I did not think he would spare his own to interest himself in our affairs for the present. He was raising money by all means to go on his crusade, and had recently sold back Scotland's freedom to my uncle William the Lion, who had ridden down for that purpose to Canterbury.

* * *

Richard left in the following year, at last for the Holy Land. With him went many of my dear friends and supporters; brave Raoul de Fougères, my husband Geoffrey's chosen seneschal; the count of Mayenne and the Sieur de Vitré, which last left his young daughter Anne in my care. The vicomte de Léon, old foe of Curtmantle, went also; in such a cause differences seemed healed among the Crusaders. They did not all return.

17

WE heard of the adventures of King Richard from time to time by way of the knight Aimery de Thouars, who had gone on the crusade and would send messengers twice or thrice a year to his brother Guy, left in charge of what remained of their Poitevin estates. I can remember my son Arthur listening intently, the tales of foreign daring enthralling him as they would have done any small boy. He desired, he said, when he grew to manhood, to follow his uncle and fight for Christ. I can remember his fair head as it shone from where it leant against my knee in the solar, and his eyes, bluer now than the sea — I have never seen eyes of so deep a blue on anyone — fixed on the speaker, who would have laid aside his helm and coat of mail and be seated at ease with us, drinking wine of Poitou.

★ ★ ★

We heard how the two kings Richard and Philip, close friends still, had set out for the Holy Land but had been detained in Sicily, where Tancred its king, who came of Norman pirate stock, made peace with them by giving up my old friend from Woodstock days, Princess Joanna, Richard's sister whom he had detained. Arthur himself — and this news hardly interested him — had then been betrothed by Richard to Tancred's daughter. This showed that Richard regarded Arthur, then, as his heir. I was pleased to learn that far-flung places we did not know, soaked in a sun I would never see, had heard the name of Arthur of Brittany.

That was before Richard married.

When I heard of this marriage, to a beautiful Navarrese princess, I was at first incredulous, then angry. Richard and Philip fell out again over the matter; Philip still, unbelievably, assumed that Richard would marry the much-used Alais on returning home. Then, beautiful as Berengaria of Navarre was said to be, I became increasingly certain that the marriage was one in name only. I had known Richard too well and too long to suppose that his nature would alter for any woman's sake. No doubt he made the marriage for the sake of alliance with her father, King Sancho, or to avoid the possible necessity of Alais.

There followed more quarrels in Cyprus. The new emperor of the east, Isaac Comnenus, treated Richard discourteously and was by him briskly deposed. The crown of Cyprus was given instead to Guy de Lusignan, Sibylla of Jerusalem's husband who had lately lost that city for Christ. It was hardly a good omen; and a far cry from the days of the brave leper king, who with the flesh falling from his bones beneath his armour had ridden out at the head of his troops at Montgisard, crying *Christus vincit, Christus imperat*. The later defeat at the Horns of Hattin had followed, after Baldwin's death and under the same Guy de Lusignan Richard now trusted. However Richard himself thereafter landed at Acre, marched on Joppa, and all but beheld Jerusalem.

"He never did see the Holy City," said Arthur sadly, at last.

"No," said Guy de Thouars in his

gentle way, "but maybe you yourself will, little duke, when you are a man."

★ ★ ★

The passionate friendship between Richard and Philip Augustus had burnt itself out over the matter of Alais. Richard decided to return home alone, and was shipwrecked in the Adriatic. What he did then was for long a mystery, as was his whereabouts. Later we learned that he had wandered in disguise through the lands of his sworn enemy, Leopold of Austria, whose standard he had degraded publicly in Palestine by trampling on it. With Richard's height, broad shoulders, yellow hair and high colour he was difficult to disguise, although he had adopted strange dress. They found him, captured him at last and in the end, handed him over to the emperor Henry, who imprisoned him and demanded a heavy ransom for his release.

Lackland, left in charge of affairs in England, was in no haste to have his brother freed. The English people loyally raised the ransom, with more eagerness by far than they had displayed over the Saladin Tithe; but the money was not sent, or not yet. It was not known even where King Richard was held in prison. In time, a young Picard minstrel named Blondel found his master by singing aloud a song they alone knew, *Richard, ô mon roi*: and the king's deep voice answered from his cell.

18

THE proudest moment of my life was when my son Arthur, not yet nine years old, was acclaimed duke of Brittany at the assembly of the estates-general in Rennes in 1196. All eyes were on the slender gold-and-white figure of the boy whose father they remembered with affection, whose own posthumous birth had been like a miracle, the coming again of the great hero of the sword Excalibur and of Lyonnesse. This also was the heir of England, making it seem again as if, as in time of old, there was no sea between. The hatred of England as a foreign power, seizing by way of Normandy what was not hers by right, would surely cease when this child was a man. He would be reared meantime as a Breton; and would soon take my place and rule.

On one hand walked his tutor and governor, Guéthénoc, bishop of Vannes; and on the other Alan of Dinan, the

389

seneschal who had replaced Fougères when he later went off to the Holy Land. It was as though light played about the little duke's golden head, making him a figure like that of some saint. Women in the crowd called blessings after him, young girls threw flowers. It was known that he was to marry the daughter of Tancred, king of Sicily, and that his name was heard already beyond seas. What a ruler he would make, beautiful, courageous, high-born, beloved of all! The bishop of Ely, England's regent, had already written to acknowledge Arthur as heir-presumptive, and so had the king of Scots. The future was bright as he passed by. My own eyes were full of tears, but they were tears of joy. For this had I been born, I, Constance of the blood royal, daughter of the Athelings and of the line of Cerdic and Siward, widow myself to a Plantagenet. Now, my Plantagenet son had come into his own: and I was content.

★ ★ ★

I should not have been so. I should have been on my guard against danger, as soon as it was known that John Lackland, count of Mortain, was making war on the bishop of Ely, withholding the ransom that had been raised for Richard's release from prison, and had earlier caused Richard himself, with all his grand divisions, to withdraw from Palestine in order to come home and safeguard his English throne. It was evident now that Lackland desired his brother to be kept in prison in order that he might make himself king.

It was some time before his treacheries were realised. No one before then had taken him seriously since the Irish matter. Making enemies where friends had been was the act of a fool; but the evil in him was not yet as well known as it would later become. When I heard that King Richard had been released despite him, and was hastening home, I was glad; he would surely punish so treacherous a brother.

He did not. He forgave John of Mortain without conditions. I have never fully understood the Plantagenet bond; or perhaps I am unaware of Lackland's charm since he became a man. It had certainly deceived his father.

Richard, on arrival in England, wrote to me courteously, sending the missive, dangling with royal seals, by courier. He said that he would come to Bayeux, and invited me to attend him there. Accordingly I kissed my son, left him with his governors, and took horse with my women, including Berthe and her sad little Havoise, from whom she would never agree to be parted. Sad is no doubt the wrong word for that child; such innocents are happy enough, and do not live long.

The wind was with us, and we rode swiftly across the land, stopping at St. Malo where a deputation of my lords received me: then next day, still with a fair wind, we rode on to Pontorson. This was a fortress whose foundations old Henry Curtmantle had paced out for himself, thereafter discussing the plans for its building directly with his mason. It was as though his presence was not far off. I entered to the smell of newly dressed stone and lime, the rendering being not yet complete.

A bowing seneschal received me, and

asked if, when I had refreshed myself, he might have a word alone. Presently I followed him, leaving my women behind. By then it was growing dark; a torch flared orange in a holder, casting grotesque shadows on the walls. The man led me to what appeared to be a small chamber, with one high window.

"What is it you would ask of me?" I said to him. He made no reply, bowed and withdrew. I heard bolts snap shut: and instantly became aware of the treachery planned from England. What had led me to trust Richard of Poitou any more than his brother? I had been a fool, a dupe twice over now.

The bolts slid open and I saw a figure enter, without expression on his face. It was my erstwhile husband, Ranulf de Blundeville of Chester. He was evidently my gaoler. As on our wedding night, he strode forward and struck me across the mouth.

"You were Henry's harlot," he said. "Accord me the same favour now that you say you are no longer my wife."

★ ★ ★

I have said enough already about this man's usage of me, and will say no more except to mention a thing which is perhaps not known to all women. If any one of us is beaten like a dog, then lain with at the conqueror's leisure once her resistance is overcome for the time, certain things happen within her body over which she has no control. I knew, when this began, what it was intended I should by the end become, and be said by others to have become: a wanton, so that my son's very birth might become suspect, and the whisper started that his grandfather, and perhaps other men, had been more than that. I knew all this, and used to bite my lips while the ecstasy rose unbidden in my bruised body: loathing the man who caused it, and yet unable to down it, having after all lived a chaste life for eight years. Queen Eleanor, in her prison, had had other things with which to beguile her time; painting, reading, music, company. I had nothing day after day except the bringing of food and water by a silent servitor, and the recurrent loathed visits of Ranulf of Chester.

He removed me under strong guard soon, being no doubt afraid lest my Bretons would rescue me from Pontorson by some means. He took me to the place named St. Jacques-de-Beuvron, in the heart of the Loire valley, far from help. There, he put me under the care of an ally of his own and King Richard's. This man was called Ascot de Raiz. He and Chester threatened, if I would not yield quietly, to turn me over to the common English soldiery to be used as a whore. I had heard the same thing happening to Berthe years since. What could I do but submit to Chester when he came? He would ride over from Le Mans, beat me, take me, then let me hear his jeering laughter. No doubt he hoped to get me with child. If that had happened he could have trumpeted my disgrace through France, England and Brittany, no doubt saying de Raiz had been at me also: God knows.

The reason why it did not happen was due to Berthe's foresight. She was permitted, with her poor Havoise, to come and go in the Loire countryside. At harvest they commonly gather up the gleanings of wheat and rye to make black ergot. This when drunk tastes bitter, and kills any conception in the womb if it is taken early and often enough. After each visit of Chester's Berthe would bring it to me, and I downed it thankfully. Had he suspected it, or had de Raiz done, they would have had Berthe herself beaten, raped or killed. She was brave, and I have never forgotten her bravery.

I was in prison, enduring the treatment I have described, for more than two years. By the end my hair, like Guenever's, had turned white. That mattered nothing; but I was constantly concerned for my son. Long before, when I was first taken prisoner, the Breton seneschal had been permitted to see me, having ridden the long distance with a party of my lords. They wanted to know my wishes as to what must be done. On entry, the man murmured a message I knew came from my good knight Guy de Thouars.

"The duke and the hawk are both safe. De Vitré has one, and I, Guy, have the other."

Ears were listening, and I made no sign except to smile. The new followers who had been admitted with Alan of Dinan assured me of the loyalty and faith of my subjects. I had already arranged the veil I wore to hide the bruise on my cheek. No word of ill-treatment must be spread to arouse Breton anger; the only concern must be that Arthur was safe.

"Stay near my son's person whatever befalls," I told them. "Without doubt an attempt will be made to take him from you. Watch over him with care as friends, good servitors, blood kin. Above all ensure, by every possible means, that he does not fall into the hands of the English." I spoke fearlessly, knowing that that nation listened in the person of de Raiz, who had remained.

The Bretons asked me then concerning myself. I replied that it was of no importance. "Whatever God pleases will befall my person," I said. "Do what is best for Arthur my son. I will do well enough so long as I may rest assured that he is guarded without fail by his faithful subjects."

Their eyes, like my own, had filled

with tears: they knelt to kiss my hands. They swore then to offer service to their young duke, to follow his fortunes even to death, and to defend him against whoever might come. They promised never to treat with Richard lacking his consent and my own. That last I knew would be hard to obtain, kept close as I would be from now on; no further deputations would be allowed. As it was, I had time to be informed that many of the lesser nobility, who had not come to my assembly at St. Malo, joined in this latest promise. Among the members of what was by then a patriotic league — I must repeat their names — were four bishops, those of St. Brieuc, Nantes, Vannes and Rennes; the counts of Penthièvre and de Goëtol, the Sieur de Mayenne, the vicomte de Léon, the returned baron de Fougères, that last having fought well at Acre; Alan de Rohan, the lords of Lohéac, de Chateaubriant, de Malestroit, de Montfort and de Chateaugiron, de la Guerche; many more.

They left me heartened, and thereafter I endured my fate.

Richard himself had meantime advanced as far as Rennes. No doubt he hoped to seize my son's person. I heard all of it afterwards; how the Sieur de Vitré had risked all he had, safety, castles, fortune, even life in my son's service. In the end the Lion Heart, discomfited of his prey, returned to Normandy. Later he gave orders to one Robert de Tournehan to ravage all de Vitré's lands, even to burn the houses of the peasants, to smoke them out of the caves where they hid and then to put them to the sword. We do not make a hero of the Lion Heart in Brittany. De Vitré by then had conveyed my son to the furthest point south, the castle of Brest itself, hiding him there.

Worse was to come for the Bretons for their loyalty to their duke. Richard might have retreated in person to Normandy, but the new bishop of Rennes, sent shortly to negotiate for my freedom, failed. The old cat-and-mouse game began once more; Richard gave the appearance of consenting to my release provided neither I nor my son acted in any matter without his advice. He also demanded hostages. These were found, the gallant de Vitré including his own daughter Anne among them. Remembering by now the fate of Alix de Porhoët, and knowing my own, I trembled when I heard: but Anne de Vitré's freedom and return, and those of the rest, were promised should I not be freed by the ensuing Feast of the Assumption.

Matters hung fire then, as always. I took Anne in my arms when she was put, like myself, in ward with Ascot de Raiz. However he vowed to return her to her father within seven years, come what might. This was small comfort. Thereafter Anne was permitted to be with me occasionally, and even allowed, which I was not, to go into the main chapel beyond the grille. When my so-called husband visited me, Anne would be taken elsewhere; and afterwards her presence consoled me greatly. Many distinguished names were meantime added to that treaty of promise of release, which in the end availed nothing; the English refused to release either myself or the hostages, having gained the latter.

A fearful war threatened to break out in Brittany over all of this, and I sent word once again that I was resigned to my fate. I hoped that this would avert disaster, but the proud barons of Brittany sent a herald to King Richard accusing him of breaking faith. This roused the Plantagenet anger, and war was resumed.

I have said that the man Tournehan had been sent to ruin de Vitré's lands. Now, with my son safe hidden in Brest, a worse scourge still appeared, in the person of a hireling of the name of Mercadet. His brigands were known as Cottereaux, and had already made France desolate. It was the Rouptiers over again, but worse. These latest visitants lived by crime, were known never to attend mass — like Curtmantle's ancestress they would have vanished at the elevation of the Host — and they were well paid by their masters so long as they did harm. They would seek out priests and monks and massacre them, having pillaged the churches. Unspeakable sacrilege was a daily event. The profaning of the sacred vessels was the least of it; I heard the rest later. Such were the scoundrels released by the Lion Heart throughout Brittany. My land will not forget.

There was of course search made everywhere for André de Vitré, known still to be in charge of my son. The vicomtes de Rohan and de Léon took up arms then, the people of Cornouaille who had seen Arthur ride through; Tréguier and Vannes banded together, a thing unheard of; Fougères once more, du Faou, de Dol, de Montfort and de Lohéac marched against this cruel horde, and met them near the ancient place of Carhaix, once the palace of the wicked princess Ahès who had caused the sea to envelop Ys. They charged, and with the first assault routed the Cottereaux cavalry.

Night prevented the latter's total destruction. Next day the remnant rallied a little in retreat, and went their way pillaging, burning, killing, and ravaging all the countryside.

It was at this point that my Breton lords, as I learned later, decided that there was only one way to ensure the safety of their little duke. They sent my son Arthur, with his governor, bishop Guéthénoc, to the safety of the man who had once been Richard's friend and was now known to be his enemy; Philip Augustus of France.

19

I HEARD of it by this means; the worst whipping my husband of Chester had ever given me since our forced marriage. I do not think there was a single part of my body which was not covered with weals when he had done. As a rule I would sink my teeth in my forearm meantime to control my sobbing breaths; this time, I could not. I lay prone on the floor when he had finished and heard him turn to go.

"Your tail must needs cool itself; I'm off to England." He unbolted the door, then cast back "Your devil's spawn is in Paris. A horse kicked out his father's guts there. Perhaps the same fate will befall him. I pray for it."

He went out then, not troubling to bolt the door. I heard him go down the stone stairs and slowly, painfully raised myself to my feet. I could hardly stand, but his last words had given me a glimmer of hope. Had Arthur indeed won to France? They must have covered his bright hair, or else ridden by night on the way. He was now known through all the countryside by his golden fairness.

I remembered then that Berthe's little Havoise had died the day before, as such folk do, still young. Nevertheless Berthe was inconsolable and would not leave the coffin. When I dragged myself down to the grille, I saw the mourning women kneeling round it. My strength gave out then and I lay on the stone, my cheek against its coolness. I tried to think of Arthur in Paris, and wonder if King Philip had welcomed him as his father's son.

I became aware of a woman's breathing near me. She was one of the mourners who had come from the fields about St. Jacques. Berthe and her child had become known among them. She knelt and made pretence to tell her beads, but I heard her speak to me beneath her breath.

"Madame, your son is safe in the French king's care. I bring word of it from the vicomte de Thouars. He has often tried in vain to reach you. When we heard of the child's death here he sent me to Berthe with the news, but she will hear nothing for grief."

She fell then to her paternosters, for there were others in the chapel. I breathed thanks to God and felt a great lifting of the heart. My son in Paris, and de Thouars near! King Philip would cherish Arthur, would make a knight of him soon; how old was my son now? Time had passed so slowly in my prison I had lost count of the hours and days. I felt blessed oblivion overtake me, and woke — it must have been much later — to find one of the servants plucking at my sleeve; it was dark except for the sanctuary lamp and the candles. The other mourners had gone, but Berthe still knelt on by the coffin, her face lined and yellow in the fading glow. No doubt she would kneel there till morning.

"I am recovered," I said to the servant; they all knew about my beatings. "You may aid me upstairs."

★ ★ ★

After little Havoise had been buried Berthe returned to her duties about me, but was never the same. She related monotonously, as if it mattered nothing, a tale of great heroism from Brittany. The lord of Vitré had taken my son as I said from castle to castle, hiding him from the search parties Richard, De Blundeville and others caused to be sent out. It was not till after that that I heard of King Philip's joyous reception of my son, both for his father's sake and to goad Philip's erstwhile friend the Lion Heart. Almost at once, having left Arthur in safe keeping and with those about him who would continue his education — this had suffered, naturally, in the hustled journeyings with de Vitré up and down the land — Philip Augustus hastened to besiege Aumale, with the intent of pulling Richard's forces out of Brittany. This made heartening news.

Richard then, always foremost at presenting himself as a figure of chivalry, challenged King Philip to a duel. I believe prodigies of valour were performed by both if the version I heard is true. Richard fought as a simple knight, though his great height and breadth of shoulder made him unmistakeable. Meantime Alan of Dinan, the same who had led my son Arthur to his ducal enthronement at Rennes, had withdrawn from the affray to repair his casque. Forgetting a similar encounter in which he himself had reproached William Marshal for exactly the same thing, Richard hurled himself, lance lowered, on the half-armed man. Alan mustered his defences as best he could, but his arms were in disarray and Richard's lance broke his shield. Nevertheless Alan's attack was so vigorous that the King of England was sent flying, and his horse likewise. The English hastened to his aid. Furious, Lion Heart pursued Alan in the confusion as soon as he might, and wounded him so severely that a surgeon had to be called. The king of England's temper flared nonetheless and would not be controlled; but Philip had won, with more than thirty distinguished captives for ransom. He seized the town of Aumale then under the very eyes of the king of England, who was forced most shamefully to retreat. This he would never forgive.

It was nevertheless clear by now even to the Lion Heart that he must sue for peace. It was at this time, at last, that he set me free.

★ ★ ★

There were rearrangements, naturally. Richard promised my lords to forget the past; whether they themselves could do so is another matter. He gave them the choice of serving myself or him. De Vitré was given back his lands and ruined castles, both in Brittany and England. His brother Robert, a parish churchman, received a pension of a hundred marks of pure silver yearly. Several of the Breton lords took the opportunity to serve France, because it meant serving their little duke. Every adversary of Curtmantle and his sons was recompensed, except in one instance; Anne de Vitré remained a hostage in the hands of Ascot de Raiz. This disturbed me greatly, but all I could do at the time was to renounce, on behalf of Anne and her successors, any right the dukes of Brittany held over her territories. Later, when she was at last freed unharmed, she was married to the vicomte of Chateau-Gontier. I have been grateful to her all my life.

There was a truce of five years then, and I resumed my regency. Once again, at this point, the pope chose to preach a crusade. The Lion Heart however took himself off to Poitou

★ ★ ★

I must speak now of myself for a little. Among those who were waiting to receive me on my emergence from prison at St. Jacques-de-Beuvron was my good knight Guy de Thouars. I walked past the grand seigneury and went straight to him.

"Take me away to where we may be alone," I said. "I find the sudden world too large."

Later he said to me that I had always had his heart. "I did not dare lay it before so great a lady," he said in his unassuming way. I laid my hand on his.

"I know I am no longer beautiful," I told him: it was the truth. He smiled, but I had seen myself by then in a burnished mirror; there were lines between nose and mouth, my eyes were shadowed and my hair, as I have said, was white, an old woman's. Guy himself was older also, grey of head, grim-faced, with the long wars and hardship there had been since his youth, and his constant fruitless efforts to send word to me in enemy country. We turned to each other; I laid my head to rest against his shoulder, and in the saddle leaned against him like a child. We have never since been parted. Love can be gentle, a shared quiet contentment one with the other. I have found this, and am filled with thankfulness to God.

20

I BORE my love Guy de Thouars two daughters during the years we lived in what the world calls sin. How could we have been expected to wait once again for the decision of the Lateran? Life is short enough. I was not however without ambition for my son, and for his sake I hid my condition twice over from the world.

Arthur is without doubt the true heir to England. His father Geoffrey was the fourth son of Henry II; John Lackland is the fifth. For Richard to change his mind on his deathbed, out of pique concerning Philip Augustus and his meantime protection of my child, was iniquitous; what else did he expect to be done to save my heir? He himself had made the betrothal with Tancred's daughter earlier, and had made it clear to the world that he recognised Arthur's rights; then at the last moment acted with treachery, as was always his wont.

I doubt if he was thinking of the welfare of England, rather of his precious Poitou and the possibility of its falling to Philip's hands. Would that have been a worse fate for the Poitevins, or the English either, than being exposed to Lackland's own idleness, folly, cruelty and lechery? The refting away of Angoulême's daughter, the child betrothed already to Hugh de la Marche, is a case in point; there was no choice for the bride or her family, as Lackland was their overlord and would have seized Angoulême by right if he was thwarted. He abandoned his first wife Hadwisa over the business, while of course keeping her lands. This is the manner of man who now calls himself king of England. Richard the Lion Heart is dead.

★ ★ ★

How did I hear of all this? One day I was in my solar, sewing by the last light of the late sun; soon it would be time to bring in candles. The little girls had been taken off to bed; they were quiet obedient children, not notable, resembling their father in nature and in looks. Guy's footsteps sounded on the turret stairs and he came in, his lure over his shoulder; he had been hunting all day in the great forest that surrounds Rennes. When I asked what the day's tally had been he did not reply. Instead he came over and took my hand.

"King Richard is dead," he said, and told me how an archer's arrow had pierced the king's shoulder at Chaluz, where he was making war on the king of France. "He has lain these many days in pain, dying. Now — "

I had risen, joy in my face and my heart. "Then my son is king of England," I said. "We must send word there quickly; or has it already gone?" It might be, I thought, that they had ridden straight from Chaluz, through enemy country; but that news would suspend the war.

Guy had not let go of my hand. "There is worse to come," he said quietly.

"Arthur? My son?" My thoughts were always with him, fearful at times; a fever, an accident, even a mock tourney like the one which killed his father; or else enemies lying in wait. "Tell me, for the love of God," I said. "I must bear it, whatever it may be."

"Arthur is unharmed, but he is not king of England. Richard changed his mind as he lay dying, and instead has named Lackland his heir." Guy's whole expression was for me: the news meant little to him otherwise.

"He cannot do so," I said incredulously. It occurred to me, even then, that Lackland would make the worst king England had ever had. "The wound in Richard's shoulder must have driven him mad," I said. "Surely he remembered how Lackland withheld his ransom to detain him in prison?" I felt the coming child heavy in me; I turned restlessly.

"It may be that the people of England will call for Arthur to be their king in the end," said my husband quietly.

"Ay, when he is an old white-haired man, worn out with betrayals." I seized my own hair, pulling at it, hurting myself. Guy tried to comfort me. "Bear it, my own dearest, for the child's sake," he said.

"The child? Why bear children? I think this news will kill me at the birth."

I am still of this opinion. I would sooner die than think of Lackland with Arthur's crown on his head. I would sooner die.

* * *

It soon became evident that I must die in any case; after all, we can expect nothing other. In my instance, however, there has been particular horror.

I have spoken of the brave boy king in Jerusalem who became a leper. It was discovered because, when he was a child, they competed to see who could endure the most pain. Baldwin could endure pins stuck in his arms and hands, pinching of his flesh, other such things, better than any of the rest. It was realised then that he could feel nothing; this is an early sign of leprosy.

The later signs are so terrible that none will go near the leper, and at all times they have been banished from society and compelled to live far out in the wilderness alone. Churches have a leper window through which these unlucky creatures may gaze at the Host and hear mass, not mingling with the rest. Their lives are lived out so, and only Christ can heal them. The power of Christ, his lack of fear, was in the Franciscan brothers who were the only ones to remain with the dying king Baldwin IV to the end, caring for him in all ways. I myself owe all things to my love Guy, who has stayed by me despite everything; also Berthe, who no longer cares for the world. Guy says he loves me, mind, body and bones, and that when I have become a skeleton he will still love it because it is mine. That is my comfort, even though I can never clasp my son again. As for the child growing in me, I trust in God that she will have escaped my disease.

★ ★ ★

Left alone often as I am, I think of the Lion Heart, dead by an arrow at Chaluz. Did he, in that year of 1199, know that he was the green victim, like Rufus royal and doomed? They say Richard forgave his slayer, though others say he had him burned alive at the foot of the deathbed, and still others that after his death, the rest took the young archer and flayed him alive, then hanged him. At any rate, he is dead. I have never forgotten the kneeling Richard at Rufus's hidden grave at Winchester, long ago; it was as if he dedicated himself then to the sacrifice, though at times he became devoutly, almost violently Christian, as if the two religions warred within him, the old and the new.

Who will be the next victim, in the coming century? I shall not live to know, and the voices which used to speak within me are silent on that matter. I wait only to die, having first to give birth.

★ ★ ★

Queen Eleanor will send me no gift this time; she is my enemy now since I sent Arthur into France. Her support weighs in the scales for Richard's choice, her own youngest son, not for a grandson she has after all not yet seen. So old a woman is still valiant; on news of Richard's death she spared no time to mourn, but commanded the people of Aquitaine and Poitou to subject themselves to

Lackland. Normandy also acknowledges him. Maine, Touraine and Anjou were different, and declared for my son. However Curtmantle's treasure, guarded once more at Chinon in the care of that devil de Tournehan, enabled Lackland to bribe right and left. In England, the archbishop of Canterbury crowned him, Saumur then followed Chinon in acknowledging him as its master. As was said in the time of King Stephen, a crown ends all argument.

King Philip meantime was not idle. He sent my son to loyal Angers under the care of Guillaume des Roches. Oddly, Tournehan's own nephew Thomas de Fumes received them with great magnificence in the ancient stronghold of the devil; the townspeople crowded beyond the moat to acclaim Arthur, whose shining beauty enchanted them when he appeared on the walls. The seigneury of Anjou came then and knelt in homage to the heir of Henry Curtmantle, of Geoffrey Le Bel, Black Fulk and the fairy Melusine. Old Le Mans, rebuilding still after the late burnings, also received my son with joy. A few days later he was honoured in the cathedral of Tours itself, vested with the habit of a hereditary canon, this itself being a dignity crowned heads covet and do not often obtain.

I was present, cloaked to hide my second pregnancy by de Thouars. I handed my son in person to King Philip, gazing for the only time into the cold Capet eyes beneath the thick hair. I cannot say I would have trusted a man of his appearance, except that I knew I must.

At that time, having taken twelve years to achieve it, the Lateran dissolved my loathed marriage to De Blundeville of Chester. Guy and I were made man and wife at last, but not in time for my little Cathérine, like her elder sister Marguérite, to be born other than bastard. It matters little; Guy is respected, and the marriages of both children have been arranged; one into the brave de Vitré family, the other to the de Rohans.

* * *

There was treachery soon enough elsewhere, whether or not by means of bribes. Hardly had Arthur quitted le Mans than Guillaume des Roches, who had conducted him there and whom my son had entrusted with its captaincy, handed the town over to Lackland and embraced his cause.

All this, and what followed, can hardly be put down to Lackland's charm, which however deceived his father to the end of the latter's life; it was all done by money. The Chinon treasure was in fact so well employed that Lackland's next device was to ask for an interview, in person, with the King of France.

From the beginning, at this rate, the plan made between them was easy enough. Lackland agreed in readiness to abandon such castles to France as had been taken in Arthur's name. My son, aged not yet sixteen, became in this way little more than a peg on a board. The sums of money said to change hands at that time were immense. A marriage was arranged then between Philip's own young son Louis and Lackland's niece, the younger Eleanor's daughter Blanche of Castile; they say the girl is extremely pious, which is more than her mother was. Again, Lackland promised all his lands this side the sea to young Louis. There was nothing he would not promise, and little he would not pay.

I blame King Philip. He should have paid heed to his own soul. The Angoulême marriage of Lackland's however displeased him, and I hear that the young Comte de la Marche is demanding vengeance. There are disputes already between France and England regarding fiefs; that matter has not been heard the last of. The two kings met at Angers, and were to meet again at Loudun, but Lackland did not appear. No doubt he would not face the angry young Comte de la Marche, who was present, determined to avenge the taking of his bride. I still have a picture before me of the bed-curtains of the married pair drawn till midday, and the bride not yet twelve years old.

These squabbles, at any rate, have caused my son's affairs to take a turn for the better. Lackland has shut himself up in Rouen, where he feels safe. A concourse of Breton noblemen have taken back certain fortresses in Normandy from his ally King Philip. They besieged Gournay, razed the fortress of Boutavant, and in other words thumbed their noses at both good friends. Lechery, greed and anger were said, with some injustice — he was not lecherous, merely treacherous — to be the vices of Richard the Lion Heart. His brother Lackland has all of them; his whole nature is evil and he will come to a bad end, if there is any justice in heaven.

* * *

My labour pains have started, no doubt with the shock of the news of Lackland's coronation. As I lie in childbed for what is after all the fifth time — and I am thirty-eight years old and with a wasting disease as I have said — the bitterness of all things overcomes me at last. Had I never known Arthur sent to France for his greater safety, had I kept my son by my side, he would have crossed the Channel by now, he would have been greeted by the waiting crowds on the white cliffs, with a shout the like of which Lackland will never hear, for they loathe him already. Ah, this labour is worse than any, and may I soon die! I have thought, and told my husband of it, that if this child lives she is to be christened Alix, after that young girl who succumbed to Curtmantle, as I myself did, long ago. Had she lived, she would have inherited Brittany. Will any in my land remember me as they remember her? *Her smile is in the crystal waters; the virgins put flowers on her tomb*. So said Berthe. A tomb matters nothing. Fair Rosamund is in hers, and I shall soon be in mine. Ah, the pain now in my ruined body! The pain!

Guy will no doubt grieve when I am gone. Others will forget; everything is changed now from the world I knew. Only old Eleanor of Aquitaine lives on, and my young Pearl of Brittany I shall never again see.

Old Eleanor, travelling to visit her daughter as far as Spain . . . our own pious Breton duchess Ermengarde, long ago, travelled to Jerusalem. Richard, for all his crusading, never saw the Holy City. How far will I travel now alone, how far? I shall perhaps in the end see God.

The pains have ceased. I can no longer feel Berthe's hands about me, though I can hear my daughter's new crying. I know without being told that she is a daughter. I will never bear another son.

Arthur is almost sixteen. At news of my death, when it comes, he will ride to Rennes, and my chancellor Pierre de Dinan will place the crown on his head. Thereafter his fate is in his own hands, and I wish him good fortune. I may still live for a little while. It is of no importance.

Part Four

The Testament of Guy de Thouars, 1213

1

THIS witness is by me, Guy de Thouars, knight: written at Chémillé in the year of Our Lord 1213, to be delivered into the keeping of my good friend and brother, the vicomte Sieur Aimery de Thouars, sojourning now at Poitiers. I ask that he pray for my soul as I shall soon die. This I send by way of the clerk Jehul.

The marriage of my daughter Alix to the knight they call Pierre Mauclerc, of the house of Dreux, has been contested by many, who would have preferred her former betrothed, the Breton Henri de Penthièvre. He was nearer her age, it is true. However in the knowledge that my dear wife Constance, Alix's mother the late duchess twelve years dead, whose soul God rest, would have wanted above all things the safety and peace of the land, I decided that it was best to break off the Breton betrothal to strengthen links with France. We have suffered

429

enough from England, the rival power who has no mercy; even now Lackland, as usual full of insensate rage, has taken sides with Louvain, Brabant, the emperor and others and will no doubt invade us in course of his persistent wars against the king of France. Lackland will come to an evil end, certainly after his death if not before.

How we have suffered from them! As all know, our true princess Eleanor, the Pearl of Brittany, own sister to the young murdered duke, has been kept by them first in a tower at Bristol, then in a convent which has remained her prison. It is unlikely that she will be seen again by the world, let alone permitted to marry into Austria as was at one time suggested: she is fortunate to be let live. My Alix, therefore, was selected by a convocation of my lords to inherit, as being of the old blood although she is my daughter and not that of a prince. Mauclerc will rule well for her. I had my doubts about him at the beginning, as it is my nature to weigh everything. From the look of his mouth I was certain he could be cruel, but his manner to Alix is tender; and he writes poems. He began as a cleric, then forsook it for the army. A soldier such as he will make a sound bulwark behind my Alix, whom her mother named after that earlier girl of whom she used to speak, who was ruined by Henry II, King of England. That man also had much for which to answer and before he died, said he took his heart away from God. I hope God will forgive this blasphemy.

I hope also that I have acted wisely concerning this present marriage. Mauclerc is twenty-three, my Alix thirteen; but the matter had to be settled before my death. By discarding the Penthièvre alliance, I lost myself the supposed lordships of Cornouaille, Vannes and Nantes as promised in that betrothal contract. All of those places are however troublesome, my other daughters are provided for by their marriages, and I do not expect to live long now.

While I may I want to remember the past, and the woman I loved better than broad lands, which in any case I lost in youth on an earlier occasion. Constance herself is without doubt reunited with her son Arthur in heaven. She grudged him sorely to France, but by the mercy of God never knew of King Philip's betrayal by reason of Lackland's bribes, and of duke Arthur's end. They say, in the smooth English manner, that there is no certainty of the manner of his death at sixteen years old, after being captured while besieging his grandmother at Mirebeau. They murmur that he may have died in Rouen tower, or else drowned in the moat there, trying to escape. Our countrymen here know differently. Those who scratch a living from the scant earth by the sea-coast, those who make their living by fishing for *goémon*, have found strands of golden hair caught in their nets. No more of duke Arthur was ever found. It is a pity that the King of France, who presently betrayed him, suffered Arthur, young as he was, to lead an army to besiege old Queen Eleanor. Naturally she sent word to her son Lackland, who came with a rival army and defeated and took the boy, whom he had long determined to destroy as his rival with a greater right to England and the Angevin empire. They say — I heard this also by way of yourself, my brother, for you have spoken with those who witnessed it — that after shutting the boy up in prison in Rouen he sent men to geld him and gouge out his eyes. Those blue eyes like the sea, that young manhood newly grown! The thought itself is unendurable; but it did not happen. Arthur got himself behind a low wall, and his screams brought in haste an Englishman named William de Braose, then in the service of Hubert de Burgh the justiciar. This same de Braose was later starved to death with his wife and children at Windsor by Lackland, supposedly for refusing the children as hostages. The same fate overtook most of the knights who supported young Arthur himself and his ally, Hugh de la Marche, whose young bride Lackland had reft away and married for himself, so Hugh sought vengeance.

Later, duke Arthur was removed by night from Rouen, Lackland having come for him in person with a train of men. There was a man among them named Pierre de Maulac, whose testimony is as good as anyone's. Arthur was by then weak from prison and from his terrible experiences. They put him in the saddle and rode with him to the coast, telling him they were making for Cherbourg. Then, at a place where there are jagged rocks above the sea, making a precipice, they dragged the boy down, some say into a boat, others on to the ground. He struggled and cried out piteously, offering Lackland all his lands if only he might have his life. Lackland then seized him by the hair, dragging him also part of the time by the foot, perhaps into the boat and perhaps not; plunged his sword into the boy's stomach — a most cruel way to die — then struck off his head with two blows. Thereafter he caused the body, weighted with a heavy stone, to be cast into the sea. No more is known, and even that is not much spoken of as men are afraid.

My wife Constance used to speak of the lost city of Ys. Not far off, washed by the tides, lie the lost bones of her beautiful only son, who should have reigned over Brittany and England. Was he the green victim my wife used also to speak of, again, in 1203? All of the victims have been young, male and royal, and killed by sharp metal, the arrow, spear, or sword.

All of that, at any rate, is over. Now there is this Pierre Mauclerc my daughter's husband to come after me. I have remembered a fragment of one of his poems: it concerns Our Lady.

Dame dou Ciel qui portastes Jhésu
Par que ce mont fut tot enluminé,
L'heritage qu'Adam avait perdu,
Par son péchié, fut par vous recouvre
(si com ge le croi et il est vérité),
Deffendez moi, que ne, soie vaincu
Par l'ennemi qui est fel et desve.

I am pleased, my brother, that I have remembered all of it. Such a man will doubtless make a kind husband to Alix while remaining a firm ruler of Brittany.

I pray for your continued health. Mine is no longer worth mention. I hope to leave this world soon to be with those I love, but God disposes. Meantime, the king of France, betraying the betrayer, has regained all of Lackland's former territories on this side of the Channel, making the murderer again worthy of the name by which he will be always known.

Completed at Chémillé, on the eve of Our Lord's nativity, this year of 1213.

★ ★ ★

Guy de Thouars died in April, his death passing almost without notice. The following chronicle is added by an unknown hand.

★ ★ ★

It was said by the enemies of Mauclerc that young Henri de Penthièvre died of grief after failing to espouse the Breton heiress Alix; but in fact he lived on to old age and in the end took the habit of the Cordéliers at Dinan, which order he had founded. Pierre Mauclerc himself, Alix's husband, greatly aided the building of the famous cathedral at Chartres. He reigned well on behalf of his wife, who died in 1221, and then for their son, to whom he made over the government in 1237. Pierre himself survived his beloved wife Duchess Alix by almost thirty years. Their son, Jean, being red-haired, founded a ducal line which endured till within five years of Crécy.

★ ★ ★

Lackland himself had died at last in 1216. He had lost the respect of his nobles and all his worldly goods including his crown, which sank in the sea off the coast of East Anglia. They say that the night after his burial in the cathedral at Worcester, nearby the relics of St Wulstan, his ghost was seen at midnight by the abbot 'surrounded by great silences'. It began to moan and beg the mercy of being removed from the holy place, as the souls of all those he had done to death were uniting to torment him. Accordingly next day, the corpse was taken secretly out of the tomb and buried in a nearby field, where thereafter no crops would grow. This is the tale, at any rate.

It was thought to be a most singular instance of God's justice that the crown which rightly belonged to Arthur of

Brittany should have vanished at last in the sea. Our old fishermen have a legend that Arthur himself reigns now in the lost city of Ys, beneath the waves, wearing his rightful crown which has been thus returned to him. The latter was certainly never found by the English, despite much searching by them through the centuries; nor has any of the regalia, except for a blackened helm, discovered at last in an East Anglian ditch.

Author's Note

French and Breton sources differ wildly as to facts, although dates are on the whole firmly accessible. Certainly Constance of Brittany died in 1201, but the nature of her disease may not have been as stated in French sources and suppressed in Breton ones. The term leprosy, in the twelfth century, covered a number of diseases now separately recognised, which could mean most things except syphilis, that last making no appearance in Europe until after the voyages of Columbus. It is no more certain that Constance, any more than Robert the Bruce, died a leper; but it is possible, was the prevailing belief, and therefore no doubt also hers. The leprosy of Baldwin IV of Jerusalem is however without doubt. Nevertheless the date of Constance's death, and the fact that it was not in childbirth, poses difficulty as to the recorded marriage of her so-called eldest daughter by her own third marriage; Alix, stated to have become the bride aged thirteen, in 1213 of Pierre Mauclerc, who thereafter ruled Brittany on his wife's behalf. Her mother's previous marriage had not been annulled till 1199 owing to delay at Rome. I have suggested therefore that this second Alix, probably called after Curtmantle's earlier prey, was in fact the youngest, not the eldest, of the three girls born to Constance by her love-match with Guy de Thouars, who became her third husband during the few years preceding her death, and that Alix was adopted as heir by reason of being the only one of the three born legitimate: also of course because the true heir, Eleanor, remained unavailable in a convent prison in England, from which she was never released. The fate of her brother Arthur is only too well known.

P.H.

TO FIGHT THE WILD
Rod Ansell and Rachel Percy

Lost in uncharted Australian bush, Rod Ansell survived by hunting and trapping wild animals, improvising shelter and using all the bushman's skills he knew.

COROMANDEL
Pat Barr

India in the 1830s is a hot, uncomfortable place, where the East India Company still rules. Amelia and her new husband find themselves caught up in the animosities which seethe between the old order and the new.

THE SMALL PARTY
Lillian Beckwith

A frightening journey to safety begins for Ruth and her small party as their island is caught up in the dangers of armed insurrection.

THE WILDERNESS WALK
Sheila Bishop

Stifling unpleasant memories of a misbegotten romance in Cleave with Lord Francis Aubrey, Lavinia goes on holiday there with her sister. The two women are thrust into a romantic intrigue involving none other than Lord Francis.

THE RELUCTANT GUEST
Rosalind Brett

Ann Calvert went to spend a month on a South African farm with Theo Borland and his sister. They both proved to be different from her first idea of them, and there was Storr Peterson — the most disturbing man she had ever met.

ONE ENCHANTED SUMMER
Anne Tedlock Brooks

A tale of mystery and romance and a girl who found both during one enchanted summer.